SUNWARD SKY

HENRY NEILSEN

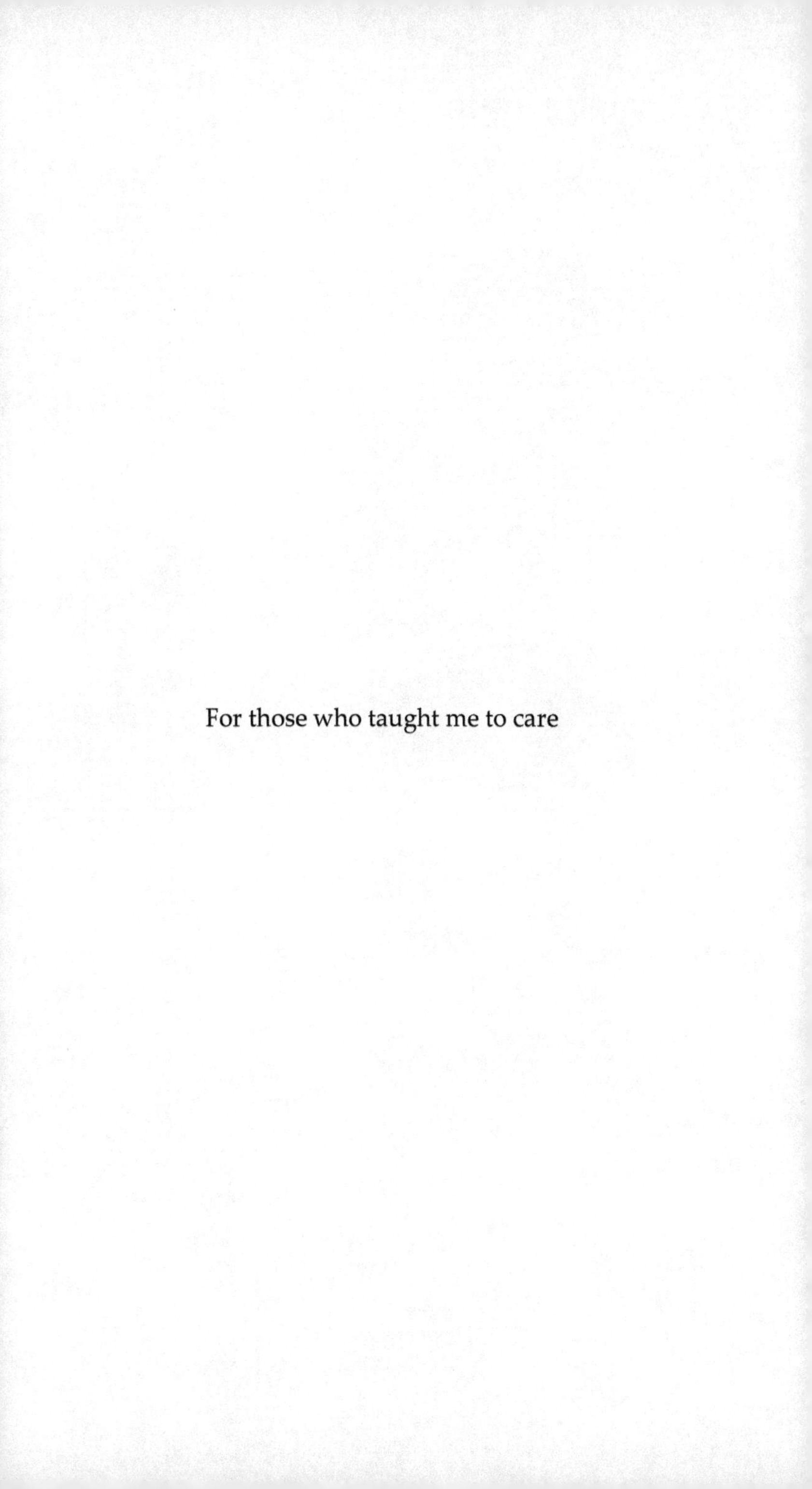

For those who taught me to care

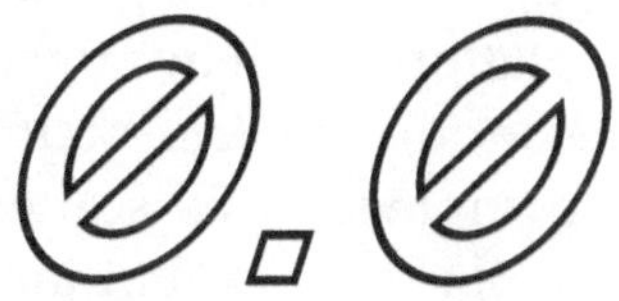

PROLOGUE

The surveillance drone crested the crater from the west, and for a moment the unfiltered sun flared its sensors before the signal corrected for the glare. Its ceramic body transmitted data through the net, which for the most part would be ignored, especially out here. Barely anyone bothered to watch the launch sites anymore. There was nothing to see. Miles of near-white, near-featureless crater bouncing the rising sunlight harshly off the Earth and into space. Into the bright white lay jagged, dark stripes like the veins of an eye. Tracks broke the harsh luminance of the rest of the crater with dark lines, splitting the terrain to make way for the semi-submerged railways and bullet-shaped locomotives with tinted glass and cracked hulls.

The drone flagged a note; the rail was stationary. Its systems expected to detect movement along the rails, the frantic ferrying of equipment and materials and crew to the centre of the crater, but it found none. Something was off task.

A recording device flipped on, and the drone moved further into the crater. Here, scorch marks overlaid one another, splaying out haphazardly from a raised square platform with two towering armatures on either side. Gantries, control rooms, bunkers and abandoned construction equipment was scattered around the site like blisters on a sunburnt back, but the drone sent no life readings back along its signal path. The platform was deserted, and its only occupant was the spacecraft.

The *Sunward Sky* wasn't new. Amongst the gleaming white of the launch crater and the industry of its platform it looked tired, ready to be scrapped, but it still towered over everything around it. The trusses of the two armatures held it aloft, squatting over its triple thrusters and a central shaft that jutted skyward, its nose cone reaching upward as though in defiance of the Earth's pull. A series of interlocking arms connected to the three wings of the spaceship, which curved around the main body and ran its length, only tapering toward the top to break the air when it was in flight. Red letters, running down the centre of one of the wings, identified the ship. The letters lay unread; painting the names on ships was for tradition more than identification these days. The words *Sunward Sky* sat inset to a rhomboid of the same colour. It stood out starkly against the blackness of the rest of the ship's detailing.

As the drone flew past, it noted the movement of a robotic arm at the base of the ship, waiting expectantly for its delivery. The sensors and cameras logged and flagged it and moved around the wing of the immense spacecraft to cut a chord to the other side of the crater.

The drone wasn't to know, but a series of electrical signals were being sent, silently, warning that the launch sequence was not occurring in order. A simple flag, autocued and sent out like the "Hello, World!" of early computer programs, was delivered through the tunnels. It was trying to reach through the earth of the crater and into a control centre so sophisticated, and so full of black-box adaptive software that no single person could understand its machinations.

This time though, it was interrupted.

Something picked up the digital signal, and in an instant flipped the warning flag to become nothing more than a notification of an unscheduled delay. The operations centre knew no reason to dispute it.

The drone reached the outer edge of the white disk of the launch crater. The hot red dustbowl of the Earth stretched out in an endless expanse, rising slowly to meet a sky that was twice as dark but just as deadly. Plant life struggled, gnarled roots casting long morning shadows that fell like threats across the plains.

Rotors screamed as the machine crested the top of the crater's walls, rising past the operations centre that overlooked the launch site. It was a hodgepodge of buildings; old petrol stations and rusted vehicles next to abandoned fuel pumps. Reconfigured office buildings and warehouses, and disused homes with faded curtains howling in the morning breeze. These were all linked together with an inelegant series of tunnels, canopies to protect from harsh solar radiation.

The building on the edge of the crater was newer than the rest. It was hundreds of metres long and stretched across the crater's lip, staring gloomily to where the *Sunward Sky* lay dormant. Its gunmetal roof was pockmarked with solar panels and turbines, and it had a series of rigid steel shutters on large actuator assemblies that would shutter the windows at any moment.

The drone couldn't see Alyssa inside. She sat, back against the wall, eyes closed, waiting patiently to be taken down to the pale crater to board the *Sunward Sky*.

PART

ONE

1.1

DELAYS

She knew the danger, but she still dreamed of spacewalking. That was the image that played against the black of her inner eyelids as she waited to board the *Sunward Sky*. To dance in the void of space, careless and alone, a tiny speck in an endless universe.

That might make it all worth it.

An announcement had come through the crackling loudspeakers of the launch system a few minutes earlier. *An unscheduled delay has occurred on the outbound launch of the* Sunward Sky, *please remain in the terminal for boarding.* So she'd waited, imagining weightlessness, and feeling the drag of the Earth's bulk against her and her clothes in the spaceport. Soon enough her imagination gave way to her frustration, and she stood up, disconnected her hand tablet from the charging station, and walked along the terminal. The corridor was gunmetal grey, and dark glass faced toward the launch crater where she could see the ship waiting for her. She found a door that had been left slightly ajar and surrounded by signs in both Mando and Anglo with threats against trespass.

Never one to leave a curiosity unexplored, she glanced around furtively before ducking through the door. A thin, even layer of dust on the floor shifted as she walked down along the corridor. After a few metres, the walls around her disappeared and she found herself in an old annex fitted with layers upon layers of overlapping and abandoned technology.

It was like a museum that had been ransacked, cannibalised and refit to within an inch of its life. A kiosk in the corner with fading plastic counter tops and broken fibreboard piled in the corner overflowed with ancient wiring. Alyssa thought it looked like an old terminal hub, the wires having once belonged to screens for self-service and purchasing until synth-chips and link payments had become the norm. As she rounded the corner, she saw one of the screens, shattered, abandoned and covered in grey dust. The faded signs above the kiosk only had old Anglo instructions on them, which she couldn't read. There had been something bolted to the floor. Several somethings, and there were old pictures of desert landscapes and groups of pointing people. They were outside, in direct sunlight and not wearing skinsuits or heavy parasols.

This place is old, Alyssa thought, *it's amazing that it still exists.* Usually, any useful materials were ripped out for reuse and anachronistic buildings such as this terminal, whatever it was, were torn down for new construction. Alyssa suspected this place had only survived so long because of its proximity to the launch pad. Space Palsy wasn't contagious, but people were superstitious; nobody came to launch sites unless they had to.

Except you, she said to herself.

The door behind her creaked open, and a man wheeled himself in, then stopped as he spotted her. He asked what she was doing here and she froze. The signs in the main terminal forbade her from being here, but surely that applied to him as well?

"I'm looking around. Same as you," she couldn't tell his age. The wheelchair was in bad repair and too small for him. His skin had the marks of a man used to smiling, but a dull ember of something like anger hid beneath his eyes, and he wore a pained frown. There was more grey in his hair than black.

He wheeled toward her. Had he stood up she got the impression he'd tower over her, with broad shoulders and limbs that stuck awkwardly from his mobility device. He listed to one side as he brought the chair to a halt, and several carabiners hanging from his coveralls clinked with the change in momentum.

"Aye," he said, and the slight trace of an old Scottish brogue crept through, "I am having a look, just an explore. Sitting still in high-grav makes the old body seize up a bit," he slapped the wheelchair and grinned - the tungsten carabiners clanked - and Alyssa relaxed an inch. He seemed safe enough.

She pointed at the carabiners, "You're a mechanic or something?"

His laugh was gruff and gave way to a small fit of coughs before he was able to answer. "Started that way, but nothing came of it. No, I'm a medic. Ships doctor, or something like it. And you?"

A medic, she thought, *that might come in handy. Though hopefully not.* "I don't know yet" she said, shrugging, "It's my first time up."

Just for a moment, she saw something in the older man's eyes. A hardness. A flame still burning. A mote of fury that snatched a moment as his smile faltered, but then it was gone and he was talking again.

"Oh. Well. Probably gonna be my last," he said, "And the *Sunward Sky's* too, come to think of it. We've both been in rotation for a bit longer than what's good for us," as he said it, he thumped feebly on the floor with one boot. It clanked against the ground. "Name's Healy," he said, and offered a hand so pale it was almost see-through. Alyssa felt, more than saw, the delicacy of the veins within as she shook it.

"Alyssa," she said, then looked around the room, trying to find something to talk about with this stranger and failing. Healy, for his part, eyed the old Anglo signs, eyes darting back and forth. *He can read Anglo?* Alyssa thought, and tucked it into her memory. "You've never been in here before, then? Looks like nobody has in a while," she kicked at the floor, sending up a puff of dust.

He shook his head. "Don't spend a lot of time dirtside these days, if I'm honest. Makes my feet a little woozy with all the g," he held his hand out. It was shaking, twitching. Alyssa knew it as soon as she saw it. Space Palsy.

"Last time I spent any appreciable amount of time on the rock was when we still launched out of Canaveral. Since then, I've been old ironsides down here in full G, and only for a few hours or days between launches. They only spin the crew on the *Sunward Sky* up to about a quarter, thankfully."

Alyssa tried to hide her surprise. He'd been at it a long time and was in surprisingly good shape considering. Cape Canaveral had been the home of space launches since before the Apollo program in the 1960s, but it had been destroyed by a category six hurricane years ago. What hadn't been washed into the sea was now far too unstable for rocket launches. It was amazing he was able to survive on the surface now at all.

He twitched as he redirected his eyes back to Alyssa, looking her up and down. The carabiners clinked softly and slightly out of time with his movement.

"Tell me something," he said, and the lightness was gone from his voice. "Why are you going up?"

"What do you mean?" Alyssa replied, but she knew what he meant.

"People. They don't just *go to space*. This isn't a job people *volunteer* for," he pointed at his translucently pale hand, and nodded at the twitching. "It affects you in ways you don't understand. Sure, the view is incredible, but it messes with your mind. That ship, out there?" he gestured back across to the main terminal, toward the *Sunward Sky*, "It's a tin can. There's a void around you. Your muscles deteriorate, your coordination goes. You have to shit and piss in a bag. You're one angular miscalculation from burning up in the atmosphere or being flung into the depths of space. And there's other things. Worse things," he wasn't quite looking at her. He looked haunted, and his skin seemed to hang down, heavy and weary beyond his years. He looked as old as the terminal they stood in, and just as bereft and abandoned. His eyes spoke of eons of loneliness, horrors, and of a lifetime of terrified silence. A wave of remorse came over Alyssa.

"I just… I always thought space would be amazing to see," she lied.

Healy composed himself and forced a smile. "I see. Well, there's something to it. The grav hurts less up there, at least."

His eyes started roaming around the room again, and he gestured to the sign. "Old tourist terminal. You know, before the launch crater, there was a big lake here? People would come from miles around to see it. Sit in here, then get on a transport, and walk out. Sun wasn't so hot back then, you could go out without a skinsuit. They'd be outside, looking like that! Damned if I know how they didn't all burn up," with that, he wheeled himself around and headed back to the door. "I'm sorry, I need to find a place to lay down, my spine is having trouble with its own weight. I shall see you aboard the *Sky*."

Alyssa watched him leave, thinking of what a powerful man he'd have been had he not spent the best part of his adult life in space. She considered following him briefly, to ask him more about his muscle degeneration but thought better of it. She hadn't liked the darkness in his eyes when he'd talked about it. She therefore turned and wandered through the undisturbed dust, small puffs jumping at her feet and leaving a trail for her to go back by.

Say what you could say about space, she thought, *at least you weren't stuck in the muck of a dying Earth.*

1.2

CARGO

There hadn't been any further announcements about the launch, and Alyssa was still restless. Instead of following Healy through the main door back to the terminal, Alyssa ambled to the other side of the room. She found a door on the other side and tried the handle. It cracked open and left an arc of dust on the floor. She bit back a sneeze. Anglo and Mando signs warned intruders to keep away, and Alyssa looked at them closely. The signs themselves were out of use and out of date, peeling and corrupt at the edges, with bubbling paint and scratches all over. Nonplussed, she walked further into the abandoned facility, her curiosity getting the better of her.

Healy was right. She didn't want to be going on this flight. For all her romanticism about space walking and drifting in the endless ether, she knew exactly how dangerous it was.

For a while, space had held such promise. The stars were calling, even as humanity continued to burn through Earth's precious resources, and there remained a hope for a diaspora to the stars. Tales of generation ships heading to habitable planets in other systems had been told, and untold trillions had been spent to get humanity there.

It wasn't to be. Stories of sickness, of a degenerative disease that started affecting spacers within a few short months, became prevalent. It didn't matter how much space flight advanced, how good the technology got, space flight was still a dangerous and risky profession that would result in people being unfit to live in full gravity. People like Healy were quite rare. Most of the time musculoskeletal and cardiovascular problems killed people long before old age did, and those who made it to his age couldn't survive on the surface for more than a few hours. Any medication developed so far was ineffective; the Space Palsy seemed inevitable. Any travel to a new place in the sky would take too long. Once people got there, they wouldn't be able to return to high gravity. It seemed as though space was just too inhospitable for humans to endure for any length of time, but there was demand for space travel all the same. Global interconnected satellite networks ran everything; GPS satellites to keep automated shipping lanes moving, communication satellites to keep the world's entertainment feeds flowing, defence satellites that kept the cold threat of violence from reaching into the void. It had been declared unconstitutional for governmental bodies to send prisoners into what amounted to a death trap. So space travel, once the dream of billionaires and scientists, was now little more than a sweatshop. The people who did it were desperate, needing something to keep themselves alive. People down on their luck, in debt, sleeping rough, and needing something immediate that made the long-term consequences almost worth it.

Why are you going up? Healy had asked her.

She had her reasons. Not that she was going to tell a perfect stranger, but she had them. She was making a plea bargain with the universe, and hoping she'd be able to make something happen. She sighed and pulled a door open to reveal another antique room.

There was a break in the layers of dust. A sleek, clear line in the cracked linoleum floor where something had been dragged from one side of the room to another. The boot marks on either side of it were closely spaced. *Whatever it was, it was heavy,* Alyssa thought. The door on the far side had cracks and scratches on it. They were fresh.

Her heart quickened in her chest and grew louder as she closed the distance to the door. This part of the terminal was abandoned; it seemed so strange that anyone would be using it that any activity felt intrusive. Like her space had been invaded.

The door was still slightly ajar when she reached it. Inside it looked like a workshop, albeit smaller and older than any she'd seen. It wasn't big enough for full-size transport pods or goods trains, and the machinery was worn out and disused. Rubber tires in the corner had degraded so much that she could see rusted radial belts beneath. Shelves lay empty but for the dust that was everywhere. In the corner she could see the crate that had been dragged through the room. It was metallic and black, and not quite rectangular. The edges were scraped and covered in the paint it had peeled from doors it had been dragged through. As Alyssa's curiosity got the better of her, she heard men's voices.

"This the only one this time?" one of them said. Beyond the crate, Alyssa could see a helmeted head bobbing as it talked.

"Reckon," there was an undercurrent of boredom surging through the syllables, "reckon it's the last one, too," Alyssa couldn't see the source of the voice. He was hidden behind the crate.

"You ever gonna tell me what's in 'em?"

The second man chuckled. "No, I don't reckon. This one is the one we took off, anyway. Just hoping we made weight properly," he sounded dismissive, like the first man was an inconvenience and not a friend. "Anyway. This is the last one. Last time you'll have anything to do with *Sunward Sky*," there was a shifting sound as one of them scuffled their feet toward the other end of the black and silver box. "And about time too."

The helmeted head bobbed and started moving toward the opposite end of the crate. Alyssa ducked back out of the way. If she'd stayed there he'd have looked straight at her.

He leaned down as he reached the end, looking for something on the box. "Wait. Brett, did you replace the - what was that?"

Alyssa's foot had slipped as she'd crouched down behind the door, and the canvas siding on her shoe had squeaked against the aged linoleum on the floor. The sound had rung out through the workshop like an alarm.

"There's someone over there," he said, "Brett. Get here, grab a crowbar."

A padding of feet and a rustling of tools, and Alyssa's

already thudding heart went into overdrive. She could hear them walking toward the door, with the sound of a crowbar dragging along the floor with them.

"Who's there?" the deeper voice, Brett's. His voice growled across the floor. Alyssa's feet scuffed along the floor, and she heard their pace quicken. A few seconds later they pulled the door open, Brett in the lead brandishing the crowbar as the other man held up the rear.

Alyssa had already gone.

Without speaking, the two men worked their way through the room, checking behind every shelf and all the equipment in the workshop. Satisfied that it was empty and that the intruder hadn't stalked their way *into* the room, they slipped into the tunnel that connected to the next building. Brett dragged the crowbar across the floor, as much a threat as it was a display. When they reached the end of the tunnel, they nodded at each other and sprang through into the waiting room where Alyssa had spoken to Healy minutes before.

The place was as deserted as it had ever been. White hot sunlight slashed through the windows, sparking off the recently disturbed dust that was now floating through the air. It was the only movement they could see, and they couldn't hear anything but the hum of the air conditioning.

The two men glanced at each other, their faces and expressions hidden by the helmets of their skinsuits. Brett held up a hand and made a sign, and the two of them stepped into the room to search.

At that moment a voice came over the PA speaker, filtering down into the abandoned lobby where they stood.

"For those boarding the Sunward Sky. *The ship is now ready to commence boarding. Make your way to the departure terminal and*

board the shuttle train at your earliest convenience. Launch is imminent."

The two men looked at each other again. Brett smacked the ground with the crowbar in frustration. Their time was up. They turned and walked back the way they'd come.

If they'd stayed for a few more seconds, they may have seen a small trail of bootprints in the dust. They led out of the door. A confused flurry of prints ten metres into the room showed where Alyssa had been been confused and out of time.

On the kiosk, the cords that had lain undisturbed for years were shifted, and a clear mark had been drawn through the dust on the countertop. Behind it, Alyssa sat, sweating. She held her hand over her mouth to quiet her breathing.

She'd escaped.

She waited for a few minutes, to ensure they'd left the room. Only when the second boarding call filtered down from the terminal did she slide out from under the kiosk. She patted herself down carefully and walked with deliberate calm back to the terminal. Before long, she was aboard the shuttle train, reeling, barely prepared for her first ever space flight aboard the *Sunward Sky*.

1.3

LIFT OFF

The trip to the launch crater was nothing like she'd imagined. Old vids she'd seen back when there were grandiose dreams of populating the solar system always showed open bridges with a bright and welcoming hatchway. She'd expected elevators running through the centre of the ship from the rocket boosters all the way to the crew cabins.

In reality, her view of the *Sunward Sky* from within the terminal was better than what she could see while in transit across the launch crater. She and the other crew had been paired up and ferried onto a thin carriage with no windows and washed out, faded lights.

The woman that had been next to her had staggered toward the seat, barely holding herself up in the high-grav environment. She wasn't the only one. Most of the crew showed signs of the same Space Palsy that she'd seen in Healy.

Alyssa swallowed. Everywhere around her she could see dark anger or hopelessness in the eyes of the crew, and even while sitting in the chair most of them twitched. Even the young ones had white hair. The palsy aged them before their time.

As soon as everyone was aboard, the doors to the locomotive hissed shut, and a low electrical whine permeated the cabin. They were moving.

"First time up, eh?" the woman next to Alyssa asked, and her head snaked to and fro as she turned to face her more fully.

Alyssa nodded, but she was distracted. She wasn't sure if the two men chasing her were on board, or whether they were ground staff. She didn't think they'd got a good look at her, but the sound of a dragging crowbar still played on her mind. They'd been wearing helmets, too, so she wouldn't recognise them if they were on the ship unless they spoke.

"Ah, still a Terran then," the woman seemed to spit the word *Terran*, but seemed kind, almost sympathetic, when she continued. "Not to worry, sweetie. First time's always rough, but you'll be okay. Whatever got you to us here, we can take care of you. We take care of our own, and we don't need to go dirtside. Just wait til you see."

"See what?" Alyssa asked.

The woman looked at Alyssa. "The Earth. No matter what anyone says about the palsy, the conditions, the dangers of space travel, it's worth it to look down on the world."

Alyssa gestured to the woman's shaking hand, "it's worth that?"

The woman placed her other hand over her arm, and consciously tried to stop the shaking. "Space Palsy ain't so bad so long as you stay in space," she said, "It's having to come down that's the trouble."

Again, Alyssa felt an anger radiating from the woman. She'd heard about spacers getting that way about the Earth. Some called it *Terraphobia*, but Alyssa thought it was completely justified. Looking around, almost none of the crew looked as though they could survive on the surface. They had been driven to this by their work. Their sheer need to survive had broken them, and they'd been unlucky enough to have no choice. She considered asking the woman when her Space Palsy condition had first set in, then decided against it. She didn't want to know.

"What's your name? I'm Alyssa," she said.

"Ellyse."

They didn't talk any more as they plunged into the launch crater. Had there been any windows, Alyssa would have seen the edges of the crater looming over her like a mountain range, the terminal shrinking behind them like a tiny speck until it was only a glint of steel and glass on the rim.

Alyssa tried to stay calm, to control her breathing. Despite the advances in technologies and the growth in requirements for regular space travel, launches and landings were still fraught with danger. Launches were so loud that they would rupture eardrums of anyone nearby. The blast from the engines would fan out with devastating violence across an enormous radius. The forces against the ground, the heat, and the danger to the surrounding atmosphere made launches something best experienced only from afar. Alyssa had watched so many vids of spaceships launching from small plazas inside mud buildings, but now it was accepted that this was never going to be practical. This was especially true as no company on Earth was interested in making space travel a more comfortable experience for the minimum wage labourers that crewed the craft. Launch craters were instead located in the growing number of inhospitable, arid wastelands that humanity was creating.

The shuttle stopped, and a light above the doors flashed green. The crew stepped out into a box platform. On one side was a lift door. Most of the crew, including Ellyse, staggered onto it. A few of the others, those who could walk in the full grav of Earth, were directed by flat-faced ground crew up a set of stairs.

Alyssa walked up silently, trying to enjoy the screaming feeling in her legs as the stairs ascended further and further up the face of the spacecraft. She didn't know the next time she'd feel the weight of her own body pushing against her muscles. She felt the lactic buildup, felt the sweat in her pores, and tried to relish it.

When she was halfway up, the stairwell opened out. A series of windows were fitted to the side of the stairwell, and Alyssa got her first close up view of the *Sunward Sky*.

It was black as pitch, and matte. The outside was smooth except for a networked lattice of lines running all over the hull. Here and there were well-disguised hatches, with white and red text spelling out codes that made no sense to anyone but the engineers assigned to them. The ship was enormous. Alyssa had read specifications about its height, and the diameter of its wings, but it was all just numbers until she was standing next to it. The vast blackness of the thing stretched above and below her further than she could see, and the mass of the ship blocked everything from view in the window. She gawked, amazed. If she peered out to the left she could see the minor break in the patterning where one part of the enormous outer drum split, and an edge of a red stencilled letter longer than the shuttle that had carried the crew out here.

A voice behind her hurried her along, and she continued ascending, staring out at the *Sunward Sky* whenever a new window came into view. A ship this size was big enough that it should never have to land. It had enough biomass and water treatment to be self-sustaining, but the company that owned it and the satellite companies found it cheaper to send the crew down every few months to resupply rather than building smaller craft to restock it when necessary. In doing so, the crew were subjected to the worst parts of the palsy, repeatedly, but it still ended up cheaper to replace labour than machinery.

A few minutes later, she reached the top of the platform. The harsh artificial lighting was back, and she fought the urge to itch her eyes as she was shepherded into the tunnel of the entrance gantry.

The hall seemed to last forever, and after a while she thought to herself *where's the entrance to the ship?*

With a start, she looked again at her surroundings. The walls had changed. They seemed older, but somehow sturdier, and the powdercoat had a satin sheen to it. The colours were less uniform, and the lights were warmer than they'd been in the journey to the crater or in the terminal.

I've boarded a spaceship, Alyssa said to herself, *I've boarded a spaceship and I didn't even notice it happen.*

Some of the more experienced crew members, sitting

down to save their muscles, were guiding the newer crew in.

"Launch couches are through here. You will report your condition once the launch sequence is complete."

Alyssa stepped into a wider area, a circular room arrayed with cot-like beds that were nailed on gimbals to the floor. A lot of them were already occupied by spacers.

Everywhere, the ship showed signs of its age. There were indicator screens with huge stripes of dead pixels. The couches themselves were covered in sweat stains and torn off sections of memory foam. The foam was pressed into humanoid divot after so many high-g scenarios. The once sleek instrumentation looked clunky and patched where things had been broken and fixed and broken again.

Alyssa found Ellyse on one of a pair of couches toward the back of the room. She nodded at the spacer before lowering herself in and staring straight up at the grating above.

"Make sure you're not hanging over the top of the couch anywhere," Ellyse warned, "It's the fastest way to find out where the infirmary is, having your forearm snap because of the launch G's. That happens, you're stuck there until launch is over, and you'll be in a heap of pain the whole time. Nobody can help mid launch."

Alyssa pulled herself in from the edges of the launch couch and made sure to fasten the safety around her waist. Her heart was in her throat as she watched the crew filter through the door. She spotted Healy, heading to a larger launch couch on the opposite side of the room. Over an unseen intercom, a *T minus five minutes* came through the sound system. The crew started moving faster, and a few of the other first timers started looking panicked as they tried to find the last of the couches in good repair.

A voice broke out over the intercom shortly after the *T-minus two minutes* call. It was the ship's captain, a man who introduced himself as Sharma. Far from the clipped and professional tones of a pilot, Sharma spoke with the casual voice of tired experience.

"Hi all. We've got quite a few new dirtsiders on board this time round, and a few experienced crew members who haven't been aboard *Sunward Sky*. If you haven't been aboard before, welcome. If you have, welcome back."

A deep hum had begun reverberating through the entire ship, and enormous metallic thuds echoed in the room. "Apologies for the delay, by the way. Cargo got loaded up, but the dockhand forgot to sign it off. Seems to be all sorted now though, and we're only a little behind schedule. We're off soon, make sure you're strapped into your launch couch."

Something niggled at the back of Alyssa's mind. The cargo, and what Sharma had said about it.

It hit her. The captain had said that the cargo had been loaded up properly, but the two men she'd seen had definitely mentioned something about loading up the *Sunward Sky*. The crate had to have been taken from somewhere, and it sounded as though Captain Sharma didn't realise it had been taken at all. *Dockhands forgot to sign it off* wasn't what you'd say if there had been a change to the cargo manifest. You'd just say there'd been a change. And the two men in the skinsuits had *chased her*. Which meant they were hiding something.

Alyssa's heart dropped. There was something on the ship that shouldn't be. The engines started to scream.

"Ellyse!" she shouted. The other woman was laying with her eyes closed with a pair of earmuffs on. She couldn't hear Alyssa's yelling. Alyssa ripped off the buckle she'd just finished doing up, and sat up, noticing her own pair of earmuffs on the edge of the couch. She reached out to shake Ellyse. Ellyse opened her eyes, which widened in horror as she saw Alyssa's crouched pose on the edge of the launch couch.

"What the *hell* are you doing?" Ellyse screamed, pushing Alyssa's hand away and throwing it out of her own couch. "Lay down, we're about to launch! What's wrong with you?"

T-minus thirty seconds.

"I saw something!" Alyssa screamed. The sound was overwhelming now, and there was no way Ellyse could hear her, "They took something, and they replaced it in the cargo! I saw them in the old abandoned part of the terminal! It was a massive flight box, and they were talking about making weight for something! Ellyse! *Something isn't right!*"

T-minus ten seconds.

Alyssa was crouched on the corner of her couch, with one foot on the floor.

Nine.

Ellyse was yelling something but the thrum of the deck was too loud to hear her.

Eight.

Alyssa flung herself back onto her couch, scrambling for the safety belt.

Seven.

The beltclip was under her body. At launch when the G-forces exploded into her, the small metal clip could cause a separation in her vertebrae.

Six.

She ripped the clip from under her back, and tried to manoeuvre her hands in such a way that the clip could get done up by her side.

Five.

The clip was too hard to deal with in the heat of the moment. She pushed it down next to her, at her waist. At least that way it wouldn't be a weight on her stomach.

Four.

The engines roared through the ship's fuselage, rattling the bones inside her head and sending her near deaf.

Three.

Near deaf... she wasn't wearing her earmuffs.

Two.

She twisted onto one shoulder, pushing herself up and reaching out for the earmuffs. The clip for the safety harness sat under her left hip bone, and she reached with her right arm while she propped herself up on one shoulder.

One.

She slipped the earmuffs on, and looked down at her contorted torso. One leg hung outside the edge of the launch couch and her shoulders were retracted as she held herself up by them. She'd need to shift back to a neutral position before-

The change in gravity was as instant as it was devastating. An unbelievable amount of thrust poured out of the ship's engines, and crushed Alyssa against the awkward twist of her torso. The aging launch couch sagged under the weight of her shoulder, trying to distribute the enormous point load away from her body and into the ship's fuselage, but it didn't do much. Her head snapped forward from the neck, hitting the couch and putting pressure on the top of her spine, while the leg that had been dangling over the edge was immediately wrenched so hard it felt as though it had been pulled from its socket. Alyssa screamed but no sound made it over the roar of the engines as they resonated through the metal exterior of the spacecraft. Her left shoulder jutted at an unnatural angle, and blood vessels in her other arm throbbed just under the surface of her skin. The safety clip dug into her hip bone, and as she cried in pain the tears thudded into the memory foam without splashing. With an incredible effort, she inched her leg back and to the side toward the safety of the couch's foam. Her already tired legs screamed at the effort, the acceleration making everything multitudes heavier than usual. She managed to get her leg onto the couch, and gasped with relief as that pain began to recede. Her left shoulder was still propping her up, and her neck was in tearing agony as it was forced to hold her head up against the incredible force of the *Sunward Sky's* ascent.

She couldn't reach down with her pinned left arm to shift the clip under her waist, so she reassessed. She tried twisting her elbow but it was stuck in the dent it had created in the memory foam. It was completely pinned. With an effort, Alyssa pulled her body across the couch by a millimetre, away from her left arm, aiming to flatten out the shoulder so it could spread the load out across the foam, and at least take some of the strain off her neck. The attitude of the rocket changed slightly as it continued through the atmosphere. All of Alyssa's muscles were full of lactic acid and burning, and she hauled herself millimetre by agonising millimetre away and downward. She flattened the sharp angle of her neck, and her shoulder took on a more normal geometry, slowly spreading her weight out across the couch. She only had two or three more efforts to go until her shoulders would be level again, and she could start dealing with the problem of the clip at her waist, which felt as though it was close to breaking her skin.

She grimaced and steeled herself for another movement. As she went to move herself, something shifted in the *Sunward Sky's* ascent. The movement was entirely in the wrong direction for her body to deal with, and her arm was ripped from its socket and her face fell sideways into the thick foam of the launch couch.

She screamed as the pain tore through her body. Her arm stuck hideously from her scapula, and the sudden downward force lodged the belt clip into her hip even more firmly. White pain poured into her senses. It overrode the thundering of the ship's rockets, and she lost consciousness.

1.4

ALERT

Keegan was bored. He'd landed a shift watching the launch crater of some end-of-the-earth site where nothing ever happened. Around him, fifteen curved monitors blazed with information, activity curves, expected behaviours, and overlays of real time imagery. The ops centre fed in all sorts of extrasensory data from the solar drones that were flying all over the world at any moment, but the work was still boring.

It beat being outside, though. The days he drew emergency services and had to don a skinsuit to head out to some disaster site or other, those were the days he dreaded.

The sun would beat down and feel like it was boiling you out of your skin, but you couldn't take the suits off otherwise you'd get crisped by solar radiation. No, on the whole, being inside and bored beat being outside and boiling.

He wasn't alone in the centre. Several colleagues were watching their own stations, with the same air of disinterest as him. In the three years he'd had the job, he'd never had anything happen on one of the data shifts that had amounted to anything significant. Every time he'd seen some aberration, some strangeness, it had ended up being a dust devil or some other phenomenon that the computers didn't recognise.

As he sat there, in the kind of workplace malaise that you can only get when your job involves nothing but sitting at a desk and waiting, his mind drifted. It danced off so much that it took him a moment to notice the alert chime when it sounded in his earpiece.

He sat up, searching the screens for the aberration. He skipped past the visual feeds; whatever was happening was probably not something that would be obvious to the naked eye. Instead, he consulted a complex set of graphs down in one corner. Each of these had a series of expected rendezvous points from a decentralised timing computer, along with a collection of communiques relating to any single data point in the graph. The left half was blue to indicate events that had occurred on time. The right half was yellow, indicating upcoming events. During the day this graph would slowly update as scheduled events launched successfully. But if he looked closely around the middle, around the rolling point on the graph that meant "now"…

There.

A few minutes ago, a maintenance spacecraft outbound from the launch site he was watching had missed its window by several minutes. It showed up as a red blip on the screen, with a small line connecting it to the yellow indicator of its scheduled launch time.

Keegan sighed as he tapped the dot. It floated to the centre of the screen, and a series of communiques relating to the launch popped up. He flitted through them, trying to find the standard automated release file that would have indicated that the ship had been delayed. On some of the older launch sites, these were still so simple that the system didn't pick them up every time.

After a few minutes of searching, his boredom gave way to frustration. He frowned and called his supervisor.

"What's up?" the supervisor on shift wasn't someone Keegan knew. He had rough features, the kind you tended to see from someone who spent too much time outside without a skinsuit. Pockmarks on his face from where the cancers had been removed, and the slightly shrivelled look of oft-sunburned skin. He didn't sound pleased to have his shift interrupted.

Keegan explained. "This ship, standard satellite repair thing, it went up a while ago. It was due out about an hour before it launched, right? So usually, when that happens, there's some dispatch file that gets logged automatically, saying that there's something delaying it. But it isn't there. What *is* there is a manual record saying that there was an issue with the cargo manifest. But then I check the cargo manifest," he rolled to another screen and pulled up a list of details, "and there's nothing out of place."

The supervisor frowned. "So the cargo manifest isn't changed, but the manual flag said that there was an issue with the cargo?"

Keegan nodded.

"And the ship is moving on a standard trajectory?"

Keegan nodded again, "Yeah, looks like it. No deviation from a usual flight path, and no change to thrust ratios or anything. It still weighs the same."

"So who signed the manual flag?"

Rolling over to the main screen again, Keegan tapped to pull the note up. "Nobody, by the looks of things. No official signature. It's weird."

"Weird," the supervisor agreed, frowning and turning the information over in his mind. Keegan waited patiently, until the supervisor asked if there were any imminent threats to other scheduled events in the area.

"I don't think so, no. The launch found a pretty clear window, there's not much else going on today on that side of the world."

"And is there anything we can do? The ship's in low Earth by now, right?"

Keegan nodded.

"Alright. Well, it's strange but I think you can ignore it. Log the aberration, but don't attach it to a warning release or anything," the supervisor looked around the room, as though to check that nobody else was listening, "It's a spacer ship. Captain was probably hopped up on something and sent out a flurry of files in his stupor. You know how spacers are."

Keegan stayed silent. He'd heard it all before, but he didn't think the spacers aboard the repair ships could be half as bad as what people said. He gave the supervisor the affirmative and watched him as he walked away.

Something about it niggled at him. He'd seen enough in his time at the control centre to get a feeling that *this wasn't nothing*. Whatever had happened to delay this ship, this *Sunward Sky*, was out of the ordinary. Manually logged files didn't just appear without a signature. Automatically logged files didn't just disappear. If the cargo manifest was reported as being wrong, why was it unchanged? And if it had been changed and not logged, how was the ship moving as though it was still the same weight?

He tapped on his keyboard for a few moments, logging the aberration and attaching the relevant files. Quietly, and without fuss, he also added it to a private folder, and spent a few minutes writing notes.

He had a feeling he'd need to refer to them later.

1.5

MAINTENANCE

The three giant wings that sat around the core of the *Sunward Sky* began rotating not long after entering orbit. After spinning up, the interior had something like gravity. The ship's diameter wasn't big enough to have the equivalent of Earth gravity, it would have to spin too fast, and it would induce dizziness in the crew. Instead, it span at one-quarter G, to allow for navigation and walkability but not enough to stop the onset of Space Palsy. The core of the spaceship, with the boosters, cargo hold, engineering and launch couches, didn't spin. Instead, the wings were mounted on enormous ring bearings around the core of the ship.

The outer layer of each wing became the floor, and along the edges of the wing were windows. From there it was possible to see the rest of the ship, and the earth below. Two of the wings had the crew chambers, mess, navigation, storage and a redundant bridge, while the third held enormous tanks of fuel, air, waste recycling, and food which could be ferried via the central shaft when the wings were locked, and the ship was entirely on zero-gravity float.

Inside one of the wings, Healy paced back and forth. The med bay was rudimentary, only holding a flat, long desk full of cabinetry against each wall. Three reclining medical couches, reinforced with the same memory foam as the launch couches, were bolted next to a series of aluminium IV poles and aging AMOLED displays. Now above the Earth, Healy could walk, carabiners clanking gently in the low gravity, moving in balletic arcs just out of time with his gait. The huge man opened one of the cabinets. Inside, medical devices were attached to the inside of the cabinet with velcro. He hummed gruffly, and the velcro rent a crisp tear in the near silence of the medical bay as he pulled a syringe and a small spray can from the wall. He left the cabinet open and lurched gingerly toward Alyssa, who was drugged and lying on one of the beds.

Her leg was a shock of plum-coloured bruises being held together with a lattice of medical tape. Her shoulder had been forced back into place after she'd dislocated it. Healy had put her arm in a sling and fashioned it so that it didn't put pressure on the back of her neck. Her leg, neck, and shoulder were all smeared with a healing anaesthetic foam. Healy pulled on a disposable glove and began to clear the foam away. When he was done, he cleaned the last of it with a cloth, and replaced it with new foam from the can, spreading it evenly with the gloved hand. Then he tossed the glove, cloth, can, and the remnants of the old foam in a tube next to the bed. He placed a small lid over the tube and within a few seconds a vigorous sucking sound took the contents away to the recycling unit.

He pushed the syringe into the muscle of Alyssa's bicep and massaged gently.

Alyssa groaned softly, and her eyelids fluttered open.

"...Hurts..." she breathed.

Healy chuckled as he walked toward her. "I'm not surprised. Frankly, I'm glad you're still in one piece. Usually after a launch like that, people go completely to pieces," he gestured to her bruised leg, "Though you are a mite more colourful than when I last saw you."

"What happened?" she couldn't think straight. When she tried to shake her head, her neck and shoulder spat pain at her. She'd been trying to stop the launch, but she couldn't remember why.

"I don't really know, but I can take a guess," she turned a bloodshot eye toward him as he continued. "You got into the launch sequence. The countdown. The couches. The noise. You freaked the hell out. Ah, don't stress about it. Happens to some people. Though I wouldn't recommend doing it again."

He danced gently upward in the low-g, and wandered away as Alyssa drifted back into a more natural sleep.

It was hours later when she woke up and Healy told her she was free to leave the med bay. She pushed up but wasn't expecting the low gravity and launched herself bodily from the bed, making it most of the way to the low ceiling before gently drifting down again. Feeling like a toddler trying to understand its own muscles, she clambered awkwardly out and loped across to a water fountain. Right arm in a sling, she pulled a cup from a velcro holder on the wall and turned the handle. To her surprise, the water sluiced sideways and moved too slowly, missing the cup completely.

Healy chuckled behind her, "Gotta get used to the spin, Alyssa. You're not on Terra now."

Coriolis effect, she thought to herself, *spin gravity. Of course.* She stared up at a grimy mirror. She looked terrible. Blood pooled behind her skin in black and purple puddles, and her eyes were bloodshot. Her otherwise pale skin made her injuries seem worse, like she was about to come apart at the seams.

She watched Healy as he ambled around the med bay, reattaching stray devices and supplies to the velcro walls and locking the cabinetry together with a series of tight *snikts*. He had the casual yet practised air of experience, enough that it had become ingrained. Leaving items unattended in the medical bay wasn't a matter of personal pride in the workspace though. Leaving things unmoored was a potential death trap in the event of sudden accelerations or manoeuvring. He hummed to himself, allowing Alyssa some small sense of privacy as she took stock.

Her head was still cloudy, but the frantic moments before the launch were coming back to her. She'd made a connection. Captain Sharma had said something about the cargo, and she'd remembered the men in the terminal. Something had twigged in her mind, but she didn't know what. She turned again to the mirror, a polished sheet of aluminium set into the wall, and stared at herself.

Keep yourself together, she thought, staring into the bloodshot of her eyes, *figure out what's happened, then try to talk to someone.* She counted to five, breathed in, then held for two, then out.

She pushed herself off the bench and turned around too forcefully in the low-g and sent herself sprawling and bouncing clumsily off the floor. Healy laughed again, and this time she smiled along.

"You'll get used to it," he said, "probably too used to it. Couple of months and you'll feel awful heavy when you get back down to Terra. You'll end up like me and the rest of the old boys. Then you'll be a spacer, not another Terran."

She'd heard Ellyse use that term, *Terran*, but Healy had said it without the vitriol. Healy just seemed sad, as though he was sorry at the prospect of another Terran becoming too used to life on the drift. The shaking in his hands was gone now they were in space, she noticed. She opened her mouth to speak but was interrupted by the ship's intercom system.

"All personnel, report to main decks for post-launch maintenance work allotment. Repeat, all personnel to main decks for post-launch work allotment."

Alyssa asked the question with a look to Healy, *Me too?* She gestured to her sling and shoulder covered in medical foam.

Healy nodded, "You too. We'll need everyone to be doing something, even if all we get you to do is go around and check the switches."

"I don't even know where the main deck is," she said.

"Ah. No worries, you can come with me, I'm going too. There's two actually. One in the central shaft for when the ship's under thrust, and one in the main personnel wing. We're on the spin now, so ours is just down this hall. Follow me."

With that, he wheeled out of the room and set off, his large frame seeming unburdened by itself in the spin gravity. Alyssa bounced along after him, trying to work out how to propel herself forward effectively without sending herself rocketing into the ceiling. She needed to concentrate, otherwise she found herself lapsing back into the Earthside habit of pushing too firmly upward.

"Post-launch maintenance?" she asked Healy, who continued to rhythmically *thump-clank* his way down the hall, not realising that the small woman was struggling to keep up with him.

"Oh, it's nothing serious," he said, "just… well, *Sky's* an old ship, and launches are violent things, as you've found out. You're pouring a lot of energy and thrust into something that's trying pretty hard to stay on the ground. Things break. If it was something serious you'd know already, but the Captain sends out a work party after launch to make sure it's all, uh, ship shape. Pardon the pun."

The hallway barely fit the two of them abreast. Every few metres, Healy had to duck to avoid structural steel bulkheads. The only features on the walls were the scrapes and marks built up by years of use and age, lit by the uniform glow of low-energy lighting strips. Doorways, labelled plainly, peeled off the main hall every few metres. Alyssa tried to orient herself, to understand where in the ship they were coming from and going to, but there were no waypoints, just this long spine of a corridor running up the ship.

After a short while, Healy brought himself to a stop and entered a door labelled *Crew Mess*. Alyssa followed. Metal tables folded out of the floor with underslung chairs attached. Food dispensers and recyclers were along one wall.

Over the next few minutes a few dozen people filtered

in, either behind Alyssa and Healy, or through an identical door on the other side of the mess. A crisp young woman with a severe haircut and a hand tablet walked through the door. She stood near the dispensers and waited. As people noticed her, the din in the room began to quiet down, until everyone was paying attention. She introduced herself. Alyssa only caught her surname. Waugh.

"I'll be assigning post-launch works to each of you, and we'll be completing these over the next few shifts. Ideally the majority of it will be happening in this shift, but we're aware of some noncritical fixes that will require additional shifts," she looked around the room before continuing, "We know that there was an incident on launch." Alyssa and her sling tried to shrink into the wall. "Those who are injured or unable to fulfil high intensity tasks will perform the systems checks. Those who have the ability to undertake spacewalks or major mechanical repairs will have their resources prioritised," she stepped back, "Any questions?"

A spacewalk! Alyssa tried to hide her disappointment. With her arm in the sling, she wouldn't be taking a spacewalk for the forseeable future. She wanted to ask about ship orientation and whether she'd be assigned a work partner, but someone shouted first. "Yeah, hi. What about the problem with the cargo? Did something happen? Should we be worrying about it?"

So I wasn't the only one who noticed. Alyssa shot a look across the room to see where the voice had come from and found a svelte-looking man with wavy hair and a well-trimmed beard. She drank in the details of his face and clothing; she wanted to talk to him afterward.

Waugh looked annoyed. "I'm sorry, Mister…?"

"Holding."

"Well, Mr Holding. I'd appreciate if you didn't say such things to the group. There are a number of things the Terran authorities demand of us before the *Sunward Sky* can launch. There's no reason to believe it was anything but a launch code error."

That word again. *Terran.*

Waugh had turned from Holding already. "Anyone else?" she spoke over his sputtering attempt to rebut.

Alyssa put her arm down. Something about the way Waugh had dismissed the man made her not want the attention of the crew leader. With that, tasks were handed around the room. Holding got a job on the ship's exterior; apparently a piece of the heat shield had shaken loose and needed replacing. He was paired off with a tall, thin man who had what looked like years of experience under his belt. When Waugh approached Alyssa, she regarded her sling with scorn.

"Ah, yes," Waugh stared. It was an empty look, and Alyssa couldn't read it. "We seem to have a new fish, eager to fling herself from the safety of the bowl."

Alyssa didn't respond, accepting the work orders quietly and without fuss. She was to check all the working rooms in the ship and ensure nothing had been dislodged during launch. She headed back to the hall, and offered a brief thanks to the low gravity environment. Even the minimal weight she had to bear on her knee was enough for her to tell it was sprained. In the float of the hallway she found she didn't have to do much to hide the limp. The rest of the crew rushed past her to attend to their assigned tasks, nobody willing to look idle during the work shift.

She made her way aft, toward the rocket boosters, when she saw Ellyse walking toward her. She seemed distracted, muttering to herself, until Alyssa called to her. She looked up and recoiled slightly at the state of Alyssa's bruised face, but seemed otherwise relieved to see her.

"Alyssa! I'm glad you're alright. I thought you were in serious trouble," Ellyse said. "You were screaming something at me, but I couldn't hear you over the engines. What was it about?"

Alyssa hesitated. Something about the way Waugh had reacted to the questions about the cargo had been off, and an instinct told her to stay quiet until she understood what was happening. She forced a smile. The bruising on her cheeks hurt. "Yeah, sorry. First time up, you know, I just… I kind of freaked. Engines were loud, and I was worried about, you know… being up here."

Ellyse didn't buy it, Alyssa could tell, but she nodded to feign sympathy anyway, "Still a Terran, I suppose. First launch can be rough. Well, I'm glad you're alright." Like Healy, Ellyse could now walk and didn't have the tremor in her hands now that they were out of the gravity well. Ellyse kept moving, muttering to herself and doing the same floating, dancelike walk Alyssa had seen Healy do.

The work shift went by quickly and Alyssa took the opportunity to acquaint herself with the layout of the ship. So far unable to replicate the liquid like movement of the experienced spacers, she trudged from room to room, careful to avoid further injuring her knee. After clearing out and reaffixing items to the wall in a room full of cleaning equipment, she walked back out to the hall. Above her, in the ceiling, there was a hatch, labelled *To Main - Locked in Spin*. It led to the central shaft of the ship, but she wasn't going to be able to access it while the spin gravity was engaged. She would get access at some point in the next few shifts, but for now she was to check the main crew wing, a mixture of crew cabins, med bay, and navigation rooms.

It took Alyssa a second to understand why the hatchway was in the ceiling, but then she understood. When the ship was under thrust, the floor she was walking on would be parallel to the direction of the ship's movement. The hatch would lead to a tunnel or walkway perpendicular to the thrust, and so it made sense to have it mounted that way. It would also mean that when the ship was on Earth, the cargo could be loaded in without needing to worry about it shifting under high-g load.

The various ways the ship could orient itself depending on gravity conditions was starting to give her a headache. She stumped to the next room, which was marked *Navigation - Alt*.

She was several metres into the room before she saw the windows.

She could see the the prominent prow of the ships nose cone, and the aerodynamic forward mast of the ship's wing. The nose cone appeared to be rotating quickly above her head, but she knew in reality it was herself and the other wings that were spinning around it. Beyond the spacecraft was the expanse.

The horizon of the Earth, curved and broiling at its edges with clouds and the blue tinge of oxygen-rich atmosphere, sat in juxtaposition to the endless black that surrounded it. The stars, she'd never seen so many! They painted miniature masks of fire over the dark and threatened to overwhelm the nothingness that somehow still held sway. Far off, the moon glowed, lord of its own empty dominion, shading itself from the brilliant energy of the sun. The inert edges of the *Sunward*

Sky sang alone in their lament to the universe's emptiness; a cold, sharp edge against which nothing fell.

As she stood, transfixed and brooding over the sheer enormity and scale of the universe, the Sun rose over the curved horizon of the Earth. A brilliant ray shot forth and pierced the black, and the lights on the prow of the spacecraft seemed to go dark against the will of the star burning energy through the emptiness at them. A wave of vertigo washed over her and she realised how profoundly small she was, and her mind rallied against her insignificance in the void.

She didn't know how long she'd been there when the two figures appeared next to the prow of the enormous wing. The crisscross pattern that she'd seen on the spacecraft as she'd ascended before liftoff was a series of harness rails. Both spacesuits that the figures wore had safety lines attached to them, with a spring reel at the belt to minimise slack, and a carabiner that looped around the rail. The two people rounded the top of the wing, flipping carefully over it. As she watched, they both disconnected from the safety rail next to the corner they'd just flipped over and attached to the next one.

One of the spacesuits was tattered around the edges and bore the signs of repeated mending and repair. It was larger than the other, and thinner. The second was more pristine, but sagged strangely in the low gravity environment, as though it didn't fit properly. With a start of recognition, Alyssa realised she was looking at Holding, the man who had spoken up in the mess, and his tall spacewalk partner.

Interested, she peered as the two men pirouetted through the void, slowly moving and clipping themselves from one contact point to the next. After a few minutes, the taller man halted, and floated down to inspect the hull of the ship. He thumbed a radio button on his arm, and the other man turned around.

They must have found the broken part of the heat shield, Alyssa thought. The badly fitting spacesuit of the new crew member made a thumbs up, and turned away from the taller man, as if to go and collect something. Holding pushed up and away from the craft, extending his safety line as he did so.

With a movement so fast that Alyssa barely saw it, the taller man reached down and unclipped the carabiner from the safety rail.

The spring retention on the carabiner snapped the clip back into the waist of the brand-new spacesuit, and Holding twisted to see what had happened. Alyssa saw Holding freeze as he realised he was unmoored from the ship. Within a moment, he was twisting to and fro, trying desperately to change his direction to head back toward the ship, but he'd been moving away and he had no way of changing momentum in the void. He kept flailing, desperate and useless, and drifting further and further from the ship. In any other situation, he'd have been able to scream for help, but not here. The cold vacuum of space turned his violent demise into a whispering death. Before long the man was out of sight, nothing more than an out of place speck of white in an endless field of dark stars.

The taller man stood stock still, facing Holding as he scrambled his way into the endless black. When Holding had vanished, the taller man turned back to the broken piece of heat shield, pulled a wrench from his belt and starting to work the injured panel from its mount as though nothing had happened.

Alyssa ducked underneath the sill of the window. Her breath ran hot through her windpipe, and she was trembling as though the Space Palsy had already hit her.

She'd just seen a man murdered.

1.6

MANIFEST

Alyssa couldn't sleep. Images of Holding drifting hopelessly away, dancing into nothingness until his oxygen ran out kept scrambling through her brain. Nothing felt right. The unreal quarter gravity didn't press her duvet onto her enough to feel protective. The pillows were hard but insubstantial, and the space was cool without being cold.

Her breath spat from her in short, sharp bursts.

She'd nearly screamed for help, afterward. As she'd waited under the windowsill, panicking, she'd almost run to Waugh to try to get someone out to help the doomed man.

Two things had stopped her.

Firstly, for someone else to get out to help Holding, they would have to get changed, cycle through the airlock, find where he was and be willing to risk their own lives to go out to get him. The thin man wasn't going to do it. By the time that could happen, the odds of being able to *find* Holding, much less save him, were slim.

Secondly, there had been something about the way the thin man had done it. He'd waited for the right moment. He'd executed it, furiously fast and well-practiced. He'd disconnected the safety line from the rail and then floated. He'd stared silently as he'd watched Holding float off into the emptiness. He'd killed the radio, and then he had gone back to work. The nonchalance was what chilled Alyssa, and it made her wonder if he'd done it before. If so, had someone perhaps *told* him to do it?

So she'd done nothing. She'd waited for the thin man to move out of view of the window, then forced herself back into an air of disinterested calm and continued her rounds, trying to keep it together until she'd climbed into bed. Her heart was still hammering, and she felt it thud even harder whenever she stopped to think about it. She'd lie there on the edge of sleep and at the final moment, in that lurch in the liminal space of the mind, Holding's body would float through her consciousness and into oblivion. She'd jerk awake and stare at the scuffed ceiling of her cabin for a while before repeating the whole process again.

Finally, Alyssa flung the duvet off her and twisted her body, letting her feet drift down to the cool ground. Her toes brushed the metal, and the pads of her feet seemed to almost bounce on the floor as she moved to her clothing locker.

She dressed quickly, pulling on the standard work

overalls and safety boots. A bottle of pills was velcroed against the wall.

She laughed. The whole reason she was up here, and she'd forgotten until now because of everything that had happened. She grabbed the bottle and took one of them out. It was poorly made, chalky and rough around the edges. She dry swallowed it, and gagged.

❖ ❖ ❖

I have to tell someone, she thought as she walked through the hall. She was still limping, but her knee and her shoulder were improving thanks to the treatment from Healy. It would only be a couple of days before she'd have full use again.

Who to tell, though? If the tall man had been following orders, there was no knowing who it was that issued them. If she told the wrong person, she'd be next on the list.

She shuddered, and stopped walking as a message came over the intercom. The speakers were low quality, but it sounded like Waugh's clipped tones.

"We have had an incident on board. A first time crew member, one Michael Holding, suffered an accident while on a spacewalk to fix the heat shield. It appears Mr Holding failed to properly affix his safely line to the rail appropriately, and upon realising his mistake, was unable to radio for help to his workmate. We must impress upon all crew members that safety measures are in place to ensure that accidents such as these do not happen. Ensure radios are in working order prior to spacewalks, and make doubly sure that you are securely attached to the ship before undertaking any repairs. Thank you."

The message was more callous than Alyssa would have ever expected, with a matter-of-fact tone that belied the reality of the tragedy. Not only that, she knew it was a lie. Holding's spacesuit hadn't been in ill repair, it was brand new. She'd *seen* the other man release the safety latch, and she'd even seen when he'd thumbed the radio, jamming it so that Holding couldn't call for help.

With dawning dread, she realised that not only had she witnessed a murder, she was now witnessing a coverup.

Her intuition to tell someone couldn't be trusted. She couldn't possibly trust anyone until she could understand who had known about Holding's death beforehand. She couldn't ask anyone about what had happened to the cargo. She couldn't tell anyone about anything she'd seen until she knew, beyond a shadow of a doubt, that they would believe her and be on her side.

With a start she realised she'd been standing in front of the mess for some time, and a couple of people working the second shift had stared as they walked past. She must have made quite a sight, standing there, staring into nothingness, wrapped in slings and plaster.

She turned around and stumped back off toward her cabin. Once she got there, she stripped back down to her underwear and pulled the duvet back over herself. She didn't secure it properly; her clothing lay loose on the floor. Any strange manoeuvres would result in her belongings flying around the cabin.

For some time more, her fright at her situation fought with the tiredness coursing through her body. She turned her shoulder slowly, feeling it loosen up in the sling.

Before too long, she slipped into a fitful sleep.

The motors that rotated the three wings of the *Sunward Sky* were enormous impulse driven electromagnets. A series of step-up transformers drew power from highly efficient solar cells on the hull. These sent powerful bursts of current through the electromagnets, which turned the wings fast enough for the artificial gravity to work.

Three days after the spaceflight began, as Alyssa lay in her cabin dreaming fitfully, the impulses being sent to the electromagnets weakened in both intensity and duration. The spin of the wings slowed down, gradually at first. After some time, though, the gravity change became more noticeable. Plates full of food bounced as they were set down. Walking was both easier, as it was possible to move with less effort, and harder, as it took time to readjust to the unusual movement of null-g.

Before long the wings had stopped rotating entirely, and a series of small motors engaged to align the walkway Alyssa had seen. With a loud series of *clunks*, the ship shifted around itself slowly. Finally, the entry shaft aligned with the hatch.

Four people wearing masks floated down the now empty hallways of the ship. Everyone was asleep in their cabins. They reached the hatch in what had been the ceiling of the hall and pulled it gently open.

One stood aside and held the hatch behind him as the other three pushed themselves off the floor into the shaft. Once they were through, he pulled his weight around and followed them. He pulled the hatch closed behind him.

❖ ❖ ❖

Alyssa woke up to a boot bumping her nose. Groggy, she swatted at it and sent it careening across the room. A few dazed and confused seconds ensued as she remembered where she was, noticed the lack of gravity, and tried in vain to orient herself to the room's normal orientation. The boot drifted off and clanged against the door, and by the time she'd turned herself right way up it had bounced back. It hit her square in the jaw.

She swore softly, rubbing her injured shoulder and her struck jaw, and regarded the floating mess in her quarters. It hurt less than she would have assumed considering it had only been a few days since the accident.

She pushed herself off the wall next to her bunk and floated around, collecting her belongings that were strewn in the air. She caught a reflection of herself off the burnished surface of the bulkhead. She saw pale bruise marks around hollow eye sockets, but her eyes were clear again and no longer bloodshot.

A globule of water was slowly forming around the head of the tap, the surface tension wrapping over the faucet and expanding outward in a shimmering sphere. She splashed the bubble with her hand. Water flew everywhere in droplets, and she smiled, hunting down the shimmering globes, sipping while she somersaulted through the air.

When all the water bubbles were gone, she lay back into her newfound weightlessness and drifted, lightly bumping off the walls and ceilings of her room, orienting herself this way and that, trying to get rid of the notion of *up and down* that her mind was so keen to impress upon her.

She couldn't get Holding's death out of her mind. It left her with a gnawing unease, and she kept seeing the flash of a carabiner unhooked from a safety rail and drifting into space.

If she wanted to understand what was going on, she'd

have to go to the cargo bay.

❖ ❖ ❖

The easiest way to move in null-g was to treat the structural bulkheads like footholds on a climbing wall and vault herself along with her legs, only using her arms to guide herself. If she'd done it any other way, the smaller muscles of her arms would have worn out and she'd not have had the ability to fly through the hall as easily as she did. She vaulted up and along the hallways, treating it more like an elevator shaft than a corridor.

Before long, she found what she'd been looking for; the hatch that read *To Main - Locked in Spin* that she'd passed earlier that day. It was shut, but not tight. It took a little while in the null-g, but Alyssa was able to spin the handle by wedging herself against a bulkhead and pushing with her legs. She shuddered, suddenly cold. With a glance up and down the hallway, she pressed a hand against the bulkhead and pulled the hatch open, then slid inside.

The tunnel that linked the wing to the cargo bay was claustrophobic and bathed in dim red light. Black shadows stretched out over handholds, and Alyssa guided herself down to the core of the ship. Soon, the shaft and its lights disappeared as Alyssa shot past the end of the tunnel and into the centre of the cargo bay.

She heard muffled voices and panicked.

She was drifting through the air and didn't have any way to correct her course. The voices were coming from the other side of the cargo bay, the direction she was drifting towards.

Several cargo crates, large and black, were stacked on top

of each other, not quite in her path. She reached out, grabbed the edge of one and her body pivoted in the air. She reached her other hand out to halt herself against the edge of the container, decelerating slowly by pushing against it. As quietly as she could, she scrambled down one side and hid behind the container.

There were three or four voices floating across the recycled air. Alyssa could tell they were close by and danced from container to container to get some distance from them. The crates were all tied down with heavy duty straps and hooked either to the floor or to a crate below. They were all the same size, and were fitted with locking plates to keep them from moving in the null-g. On their sides were shipping tags marked with a hex code, along with Anglo and Mando details of the crate's cargo and destination. She read the Mando side: Shipment boarding *Sunward Sky,* a date, and a code next to the destination marked "G-Sync PRC 2081". Next to the tag was an indecipherable string of letters and numbers.

She guessed that G-Sync PRC 2081 was the satellite number, and the string of letters and numbers were parts in the container. Probably solar cells or something.

The container she was inspecting was strapped to another. She pulled herself carefully upward and checked the tag. It was destined for the same satellite. *Makes sense,* Alyssa thought, *they can grab it all at once and shunt it out for install.* She moved to the next row and sure enough, they were all destined for a different geosynchronous satellite.

Keeping a close ear on the voices nearby, and making sure they didn't get too close, she inspected the manifest stickers on each of the containers. They were mainly destined for geosynchronous global positioning satellites, but occasionally one would have a code for a photographic mapping array or radar kit. Most of the contents were similar to the first she'd seen, indecipherable codes for what she assumed were parts replacements.

She didn't know what she was looking for, but something told her she'd know it when she found it. Holding had said something about the cargo, and the two men in the terminal had been moving a crate that looked just like these.

She was getting too close to the voices and she worried about being heard. Their voices were muffled, and she couldn't make out what they were saying.

It was getting too risky.

She turned to head back to the wing, then saw it.

The other storage crates were all the same size, even the one she'd seen before the launch. They were long, wide and squat. Uniform and stacked neatly for deployment. Each had the same matte black finish casting satin reflections of the red lights, and brushed steel corners that clipped into each other.

This wasn't like that.

It was all white ceramic and silver chrome, segmented and enormous, and the red light shone off it like a mirror from hell. The cables holding it in place were three times the size of those on the other containers as though the thing were apt to burst to life. Somehow it gave the impression of a coiled scorpion, ready to unfurl and strike at any moment. Alyssa stared at it. She had no idea what it was, but she knew it had something to do with everything she'd seen aboard the ship so far.

She floated, wondering what she could do. It seemed so *brazen*, the thing being out in the open like this. It leered at her in the dark, glowing faintly with red light.

I can't tell any of the installation crew, she realised, *They must all be in on it, otherwise they wouldn't be able to hold it in the open like this.* Mentally, she ticked half the crew off the list of people she could trust.

"This is the last one?" the voice was female, and *close.* Alyssa's attention had slipped and the others in the cargo bay had moved closer. It sounded as though they were on the other side of the container. Alyssa froze.

"Yeah. All the others have been in place for ages," this voice was male, deep and gravelly. "I don't think we're likely to have any more trouble."

"Where are we dropping it?"

"First dock. We managed to get the launch times right. It made the most sense for navigation to have this one come up first."

Alyssa was breathing hard. She was surprised nobody could hear her. *All the others have been in place for ages.* What others?

"We're not going to have any more issues, are we? I don't want more questions."

Alyssa jumped as the man burst into laughter. His voice rasped as he spoke, "Fucking Terrans! Nosy fucks. They snoop around asking questions but they don't fucking understand. It's too easy. Take 'em up, offer to show 'em the sights and then tell 'em to jump. After that it's a flip of a switch, isn't it? Send 'em floating off. See if they ask any more questions."

Terran. That word again. They were referring to Earthsiders as *Terrans,* and the way they said it. It was like a slur.

"Nah, that Holding was the last one who knew. We're

pretty sure that's the one Brett saw on the ground while he was swapping out the crates."

Brett.

Brett was on board.

Alyssa had heard enough. She pushed herself backward off the crate, but in her panic didn't adjust for null-g. The straps on the crate rattled and shook and a "What was that?" shot from the other side.

A series of thumps came from behind the container as the others pushed off flat surfaces and came after her. She had a head start but there were three, no, four of them. She bounded from container to container, no longer trying to be quiet, just accelerating as fast as possible back to the hatch. A few seconds later she saw it, sitting out in a yawning chasm between the crate she'd halted next to on the way in, over a walkway she'd missed before. She considered ducking down and hiding, to see if she could sneak past them but decided not to risk it. Instead, she pushed her legs as hard as she could, flinging herself desperately toward the hatch and careened into the shaft.

Two people rounded the corner as she shot into the tunnel.

Shit, did they see me? She thought, ripping herself down the handholds as fast as she could. The red lights made the tunnel into a blur, and she pulled herself down at a breakneck clip. The others followed her down, crawling like spiders, trying to reach her before she got to the end of the tunnel.

It didn't work. She burst out into the hall with a gasp and slammed her injured shoulder into the deck. Swearing, she pivoted and pushed back up to the ceiling of the hall, twisting to get into position to close the hatch. Pressing her legs against the bulkhead, she gripped the heavy door with both hands and slammed it shut. As she raced away, she heard the thud of several bodies hitting the hatch. It clicked open a few seconds later, but by then she was out of the hall, flicking her way back to her cabin. They hadn't seen her.

She was almost sure of it.

Back in her cabin, she pulled the door shut, her chest heaving and shoulder aching almost as badly as it had when she'd woken up after the launch. With a kind of frenzied determination, she stripped off her coveralls and threw them at the wall in impotent rage. She wanted to scream, but they would have heard her.

She curled into a ball and cried.

1.7

IDEOLOGY

The mess was nearly empty.

Perfect, Alyssa thought, and snuck in, moving fluidly to one of the seats in the corner and sitting with her back to the wall. The incident in the cargo hold had made her leery of the other crew members, and she'd avoided being out of her room when she wasn't on a shift.

She didn't know who she could trust.

Of the two men in the terminal, one of them was aboard. Brett. They had been taking one of the crates off the *Sunward*

Sky, which they'd replaced with… whatever that thing was. She'd been in the wrong place, and they'd heard her and tried to find her. When Holding had said that *he'd* noticed something odd about the cargo, they had brutally dispatched him to the cold, uncaring void of space.

And that would have been it. There would have been no reason to worry about being discovered, until she'd got nosy. Until she'd gone to the cargo hold, like an idiot! They'd seen someone there, and now they were looking for her.

She had to assume Waugh, the crew leader who had doled out the work orders, knew. She had to, otherwise how had Holding been allocated to the man who would kill him? Alyssa hadn't recognised Waugh's voice in the cargo hold, and there had been four voices she'd heard.

That meant there were at least five people aboard the ship who knew, plus Brett.

Six people to avoid.

She had only got one good look at the chrome thing before she'd been pursued. It looked mechanical and insectoidal, as though the segments would unfold and split like the carapace on an enormous arachnid. It loomed in her mind as she struggled to make sense of what it meant for her and for *her* mission on the craft.

She toyed idly with her food. In the low gravity, the combination of peas and the surface tension of the water droplets and gravy left the whole thing with a jelly-like consistency. Things stuck together just longer than they should, and the water didn't settle quite right in her cup when she set it back down.

There was one thing that kept her from flying into a full-blown panic. There had been no communication about someone being in the cargo bay when they shouldn't have been. No shipwide warning or public manhunt. That meant that the crew leadership wasn't involved. Or at least, they weren't all involved. Which meant that whatever they did to find her, they had to do it in secret. For now.

She rolled her shoulder back, grimacing, and continued to eat. The low gravity was reducing her appetite. She pushed the variously coloured vegetables and proteins around the plate, occasionally shovelling a forkful into her mouth.

"Alyssa?"

Alyssa snapped her head up in the direction of the voice, cursing her lack of vigilance. Ellyse had sat down across from her, so quietly she hadn't noticed.

"Oh, it's you," Alyssa said guardedly.

Ellyse ignored the cold tone, "Seen you in here on your own a few times now, and not much anywhere else. Space getting you down?"

Alyssa sighed, "Something like that." The urge to confide in her was so strong, but something held her back. Ellyse seemed so much more comfortable in space than she had in the terminal on Earth. Now she was back in orbit, the nervous tremors and wobbling and tics had gone away. She stared at Alyssa, calm and confident.

Ellyse nodded, "You'll get used to it. You're still a Terran. You still move like one of them."

Alyssa breathed out. *Terran.* She kept hearing that term. The captain had referred to people who lived on Earth as *dirtsiders,* not *Terrans.* But quite a few of the crew used the other term, and never in a positive light.

"You're not going to make many friends, sitting in the

corner like this," Ellyse said, gesturing to the smattering of other crew members in the room, "and you'd better make friends. Not too long and the palsy'll get you, too. It doesn't care if you've got a stick up your ass or not."

Ellyse sat loosely opposite Alyssa, and for the first time Alyssa saw the slight differences that made her look like a *dirtsider*. A *terran*. *Her* feet were firmly on the ground, and she gripped both seat and table edge, consciously maximising the number of contact points with something solid. It was as though she was willing her body down into gravity that was no longer there. She was tense on the chair. Ellyse's arms and body drifted to and fro with freedom like an anemone in a light tide. She would adjust her movements with minute and barely considered flicks, making sure her body stayed in the right place. The flicks and twitches seemed as ingrained as Alyssa found them uncanny. Alien, even. Nobody from down the gravity well could have moved like that.

"So when do I learn how to move properly?" she asked.

Ellyse fixed her with an unreadable expression. "It depends. Most people get it early, on their first run. Some take a little longer. Usually, by the time you've got the float down, you've got the palsy. Then you can move up here, but you can't go dirtside again."

Alyssa stayed silent. Space Palsy was why she was here, but she'd never head the other half of the story, the way you learned to move effectively in your new environment even as your muscles degraded and your bones softened. She wondered briefly why there hadn't been any research about it, but she knew; Once people learned how to move it was too late.

Until her.

"How long did it take you?" Alyssa asked.

"Three circuits. I've always been a slow learner. By the time I got back onto the ground the third time, I could dance around these halls with the best of them, but I couldn't hold myself still down there," Ellyse pointed vaguely away from the table.

Alyssa hesitated. "Is that why you all seem to hate the *Terrans*?"

"Ha!" Ellyse seemed amused at the use of the term, "I mean, that's part of it."

"Why? What has it got to do with," she bit back the word *us*. "Them?"

When Ellyse answered, there seemed to be a low, deep growl to her voice. A fury that resonated permanently just beneath the surface.

"*Everything* has got to do with them. The whole world is run from up here. You *think* about it. You want to go to your friend's house, you hitch a ride. The ride can't navigate but for the Geosync system, which is run from these satellites. You want to watch the latest vid dramas? They're streamed the world over, and they do that by bouncing off comms satellites. You watch the world decaying, and to do that you take pictures with satellites that *we* maintain. The Terrans take all this, and spacewalkers provide the means, and it slowly kills us. Silent, like, up here where the Terrans can ignore us."

"I don't know what to say," Alyssa said.

"I'm sure you don't."

"So, what…?"

Ellyse hissed angrily. "I'll tell you what. I'll tell you *exactly* what. This is the job with *the highest* chance of injury, disability or death. Of *anything*. Any job still done by humans.

We have a near *one hundred per cent* incident rate if you're on two or more rotations. People know it, but there's nothing to do about it, and there's no oversight at all. We're just the unfortunates that drew short straw. They build pieces of shit like the *Sunward Sky* and pile us on. You go a few rounds and you *know*. You just *know* that you'll be stuck on here forever. You *know* that your life down a gravity well is over. That you'll get the palsy," Ellyse's careful dance had become frantic; tiny taps and kicks pushing her body this way and that. "And for what? There are so many of us up here. Repairing the Geosync satellites. Increasing the power and bandwidth of the video networks. Clearing and resetting overloaded memory caches. Replacing solar panels. Getting sick from a known chronic disease, suffering and dying and for *what*? So the Terrans that are lucky enough to not have to come up here can have their automated deliveries and their vidstreams?"

Alyssa said nothing. The words *I'm sorry* and *that's awful* and *I didn't know* felt so wrong. The fact was that if she wasn't careful, before long she'd be one of them. One of the souls lost to the Earth forever, floating through the void, performing routine tasks that required only just enough creativity that they couldn't be automated.

She looked at Ellyse. The older woman's eyes were moist and filled with long held rage.

"I'm sorry," Alyssa said, and the words sounded pathetic and small, and felt like she was trying to absolve rather than apologise. She stood from the table, uncomfortably aware of the heaviness of her movements as she crossed the mess and threw the last of her scraps in the recycler. Ellyse stared blankly ahead and ignored Alyssa as she left the mess.

Alyssa tried to glide, to tap herself down the empty hall the way she saw the spacers do, but she couldn't get it. She trudged heavily, bouncing down the hall feeling clunky and overlarge until she got into the med bay.

"Hiya, Healy," the big man looked up from a tablet with a series of scrawled notes on it, then grunted and gestured for her to sit in one of the bucket-seat couches.

"How's the knee?" he said.

"Still stiff in the mornings. It's definitely better though, not giving me the grief it was before."

Healy grunted again, this time in modest approval. He flicked himself gently toward her; Alysssa couldn't believe she'd never noticed how lightly the experienced travellers moved before now. He checked her pupillary response, then prodded her shoulder. She gasped, and he frowned.

"Mmm. Your shoulder was clearing up well but then you ran into that door."

She'd told Healy she had run her shoulder into a closing door on her rounds, not that she'd flown at high speed out of the cargo bay into the ground of the corridor. She still wasn't sure if he bought it.

"Yeah," she said, "it hurts, but only when I try to do something stupid with it." *Like vault myself through a tube while I'm being chased.* He didn't respond, turning to a machine showing a colourful series of numbers and graphs. He frowned.

"Alyssa. Do you take any medication? Aside from the painkillers I've been giving you?"

"No," Alyssa said, too quickly. Healy didn't seem to notice. A few minutes later he shut off the tablet and turned to her.

"You've come a long way in not much time," He said. "I didn't think your body would hold up the way it has. You're not showing any of the muscle and bone degradation I'd expect," he gave her a look, "It's strange. Usually you can detect the palsy quite quickly, but not with you."

Alyssa said nothing.

"Alright. Well, aside from that, your shoulder is healing. Again, because you haven't seen the degradation I'd expect, I think your body is able to heal more like what a Terran might. Give it a day or two and you'll be right as rain."

This time, Alyssa nodded. She didn't trust herself to say anything, lest she reveal the relief running through her. This was the first indication that it was working. Healy placed his instruments into the velcro holders and threw his gloves in the recycler. Alyssa heard the door open behind her, and someone stepped into the chamber.

"Is she cleared?" Waugh demanded.

"Two days hence," Healy said, "she's just got a final—"

"Good," the crew leader interrupted, then to Alyssa, "report to the main airlock at 0700 in two days' time. We're transferring cargo to the first of the geosync satellites and it's about time you made yourself useful." She walked back out the door without another word and without waiting for Alyssa to respond.

Alyssa didn't move. The last time she'd seen Waugh send someone on a spacewalk they'd ended up drifting alone through the void.

"You alright?" Healy was still in cleaning mode, distracted, moving things, stepping hither and thither, replacing things to their proper location. "You seem a bit spooked."

No shit, Alyssa thought, but said, "It's nothing. Waugh just… she's a bit intense."

Healy laughed. "True enough!" he said, and turned back to his cleaning as Alyssa tried and failed once again to flick herself lightly down the hall like a true spacer.

Once she was back in her room, she shut the door and looked into the mirror, then turned to her wardrobe. Beneath the pile of clothes was her toiletries bag, hidden at the bottom. Toothbrush, deodorant, toothpaste, floss, and mouthwash all sat attached to small velcro tabs. Next to this was a small first aid kit and the vial of painkillers Healy had given her. And then there was the container. She pulled it off the velcro and slipped off the lid. She pulled out one of the chalky pills, careful not to grip too hard lest it crumble in her hand. Without looking, she threw it into the back of her throat, and grimaced as she dry swallowed.

1.8

DOCKING

There was never true darkness on the ship. Even during third shift, the "sleep shift", when there were minimal operational lights, infrared wayfinding lights shone at ground level, and the halls of the *Sunward Sky* glowed darkly.

The cabins were the same. None of them had windows, and complete darkness and low gravity was a recipe for disorientation. Alyssa lay, staring at the ceiling in the middle of the ship's night, watching the place where the blood red lights turned to black shadows.

The alarm she'd set began to ring, to wake her from a

sleep that had never come. She groaned and switched it off, then sat up. She pulled on the pale grey undersuit and a pair of shoes, then sat on the edge of the cot and kept staring as the lights in her room rose from blood red to cool white.

Before she'd boarded, she'd wanted to do a spacewalk more than anything else. It was the one thing she thought would make it worth it. But then she'd seen Holding murdered, and now her first spacewalk was being scheduled by the woman who had rostered Holding. The inside of the ship felt at once claustrophobic and cold as well as warm and inviting. After she'd found the monstrous construction in the cargo bay she'd have given anything to get out of the ship, anywhere but the endless hallways full of people she didn't know.

Now though, the prospect of leaving the ship on Waugh's orders terrified her.

Eight spacesuits hung from the wall. Four of them were decidedly worse for wear. These four had name tags attached and bore a series of customisations from their owners. One of them had five sets of carabiners on the waist instead of the usual two, another had what looked like a small oxygen canister sitting above the right wrist. All of them had been patched and repaired any number of times.

Alyssa was early, but one of the new suits already had a note with her name on it. She picked the suit up and looked it over. It was a flexible carbon-fibre weave on the outside with a thick layer of insulation on the inside. Sandwiched between the two, she knew, was an airtight layer. The insulation was scratchy to the touch and was pressed carefully around any junctions or breaches in the suit. Sensors on the inside connected to a panel on the suits right arm. Alyssa flicked it on and it gave off a series of error codes where there should have been life signs. She switched the display off again and continued to check over the suit for signs of tampering, even though she wasn't sure what exactly she was looking for.

She was bent to her work when the door slid open behind her. Startled, she jumped around to the man stood in the doorway. He looked at her incredulously, surrounded as she was by spacesuit parts. She'd been disassembling one of the arms, taking radio buttons, display indicators and sensors off their foam and rubber mounts. They were placed carefully on the ground in a mockup of their original positions. As the man watched, she replaced the parts one by one, then snapped the head of the casing onto the radio panel. She flipped a switch, and the air filled with static from inside the helmet that was abandoned some feet away.

"It works," she said.

"Course it works," he said. "Damn thing's near brand new." He didn't look like a spacer. He was wearing the same grey undersuit that Alyssa had on, and she could see his muscles moving beneath the skintight clothing. He wandered to the suit with the extra carabiners and began running some diagnostics himself.

"Yeah, I just thought I'd check," Alyssa said, "first time out, you know? Nerves."

The man didn't look at her. The tag above his spacesuit read *LEE, B*. "Ah, Terran girl. Try not to think too much about it. We're just upgrading a satellite. Geostationary satellite. The new instruments will be able to tell you where you are on Earth within a couple inches. If you're down there." The man's voice seemed familiar. He hummed as he checked his suit.

Alyssa was confused. He moved like a spacer. His suit was well worn and customised, and he'd used that word — *Terran* — that she'd heard so often, but he clearly wasn't suffering from Space Palsy. Not yet, anyway. She asked him about it, how he managed to stave it off.

"Ah, yeah," he said, "this is only my second longhaul trip. Before this I was doing shuttle work. You come up for between two and four days on a small ship that's sent out to fix emergencies, rather than these maintenance missions. You get enough time off in between for you to build your strength again. Four days isn't enough for you to atrophy completely." His face went dark, "I've seen what happens, though. Even if I don't suffer from it, I've been around the traps long enough. You get so sick, so immobilised, that you can't survive on Earth. They have to put you in flotation tanks when it gets really bad."

Every time any of the spacers talked about the palsy, there was a fury in their voices, a darkling anger and a shared lament. Alyssa worked a little longer, then turned back to the man.

"What's your name?"

He held out his hand. "Brett."

Ice shot through her veins.

Brett.

Brett from the terminal.

She shook his hand, conscious of the clamminess of her own. She released quickly, not trusting herself to make eye contact with him, and threw herself back into checking over her suit. Time slowed, and she felt the thrum of the ship's rotational gravity through her feet as she tried to concentrate on anything but the room she was in. Brett took one more step and opened his mouth to say something when the door cycled and three other crew members walked in.

Waugh was in the lead, flanked by the long thin man that had dispatched of Holding and a young woman she didn't recognise. The thin man made his way to the worn out suits and started checking his over without a word. The other woman seemed less certain of herself, and crept quietly to the suit next to Alyssa. Brett turned to Waugh.

"Morning, Brett," Waugh said, then turned to the young woman, "Isa may need some assistance getting her suit ready."

Brett nodded, then smiled at the thin man. "Morning, Clarke."

Isa looked very nervous. There were goosebumps on her dark skin and she kept glancing into the airlock. From their position in the aft of the ship, they could occasionally glimpse the edge of the Earth in the endless sea of stars through the porthole. Alyssa, glad for the distraction from Brett, introduced herself to Isa.

"You okay?" she asked, "you look like you're about to faint."

Isa nodded, "I've never been out before. Not sure I want to. I just drew the short straw this time."

Alyssa smiled, "That's okay. I've never been out either. Let's just have a look at this equipment, yeah? Make sure it's all holding up okay? That way at least we'll know we're safe."

Reassuring Isa gave Alyssa new strength, and she bit back her own fears and found steel. Isa nodded, and her eyes, which had looked about to pop from her head, returned to more normal dimensions as she calmed down. Together, the two of them worked through the prep procedures for the spacesuit, double and triple checking every seal and moving part. As they worked more people came into the room and soon the space was crammed and starting to slightly overheat with the warmth of the bodies.

At one point, Waugh walked over to where the two women were working on the suit. Alyssa was squatting on the floor with her elbows resting on her knees comfortably, and the crew leader stood over her. She said nothing, simply stared.

Alyssa stared straight back. She reached down slowly to the arm of the spacesuit, then keyed the button on the exposed panel. She clicked her fingers over it, and a VU meter of green lights lit up to indicate that it had received the audio and was transmitting.

"Looks like the radio works," she said. Isa nodded, but Alyssa was staring daggers at Waugh.

Waugh held her gaze for a moment or two, then smirked and walked off to speak to Brett and Clarke.

"What was that about?" Isa asked.

An hour later, they were outside the hull. Alyssa felt as though she was standing upside down on the bottom of a boat, looking down into the depths of an endless ocean of shimmering lights. The other new crew members huddled with her, carefully holding their guide ropes and double checking they were secured to the safety points on the hull. The Earth loomed in Alyssa's vision but the nothingness beyond bypassed all meaning in her mind. All her hindbrain knew was to tell her *that way means death.* A beautiful, dreamlike death, or a screaming silent death like Holding's.

And yet she felt the strange yearning, like driving on a highway at night, or leaning out over a cliff face. The urge to leap away, to swerve sharply and permanently into darkness, was as present as her horror at the thought.

One of the more experienced spacewalkers was briefing Alyssa, Isa, and the other huddled first-timers. "The safety lines *will not break* on you. They are *extremely* strong." The radio crackled, and Alyssa strained to see if she could identify it as one of the voices from the cargo hold. She couldn't tell. There was too much static.

"Your job today is simple," the spacer continued. "The four of us will be exporting cargo from the *Sunward*. We've already docked with the satellite, but we aren't in contact, we've just matched our speed and direction. You four will be taking the cargo that Brett and Clarke are shifting out," He pointed to an open cargo bay halfway along the fuselage, "and moving it to the sat. When it's all moved, you four will go back inside while we wire it all up. Clear?"

Alyssa nodded inside her helmet, then remembered that she had the sunshield down and her face wasn't visible. She and the others gave a thumbs up, and headed to the edge of the cargo bay.

A spacewalk.

She was *on a spacewalk*. She'd dreamed of it, once she'd known what she'd have to do. Nothing more than thin layers of clever materials between herself and the nothingness that held sway between the planets and the stars. But instead of joy and release, she was anxious, the image of Holding reflecting against the sunshield in her helmet. Making her jumpy, waiting for the same to happen to her. Every step she took she was double checking her contact points, looking to see if anyone was blocking the radio like she'd seen the man she now knew as Clarke do.

Isa was directly in front of her, clasping the outside of the spaceship for dear life. *She can't be more than seventeen,* Alyssa thought. Isa's frame had the dire lankness of someone chronically underfed and still desperately trying to grow. The spacesuit swam on her. It had taken several tries to pad the gloves enough for her to use her fingers effectively. Her face was hidden by the sunshield, and she was facing away from Alyssa but her body language still looked terrified.

A black fury rose in Alyssa's throat. She'd known, or at least she'd heard about the conditions on the repair ships, but she hadn't been prepared for the reality. It wouldn't have surprised her to find that Isa had grown up sleeping rough and had jumped at the opportunity for a bunk and regular meals despite her obvious fear of space.

The solar wings and tin can abdomen of the satellite floated a few feet above the surface of the *Sunward Sky*, at relative halt next to it. It looked as though the craft was hovering effortlessly, despite both machines moving at several thousand metres per second. Alyssa shivered.

For the next few hours, the new crew members ferried small items across from the cargo bay to the satellite. Solar panels, memory cache and cable patches, all delivered in the same black and silver crates Alyssa was becoming all-too familiar with.

The satellite was old. The panelling was worn and pitted by micro-impacts of space junk. It was dark, dull grey fading down to burned black. Some of these panels were replaced as well, and Alyssa took the old parts back to the cargo hold, leaving them on the lip for Brett and Clarke to stow away.

Once they were done, Alyssa and the new members were told to head back inside the airlock and were allowed to strip out of their sweat-ridden underclothes and shower in a special anteroom nearby.

Alyssa pulled on a fresh crew jumpsuit and headed back to the main chamber. Isa stood there smiling, white teeth shining against her skin, all signs of fear gone. Alyssa couldn't help but grin back.

"That was amazing!" Isa said.

Alyssa agreed, despite herself. Her fears had been unfounded. They hadn't done to her what she'd seen happen to Holding. "It was pretty cool, actually. It feels so *empty* out there."

Isa nodded emphatically and began talking animatedly about the experience of the space walk. Alyssa was bone tired, but listened politely, her own mood being lifted by the infectious enthusiasm of the young girl. They exited the prep room and started walking toward the mess.

Isa was babbling excitedly beside her. "Honestly, at the start I was *totally* freaked out about being on the *outside* of the spaceship. I mean, it's space, right? There's nothing out there to help if something goes wrong, you don't want to mess around with it! But then after a bit I realised that the safety lines are there for a reason, right, and I could relax my grip. When I was waiting for one of the loads, I started letting myself drift off, just a little bit, 'til I bounced on the end of the safety line. Then I'd float back down and stick to the satellite like an insect. It was *so* much fun."

Like an insect, Alyssa thought, and the thing from the cargo hold sprang to her mind. Hadn't she heard them say something about *First Dock?*

"Hold on," Alyssa interrupted Isa's excited rant, "I think I left something in the prep room. Let me go back and have a look."

Without waiting for a reply, Alyssa turned on her heel and jogged back down the hall. She flicked her heels underneath her smoothly, beginning to bounce in the easy rhythm of those familiar with shipboard life.

She entered the prep room, checked that nobody else was there, walked to the airlock and cycled the inner door. She sprang into it and flung herself at the window, peering out.

The four remaining workers were not on the satellite. All the parts that Alyssa and Isa and the others had painstakingly transported hung limp on wires from within the sat, gleaming and drifting in space. The satellite seemed ripped, a hopeless creature pulled apart and left gasping.

The workers were clambering over and manoeuvring the ceramic and chrome box that Alyssa had seen in the cargo bay, but it was no longer merely a box. It had unfurled, and the insectoid links she'd seen had become gigantic metallic tendrils that reached toward the satellite. As she watched, the space suits pushed the thing toward its body.

It looked carnivorous. Parasitic. The chrome tendrils pushed outward from the main body of the thing like the interlocking tarsals of a praying mantis. The crew flung itself toward the satellite and the outreaching tip of the insect pressed into the holes left where the panelling had been removed. The thing seemed to awaken, ratcheting itself inward, onto the satellite, enveloping it. The replacement panels served as cold welding points for the monstrous mechanism, and before long the satellite was subsumed. The bright metal and ceramic wrapped around it, and four tiny figures danced weightlessly back to the cargo bay.

Alyssa stepped back, and nearly ran into Isa as she turned around. Her smile was gone, and she was looking out the window at the thing.

"What is *that?*" she said.

1.9

DISCLOSURE

Alyssa grabbed Isa's upper arm and pulled her away from the window in the airlock, to cycle it before the crew came back.

"What are you doing?" Isa said, "What is that thing? What are *they* doing?"

"Shut up," Alyssa hissed, "Come with me." Isa gave in and allowed herself to be led down the hall until Alyssa pushed her unceremoniously into Alyssa's private quarters. Alyssa pulled the door shut behind her and hit the magnetic lock. It clicked loudly in place and Alyssa turned to Isa, shushing her before she could open her mouth.

"You don't want to talk about what we just saw to anyone else on this ship," Alyssa said, "Understand?"

"What? Why?" Isa was reeling, clearly still confused.

Alyssa rubbed her hands over her face. "Okay, you remember Holding?"

"The one who died in the accident?" Isa said.

"Yeah, except it wasn't an accident. I saw Clarke cut him loose, out on his first spacewalk. I'm convinced it was because he was asking about the cargo."

"The cargo?"

Alyssa told the young girl about the cargo she'd seen at the terminal. The way she'd seen Clarke let Holding drift into space. The thing she'd seen when she'd snuck into the cargo bay.

"So, there's something going on in this ship," Alyssa concluded, "and I don't know who knows, and who doesn't. That thing on the satellite is part of it, and I don't want anyone to find out that *we* know until I figure out what's happening. Okay?"

"I could help you."

Alyssa shook her head. "Not a chance. They've killed Holding. They might kill me. I'm not risking you. You're one of the ones I'm trying to help."

"What?"

"Never mind," Alyssa said, thinking of the pills in her room. "The point is, I'm already knee-deep in this and you're not, so you're best to just keep quiet and go about your business, or you might end up thrown into space like Holding was."

It was harsh, and Alyssa knew it before she saw Isa's eyes widen. Horror dawned across her face. The poor girl, Alyssa thought. She'd been so excited about her spacewalk and now the joy had been taken and replaced with the same nervous anxiety as Alyssa's. She reached out and touched her on the shoulder, pressing down into the spongy fabric of the jumpsuit to try to ease Isa's worry.

"It'll be okay. Nothing is going to happen to you. I won't let it," she stared into Isa's eyes and tried her best to hide her own worry. "Alright?"

Isa calmed down. "Alright."

"Now let's get you out into that hallway and headed back to the mess where you'd normally be right now, and you just pretend nothing had happened. You saw nothing, right?"

Isa nodded. Alyssa opened the door and watched her as she walked out of her cabin. *God, she's thin*, Alyssa thought. The jumpsuit hung loose around her. It looked almost comically large, and her hair and hands hung lank at her sides. She looked back, and a certain hollowness in the cheeks and nearly sunken eyes made Alyssa grimace. This was the kind of person they got to work up here. *Despite attempts towards equitable treatment for everyone in a world that had more than enough resources for everybody, this is where we end up.* Here, again, still, pushing people with no hope to the very edge of humanity, even off the edges of the Earth.

Alyssa sighed as she watched the girl's tiny frame disappear around the corner of the corridor.

A week later, as Alyssa was finishing a meal, a freshly showered Isa wandered into the mess. Since the incident, Isa had been seeking Alyssa out, and Alyssa was glad to have the company, even if their bond was due to a terrible shared secret. Isa spotted her and walked over. The lightness in her steps spoke more of resilience borne of a life of hardship and hiding than it did of a familiarity with the low gravity. Alyssa invited her to sit down. They ate their meal together, neither of them speaking, simply enjoying the solidarity of existing together in that moment.

Alyssa made a decision. She sat long after she'd finished her meal, waiting patiently as Isa finished eating. When she was done, Alyssa took both of their plates to the recycler and dumped them, then walked back to the table. She crossed to the side Isa was sitting on, leaned down and whispered in her ear, "Let's go talk somewhere." With that she strode from the mess with Isa walking behind her.

"Come with me," Alyssa said.

A few minutes later, after ducking through the hallways so they could make sure they weren't being watched by anyone, they were in Alyssa's quarters. Alyssa fussed around, and Isa waited anxiously. She wrung her hands and hissed through her teeth, tension in her shoulders. Finally, Alyssa turned to Isa and placed her hands on her shoulders.

"What I'm about to show you *cannot* leave this room, okay?" when Isa nodded, Alyssa reiterated. "I'm serious, it *absolutely* has to stay between you, me, and the doorway. Got it?"

Isa nodded again. Alyssa gave her a long, hard stare and turned to her cabinet. She pulled it open and extracted the makeshift pill container.

"See that? That's my medication."

Isa was nonplussed, "For what?"

Alyssa paused. "Okay. You know how zero gravity is really bad for you, right?"

Isa's blank expression gave way to worried confusion.

"They don't — they didn't — oh, *Jesus*," Alyssa said, "Did they not even tell you?"

"Tell me what?" Isa was trying to keep a quiver out of her voice.

"Isa, how did you end up here?" Alyssa asked.

The younger woman shrugged, then sat down gently on Alyssa's bunk. "Grew up in the tunnels under Baltimore. Bounced around from place to place, but nothing really stuck. You know how it is. Lots of houses, none of them homes. Ran away, more often than not. State said I had to stay for my safety, I knew I had to leave for it. Living arrangements got worse and worse, you know? Eventually, I was in this hole next to the subway tunnel where I could sleep for an hour at a time. Couldn't get more than an hour's sleep, cause the train would come through, rattling my brain, waking me," she was talking about it so calm and flat, like it had been a news report she'd read instead of a thing that had happened in her life. A thing that had *been* her life.

"One day, little while ago, a woman came down. I barely see anyone in the tunnels. Only place I'd see anyone is when I went up into the dome to steal food. Anyway. This woman, she says am I tired of living down here? I almost laughed in her face. It wasn't exactly what you could call living. When I'd had a building to sleep in, I was hungry most of the time, and now I was that and cold, probably not far off my last winter, so I said obviously I was. Tired of it, I mean.

"She arranges me to go to a hospital, somewhere. I don't recognise where. They check me out, give me some tablets and whatnot. Feed me up and make sure I can get around properly. Then they put me on this railroad. On the way they say I'm going to space, and that it means I'll have a job and a place to live. And yeah. Then they launch me and I clean and I do what they tell me but nobody talks to me. I guess this is what they meant, when I said I had a home?" she looked around, at the bulkheads and the minimalism in the room. "At least the train doesn't wake me up anymore."

Alyssa was aghast. They didn't even tell their workers what was going to happen to them. People like her weren't even volunteers, they were faced with the choice between dying alone somewhere or slowly degenerating in space. No, worse than that, their choice was between dying alone and the promise of life, with no informed consent about the risks.

Alyssa breathed out, trying to hide her slow rage as she spoke to Isa. "Isa. Look… I'm a medical research scientist from Ontario," she took a deep breath, "I'm going to have to tell you something, and it isn't going to be nice to hear. My team and I have been researching the effects of space travel for quite a while. There's a thing that happens when you go up, and it's not good. Usually, you're okay for a little while, but then you start to get the Space Palsy. You get back to Earth and can't walk, or your eyes are blurry, or you have a persistent tremor in your hand. That's why most people don't ever stop working on the ships; they can't. If they stay on Earth, they need extensive medical care, and space work doesn't pay enough for spacers to be able to afford it."

Isa's face was growing more and more horrified as Alyssa went on.

"We studied a few people that *had* come back to live on Earth. Their bone density had decreased, so it hurt for them to walk. They had muscular atrophy and catabolism, so they were weak. That was fine, right? Didn't matter. We know how to fix that. What we *couldn't* fix was the nerve death. It was like their whole neural system had shrunk back from their bodies. It meant that even when we did resistance training to improve their bone density, and we fed them protein rich foods and we gave them daily physiotherapy, they *still* couldn't deal with the effects of the gravity well. They no longer had the nerves to control their bodies. We were wondering how the companies were getting away with it, but if they're recruiting and not telling you about it, no wonder!"

Isa stood very still for a moment, processing. Firey anger burned in Alyssa, but she kept it inside, waiting for Isa to ask the question she knew was coming. She'd grown up rough but she wasn't stupid. "You mean, I'm gonna get this? This… nerve thing? Be stuck on the ship forever?"

Alyssa nodded. "They call it Space Palsy."

Isa's skin had a grey sheen to it. "Nobody said. Nobody told me."

"That's why I'm telling you now," she waited a moment before continuing, waiting for Isa to calm down. Alyssa picked up the pill container again, and handed it to Isa.

"Okay. Here's the deal. After we'd found out what the problem was, we made something that *might* be able to help people who repeatedly go on long haul space operations. People like you. In our tests it's done pretty well at halting neural degeneration. It just… hasn't been tested on humans yet."

"So… you made this… medicine stuff…" Isa said.

"Yep, we did. This batch I made up myself, it's why it's all dusty and chalky. *Nobody* we spoke to was interested in letting us go through a clinical trial process. All we got back was comments on lack of profitability. After all, it's only spacers that suffer from Space Palsy. They're a tiny portion of the population, and not a wealthy one at that. All we were told was 'We know how to avoid Space Palsy; *don't go to space.*' They ignore the fact that not going to space *isn't an option* for a lot of people."

"So, they didn't test it?"

"No. We couldn't get a trial approved."

Isa looked at the bottle of pills, then back at Alyssa, then back to the pills, before speaking again.

"You're testing them," Her voice was quiet, "aren't you?"

Alyssa nodded slowly. "If you don't get approval to test a drug, you can't test it, except if you test it on yourself. That's what I'm doing. Nobody would do anything, so I'm doing it," with that, she spread her arms and gave a hopeless sigh, "I don't know if it works. I don't know if it does nothing. I don't know if it's harmful or benign. I don't know if it causes cancer or liver failure or kidney stones or *anything.* I'm just up here *trying* the damn thing, to see if it has any effect that will stop people from getting stuck on cargo runs in a rusted old ship like this one," she slapped a bulkhead and laughed hopelessly, "and for that, I get called a *Terran* and see people murdered and gigantic metal insects and whatever the *fuck* is going on on this ship."

Silence fell over the room, and the two women stared at each other. Then Alyssa fished a second container out of her cupboard. This one was smaller, but she poured out half of the pills and handed it to Isa.

"Isa?"

"Yeah?"

"You can't tell anyone," she said, "This stuff is contraband and if they found out it might be a cure for Space Palsy, they'd take it and either kill me or I'd get my research license revoked for letting people other than myself have it. Neither of those things sound fun."

Isa nodded, "I understand," Then after a pause, "thank you."

❖ ❖ ❖

Hours later, the lights were dimmed and the halls were cleared. Isa was long gone, and Alyssa was feeling giddy with relief. The anxiety from keeping all the secrets had been weighing heavily on her, and the ability to admit her purpose to another human being on the spacecraft meant more to her than she'd realised.

She hadn't turned the light on but was standing fully clothed in the infrared light of the corridor, backlit by the gloom of her own quarters. Her room was squared away again, her contraband snuck carefully back into the medicine cabinet, half as full but doing twice the work it had been.

A long, quiet shadow led itself down the corridor toward her. Alyssa slid softly into her room and pulled the door almost closed. Through the sliver she could only just make out who was walking past. He stumped around with the grace of a Terran, but he was obviously still familiar with the layout of the ship. With a start, she realised she knew who it was. She hadn't seen him since the spacewalk. She wondered where he was off to on the sleep shift. He seemed in a hurry, striding away from the sleeping quarters.

She slid the door open and skulked after Brett down the blood red corridor.

1.10

CONSPIRACY

Brett could barely see. His eyes had never dealt with infrared lighting particularly well. Sneaking around on the sleep shift was a necessary but frustrating part of the plan.

Once he was out past the crew quarters, he reached into the pocket of his flight suit and pulled out a torch. He twisted the cap on it and it flung a bright cone of white light onto the old bulkhead, washing out the infrared of the hall. He tried his best to move quietly but he knew how loud he was compared to the full-time spacers.

If anyone had asked him if he was on edge, he would

have denied it, but his breath still came in short gasps as he moved around. The operation had been in planning for years now, and they were getting close. They were now a well-oiled machine, and all the scarabs were now attached to the satellites.

He wasn't too concerned about getting caught. Waugh and Clarke owed him for lugging the scarabs in and out of cargo ships on the surface, making sure the manifests made weight and double checking that everything lined up properly. They were with him, and had enough pull on the ship to dispel any suspicions people might have had.

There were another three spacewalks scheduled on this route, two on orbiting satellites and one on a geostationary. The geostationary satellite was the first they'd noticed the design flaw on. You could attach something to it and override its functionality and nobody on the ground would notice unless they were paying far too much attention to miniscule orbital destabilisations. He'd programmed the scarab for it, the hulking metal things that attached to the outside. The best thing was, only one or two spacecraft and a select number of crew ever looked at the satellites up close enough to see the scarabs. After a while, they just looked like part of the ship, as the chrome and the replaced panels cold welded together. By the next run, nobody suspected much. The satellites just looked different to what they remembered.

He could *taste* it. The years of careful planning coming to fruition before his eyes, with him aboard the *Sunward Sky* to witness it firsthand. All they had to do was keep quiet and keep everyone's eyes off the geosync sat when they pulled up. If they did that, then the scarabs —

A sound came from the corridor behind him.

He spun, flashlight in hand, turning to and fro looking

for the source of the noise. It had been a small scrape, like that of a shoe on a grated floor.

Alyssa had waited until Brett had turned the corner and then snuck after him, keeping a safe distance between the two of them. She was thankful for his inability to move with the quiet efficiency of the career crew; Brett's stomping echoed down the halls, making it easy for her to both follow and hide the sound of her own clumsy footfalls. She kept her distance. Following was easy enough after he stepped out of the crew corridor and switched on a flashlight. He was heading fore with some speed, and she watched his black and red silhouette dance around the roving white of the flashlight.

Then the white light had gotten bigger, and she'd realised she was moving too fast. She pulled herself up too abruptly, and a loud scuffling sound rang down the hallway.

The torchlight pulled up and froze completely. With a deftness that surprised herself, Alyssa ducked behind the bulkhead just as the torchlight illuminated where she'd been standing.

Holding her breath and willing her heart to slow down, Alyssa listened as Brett walked closer to her hiding spot. The heavy, slow thud of his feet crept closer until she was certain that he couldn't have been more than a couple of metres away. Her breath was caught, live and squirming in her lungs. She was desperate for air but didn't want to make a sound.

As her lungs felt fit to burst, she heard a grunt and the light disappeared from the walls and floor. The infrared coloured the black, and the thumping of Brett's feet receded down the hall.

She breathed out slowly, not daring to make too much noise, and waited for the steps to fall into a rhythm again before she ducked out from the hiding spot. The man was hidden in the silhouette again. He rounded another corner, and Alyssa followed into the main corridor. The main hallway had fewer bulkheads along it, and more doors.

He was being far more cautious now. She crept along behind him. The deck was faded and dark, and steel rivets held down panels that had come loose. The light from Brett's torch reflected off the walls and cast pearlescent reflections everywhere. Alyssa did her best to copy the timing of the footfalls of the larger man in the hope that she wouldn't be heard.

She placed her foot down and heard the deck groan underneath it. The torch swung around, and this time there was nothing to hide behind. Caught fully in the glare, Alyssa dashed backward and flung herself through a nearby doorway.

❖ ❖ ❖

Isa couldn't sleep. After months and years of having to struggle to survive, she'd just wished that the *Sunward Sky* would have at least been safe. It didn't have to be comfortable, and she was even prepared for it to be scary. She could deal with being scared, having been terrified in the dark tunnels under Baltimore for most of her short life.

She'd got used to it, the fear. And getting used to it was almost as good as not feeling it. She'd even been excited after the spacewalk. But then Alyssa had told her what would happen to her, and about Holding and the thing on the satellite. Isa lay silently in her bed, thinking.

If it was true, and the people on the ship were doing something with that big machine on the satellite, then it had to be the people higher up in the ship. The important crew members, and all the people that knew about how everything worked. Otherwise, they wouldn't have been able to sneak things onboard the way they had.

The ship was beginning to feel like a trap. At least in the tunnels she'd been able to get out, to *escape* somewhere that would, for a while, be less threatening. Here, she was stuck in her perpetually not-quite-dark room and the thoughts of what was going on in the ship played in her head on repeat.

It wasn't fair. The spaceship was supposed to be her ticket out. That's what the lady had said. That's what she'd felt originally, and that's what she had been hoping for.

She thought back to her first day on the ship. There had been an induction, and a lady had been introduced to her. Her name was Ellyse, and she'd said that if Isa had any issues, she could come and tell her about them. *Anything at all,* she'd said.

She got up from the bed, pulled some clothes on and headed out of the hall. Somewhere toward the ship's bow, a door slammed.

❖ ❖ ❖

Brett spun quickly and his torch caught a short, dark-haired woman standing some metres behind him. Before he could react, she dashed backward and threw herself through a doorway. He swore softly and gave chase. The woman had a good head start, but she couldn't lock him out of the room. He had top-level key pass access. Still, she slammed the door behind her and he heard the lock *snick* into place. He bounded toward the door and stopped in front of it, fumbling around his flight suit pockets, trying to find his access pass.

❖ ❖ ❖

On the other side of the door, Alyssa was panicking. She should have recognised what the door led to. It was a supply room, a maze of different cleaning and medical apparatus that left no place to hide. The only way in or out was the door that she'd just come through.

She could hear Brett outside. She rushed to the medical cabinet and rustled through the inventory before she finally found what she was looking for. She pulled it out and ran across to a large container.

❖ ❖ ❖

Brett thumbed his sensor over the door lock, and heard the bolt demagnetise. He slid the door sideways and stepped into the storage room. Shelves blocked his view to the left and right. He took a gamble and headed left and knew immediately that he'd made a mistake. When he turned around Alyssa was there brandishing a syringe full of clear liquid.

"Move and I'll stick you, I swear to God," She hissed. "This is Sodium Hydroxide. I don't know what it'll do to your insides but I'm willing to bet you don't want to find out."

❖ ❖ ❖

Isa heard a commotion down the hall but ignored it. She was trying to remember where Ellyse's quarters where. She'd been shown on the induction, but that had been when the ship was lit for the day shift. The *Sunward Sky* barely looked anything like the same in the red and black gloom. Still, she managed it. She hesitated in front of the door. The ship echoed with a series of thuds, and she recognised the sound from the fights she'd heard in the tunnels.

Isa put her fist up to knock but stopped short. Ellyse's promise to help her was probably like the promises of the state workers who had shunted her from home to home in her early years. Every time someone had offered her "help" it had really meant *we're going to throw you into a new situation. Figure it out.*

You're being silly, she told herself. She took a deep breath and knocked on the door.

Nothing. No sound came from inside.

She must be asleep, Isa thought. She knocked once more and waited a few more seconds, then let out a defeated sigh.

As she turned to go, she ran straight into Ellyse as she was creeping down the hall.

❖ ❖ ❖

Alyssa tried not to shake, or to squeeze any droplets out of the end of the syringe as she brandished it at Brett. She thanked her stars that this supply cupboard was the same one she used to refill cleaning apparatus on her shifts. Brett looked incensed. Fury knotted his brow and he feinted this way and that, trying to get around the needle.

"Get out of the way!" he snapped.

"You've got some explaining to do first," she stepped toward him, backing him into the corner of the storeroom. His breath was steady but she could see his pulse racing in his temple.

"Explain what? You're the one threatening to fill me with drain cleaner!"

"You remember back in the terminal? You and a friend were lugging some box around? You took it off the *Sunward Sky*, I'm guessing."

Brett frowned. "That was you? In the terminal?"

Alyssa smiled. "Yeah, that was me. Then I got dragged onto this ship and I've been trying to figure out what the hell has been going on ever since."

Brett put his hands up, trying to placate her. "Ok, lady. You're the one with the needle. What do you want to know?"

This took some of the wind out of Alyssa's sails. For all the things that she'd witnessed both before and during her time on the *Sunward Sky*, she didn't *know* what was happening. She didn't know where to start.

"Okay. What was that thing you put on the satellite?" she asked.

❖ ❖ ❖

Ellyse was staring at Isa, who had nearly run into her as she rounded the corner in the corridor. She'd been the mentor for her when the ship had gone up. Isa shivered in fear, clearly unsure what to do.

"Tell me again," Ellyse pressed.

"Clarke, and Brett, and the other two… I can't remember their names. They were pushing along this giant insect-thing that I saw come out of the cargo bay," Isa seemed fit to burst as she continued, "Alyssa said that she'd seen Clarke *murder* a guy when they were fixing the heat shield and she told me not to tell anyone but I figured someone else had to know and *you* told me I could tell you anything so I thought…" She drifted off, suddenly awkward, tears threatening to spill. Ellyse reached out and drew the young woman into a hug.

"It's all right. It's all right," she said, trying to soothe Isa as she began to heave with sobs, "I'm glad you told me." Ellyse felt Isa's body relax into hers, felt the relief flooding her body.

"Isa?" Ellyse pulled away slightly, and Isa looked at her with bleary, tearstained eyes.

"That thing you saw? It's called a *scarab*," Ellyse swung and struck the girl in the temple, wrapped her arms around her throat and dragged her down the corridor.

"What are you going to do? You stab me with that, they're going to find my body and then find you," Brett was mocking her, feeling less out of control than he had. Alyssa had guts, but being tough and being able to kill someone were two different things.

"Tell me about the scarab," Alyssa said, still blocking the exit to the door and brandishing the needle full of drain cleaner.

"The one you saw was the last one. Thats all you need to know. We've been working on this for years. Everything is in place. You're too late."

"I don't *care*. What do they *do*?"

"They're giant, parasitic metal machines that feed into satellites. What do you *think* they do?" he was getting bored of this. She was trying to buy time. Trying to think of how to get out of this. "What does a parasite eventually *do?*"

Alyssa didn't know what to ask next. How many of these scarabs were there? How long had they been working? Who was *they*?

What *did* a parasite eventually do?

A scuffling series of thuds echoed down the hallway outside, breaking her conversation. They were loud, heavier even than the footfalls of a first-time spacer. Alyssa wanted to look behind her, to open the door and check what was going on in the hall, but she didn't want to take her eyes off Brett.

She stared. He stared back.

The two of them sat frozen as the footfalls grew louder, until they were right outside the door.

"In here!" Brett yelled, then ducked. Alyssa snarled and ran for him, needle outstretched in her hand. The door slid open behind her, and Alyssa turned to see Ellyse dragging Isa by the throat. Before she could spin to face him again, she felt Brett's hands on her arm, squeezing until she dropped the syringe. Alyssa gave in and the man wrenched her arm painfully behind her back. She went quietly as he marched her out of the storage cupboard. Ellyse followed them, and a terrified Isa looked at Alyssa with pleading eyes. They were headed toward the bow, and Alyssa had the horrible feeling that they were about to find out *exactly* what was happening aboard the *Sunward Sky*.

1.11

BETRAYAL

Clarke stood in the corner of the officer's mess, waiting patiently. The officer's mess was smaller than the crew mess, and despite its name nobody ate there. The ship didn't have officers, only senior crew. Since its first launch, the space had been re-appropriated several times, and now functioned as a meeting space for senior crew. The room was at the edge of the wing at the front of the ship, and a corner window wrapped the wall. From here Clarke could see the stars, the earth, and the ship's central column jutting out, an incursion into the nothingness. Clarke's unnaturally long limbs crept from him like a spider as he placed a hand against the thickened acrylic of the window. He held it there, leaning against it with the feeble weight of the spinward gravity.

Not long now, he thought, pushing lightly with his arm and bouncing off the window. He saw the Earth — Terra — stretched out below him, and hated that he still felt the inimitable sense of wonder seeing it. The majesty of the sun building over the orb and spreading light over its surface; a torchlight in the cavernous dark of infinity. It wasn't something the human mind was able to get used to.

He *wanted* to hate it. It was the home he'd been denied, and the people on it were the ones who had denied him. His limbs, which had always been long and wiry, were now so degraded by the palsy that there was no chance of him ever living on the surface. He was staring at the blue orb of a home he could never return to.

He heard a series of scuffles and grunts coming down the hall. He pushed himself off the window, more forcefully this time, and turned to the door, attentive. He could make out heavy, Terran footfalls and the sliding of bodies. He hoped they hadn't had to kill anyone else. When he'd been forced to dispatch Holding he'd told the rest of his crew that he didn't want to risk more people dying. Not on this trip. Not when they were this close. He'd had to repeat the sentiment after the incident in the cargo bay. Whoever it was that had been in there couldn't have found out enough to stop them, and turning the ship upside down looking for them would rouse suspicion from the rest of the crew. And a restless crew was the last thing they needed.

When the door opened, Ellyse and Brett dragged in two women. He recognised them; they'd been on the spacewalk a few weeks prior. The door hissed closed, and the dark-skinned girl sobbed quietly in the corner. She was stick-thin and couldn't have seen her eighteenth birthday yet. The other one was older, deathly pale and defiant. Her eyes were like coals, ebbing a silent fury across the room at him even as Brett tossed her onto the floor.

"And what," Clarke rasped at Brett and Ellyse, "the *fuck* do you think you're doing?"

❖ ❖ ❖

Alyssa's scalp was screaming, and her flight suit had rubbed the right side of her neck raw where Brett had pulled it taut. She kept her face set; she wasn't about to give this man the pleasure of her pain. She bore her eyes into his head, willing her vision to crystallise into shards that would pierce his feckless brain.

Clarke only gave her a cursory glance as she was dragged in. When he demanded to know what Ellyse and Brett were doing, the two other crew members stopped.

Brett spoke first. "She was following me around. Was on my way here to meet you and I heard her behind me, sneaking. She held me up in one of the supply closets. Was asking questions about the scarabs. Brought her down to see what to do about her."

Clarke rolled his eyes. "Right, and you?" he looked at Ellyse, who was now holding Isa by her stick-thin upper arm.

Ellyse twitched her head in Isa and Alyssa's direction. "They know," she said.

At this, Clarke hissed softly, air venting through his teeth as he grimaced. He was seething. Brett nodded in agreement and told Clarke about Alyssa trapping him in the supply closet and threatening him. He shook her as he spoke and became more and more agitated as the story wore on.

"We're going to have to get rid of them," he said.

Clarke shook his head. "No. We can't. The Captain would ask too many questions if more people disappeared. Once is an accident. More than that on one run arouses suspicion. And Captain Sharma isn't afraid to clamp down security if he thinks something's amiss." Clarke was pacing back and forward in front of the two women now, and Isa's bottom lip was trembling. Finally, Clarke made a decision.

"Lock the door. We're still on a sleep shift; we don't want any of the officers coming in here looking for a nightcap and seeing this."

Ellyse shoved Isa over to Brett and hit the magnetic deadbolt on the bulkhead. It clanged into place. The hum of the spacecraft's engines and air conditioning systems rang through the room, droning behind the panicked breathing of Isa and the forced calm of Alyssa.

"Get Waugh," Clarke said, "We're going to have to hold these two somewhere and she'll be able to figure out where," Ellyse started moving and Clarke added, "Oh, Ellyse? Get Healy, too. We might need something to calm these two down."

Ellyse nodded, then walked out of the room, shutting and locking the door behind her. Isa burbled in the corner, tears streaming down her cheeks. Alyssa's face was like a mask. Clarke searched their names and room numbers, then walked away to the gigantic corner window and thumbed a radio under his collar.

"Ellyse, are you there?" when she answered in the affirmative, Clarke continued. "Find their rooms and search them," with that, he gave the names and room numbers.

Alyssa kept her face carefully blank as he turned back toward her and Isa.

Ellyse tapped herself lightly down the hallway and entered the tiny crew cabin. The place was squared away neatly, and all of Alyssa's belongings were in the various cabinets or containers to stop them drifting in the low grav.

She began with the bed, tearing the sheets off and checking for any incisions in the memory foam where contraband could be stored. She tossed the sheets onto the floor and once the mattress was cleared she checked that nothing was attached to the sheets like a processor or miniature radio device. Then she opened the clothes locker and did the same. She didn't know what she was looking for, but any data storage or comms device would have been a giveaway. Alyssa didn't keep a diary or a hand terminal.

She ransacked the room, strewing belongings everywhere, before heading to the door. She'd found nothing. As she was about to walk out and head to Isa's room she stopped.

I didn't check the bottom of the locker cabinet.

She turned and re-entered the room.

"You can't seem to stay out of trouble, can you girl?" Healy shot at Alyssa as he and Waugh entered the officer's mess. He leaned against the window, back to the view, and gave the two women a hard look. "You're lucky, really. That Holding fella, he's probably out there somewhere still wondering where he made *his* mistake. Not sure we can do that to you two as well."

Healy. She was shocked at his involvement. The man seemed too caring, too thoughtful and kind, to be involved in whatever was happening. This conspiracy, spread not only among the ship, but to wherever the scarabs were manufactured, to the ground crew who covered when the *Sunward Sky* was delayed.

God, Alyssa realised, *this operation must be huge.*

"Where are we going to keep them?" Healy asked, pointedly looking away from Alyssa.

"I don't care. Somewhere they can't be heard. The last thing we want is for someone to hear them and come to the rescue and blow the whole operation. I've waited three years for this, I'm not jeopardizing it now. It's a shame killing them would arouse suspicion." Clarke was pacing back and forward. Healy looked incredulous in the corner.

"It's a poor spacecraft that has unused space. You're not going to find a place you can use as a makeshift brig," Healy's voice was expressionless, and he seemed less concerned about the fate of the prisoners than the younger conspirators. Alyssa got the sense that his words were driven by practicality and not fervour. His back was against the glass, and the carabiners on his suit were clinking softly as he swung one leg back and forth. He looked almost casual.

Brett circled the two women, and the look on his face made it clear that he'd rather shove them out an airlock than anything else.

"This one's been following me since we were still on rock," he said, pointing to Alyssa, "She saw me in the terminal. We were shipping out the crate that we swapped the scarab with and she saw us. We couldn't find her," he turned to her. "that night, in the cargo bay, when we were testing the scarab. That was you, wasn't it?"

Alyssa didn't answer, just stared at him until someone knocked on the bulkhead. Clarke opened the door and Ellyse walked in.

"I inspected her room. Didn't find much, except this," She took something from her pocket and tossed it at Alyssa, who snapped her head to the side. The container bounced up and almost hit her in the jaw. Instead it hit her on the neck and fell too slowly to the ground in front of her, and she recognised the chalky pills she'd smuggled aboard.

"It's not what it looks like," Alyssa said, but she was cut off before she could finish the sentence.

"You brought drugs up here? Fucking Terrans," Waugh spat. "Space travel is nothing to people like you, is it? It's a game. You come up to play. To get a taste of what it's like to struggle. You come and dance around, see the stars and then get back to Terra before the palsy gets you. Most dangerous job in the world and *you people* are so *clueless* as to get high," she picked up the container and shook it in Alyssa's face, "what is it? Some sort of stimulant? Need an upper? Or a hallucinogen because you're just not entertained enough? We've been up here, maintaining your networks and your satellites and your information highway and that's just not interesting enough for you? Costs our lives, but you don't see the fun? *What a shame for you.*"

Alyssa stood up. Brett stepped toward her but stayed back. She snatched the container from Waugh's hand. "I know about your problems, space jockey. I know what happens when you're up here. You're screaming at the wrong person. I'm trying to help,"

She popped the lid off the container and pulled out one of the chalky pills, holding it up for the room to see.

"This isn't a drug. Not in the way you're talking about anyway. It's not designed to make you high, or spaced out, or anything. The only person it's putting in danger is me."

Nobody spoke, so she continued. "I'm a researcher. There was no active work going into space palsy. There was no money in it; the people funding the research didn't care. There was no profit motive, and the problem was invisible. You're all up here, after all," she gestured to the pills, "This is — this *might* be a cure. The only way I'll find out is to take it and see if I develop symptoms. I'm doing this so nobody has to do this again. If it works, we could have happy, healthy technicians running ships like *Sunward Sky*. We wouldn't need to fear space palsy, and spacers wouldn't become outcasts, trapped in the sky."

There was a silence in the room. Healy was staring at her strangely. Waugh still looked ready to rip the two of them apart. Ellyse and Brett were speaking in low, hushed tones, and Clarke—

Where's Clarke? Alyssa thought, and spun round as he finished sneaking up behind her. She tried to escape but the man's long limbs enveloped her and before she could react he had her in a vice grip around the neck.

The room erupted. Isa jumped up and flailed at Clarke with her fists, screaming to get the attention of anyone who might be walking by the corridor. Brett stomped into the fracas and pulled Isa off Clarke. She span round and started scratching and biting the big man to get him off her. Alyssa heard Clarke yell to Ellyse for something but didn't hear what. Waugh tried to jump in but Alyssa kicked her legs out, catching her in the chest. Noticing this, Clarke dragged Alyssa backwards and away toward the window.

Ellyse ran over, brandishing a syringe. Alyssa kicked out, but couldn't manoeuvre herself into position properly. Clarke had her locked down tight against his chest. She kicked again and cried out but Ellyse manoeuvred out of reach of Alyssa's flailing limbs. She pushed the needle into Alyssa's neck.

Alyssa's vision blurred, and she found she didn't have the strength to keep fighting. Just before she passed out, she heard Clarke's harsh whisper.

"Who do you think you are? Coming here, trying to be a saviour. Pompous bitch, we can save ourselves."

1.12

ATTACK

The satellite hovered in a mid-earth orbit, ten thousand kilometres from the surface. It, along with the seventy-one other satellites of its ilk, formed the vertices of a huge polyhedron enveloping the Earth, orbiting it at twice the speed of the Earth's rotation. Each had an incredibly accurate caesium crystal chronometer and a high-bandwidth processor able to process trillions of requests per second. At least twelve of these satellites were visible from any point on the ground that was significantly exposed to the sky. Above them, in high earth orbit, were the geostationary satellites. Below them were the low earth experimental satellites and manned space stations long abandoned after the glory and hope of eventual diaspora to space was abandoned.

The machines in this middle layer timestamped and sent back data from transceivers all over the world, tabulating response times and firing them back. The machines that had made the requests would calculate a set of triangulations and from that, work out where on Earth the device was.

Global positioning systems were ancient technology by this point. However, in addition to the weather and communications satellites, and the unmanned research probes, they were among the most important pieces of equipment still used in the sky. To work, four of the satellites needed to be visible, otherwise some portion of the signal couldn't be triangulated. With the advent of modern contemporary transport and delivery drone services, as well as personal mapping devices and other luxuries, the satellites were responsible for an enormous amount of functionality on the ground. Fourteen billion people, tapping into signals they didn't even know were there, to understand where they were in the world.

Because it was so important, the satellites had been built into a double redundancy network. The seventy-two satellites were arrayed as three overlapping networks. If one satellite was destroyed or damaged, the other two could pick up the slack. Two-thirds of the network was always on, and the other was on standby and ready to slot in at a moment's notice.

Keegan was looking carefully at the stats for each satellite but had got fixated on this one. It was due for a round of maintenance, but there was nothing overtly wrong. It still worked as well as it needed to. The memory cache needed clearing but it was another five months before that would start being a problem. It was drifting a little more than usual, and at first Keegan thought it might have just been accelerated too hard by the team that first put it up there. As he looked closer, he noted a series of differences in correction burns.

The satellite looked as though it was *too heavy*. The correction burns, the tiny bursts of compressed air that the satellite automatically made, were using more air, and moving the satellite more slowly, than its recorded weight would suggest.

Keegan was nonplussed as he logged a maintenance request to review the thrusters on the next round of maintenance. He also logged it into the growing private file he kept, filled with all the strangeness he'd noted while on shift. The late launch of the *Sunward Sky* had been the first, with its contradictory messages of changes to manifest but no change to lift off weight. He'd tracked down pre-launch drone footage that had shown the ship on the platform and had made a few notes as it had continued through the sky. Other than the strange launch, he'd noted an unscheduled spacewalk. It had also spun down its wings once, too early, and for too long. He couldn't shake the niggling feeling that something was amiss.

He didn't have a *case*, though. He didn't know if he was being stupid about the ship, but now there was something off about the satellites, too.

He ran off a query for all the satellites of the same type. When it came back, he frowned. The same weight-to-fuel burn differential was happening in almost all the sats. He logged that, too, and lay back, trying to think about what could be causing it. A faulty sensor? On several dozen machines, all at once?

It seemed unlikely.

The one thing he didn't have, for all his access to

acceleration data and fuel levels and digital reports, was a *telescope*. He couldn't actually *see* the thing he was trying to understand. It was like trying to find a branch in a forest while having it described by walkie-talkie in a foreign language. He could see the numbers, and none of them made sense, but he couldn't see what was going on.

Far above, wrapped around the first satellite Keegan had noticed the anomaly on, was the first scarab devised. Far from the slick machine that Isa and Alyssa had seen some weeks ago, this was gnarled wires, clips, and bands of metal riveted together. It was a prototype, and it had been working for years, and was as pitted and scarred as the satellite it had consumed. The opening move in the chess game being played by the spacefarers that referred to themselves as "Project Blackout".

Accelerating five thousand kilometres above the hobbled satellite, the *Sunward Sky* span inward from a high Earth orbit, where Project Blackout were preparing their checkmate move.

Alyssa woke in the med bay, tied to the adjustable chair that she'd found herself in after the launch. Her head felt as though someone was packing styrofoam into it with a brick. Her eyes were bleary. She could see a dark blur on the couch next to her. *Isa,* she thought. Turning the other way, she saw the dark outline of two crew members and heard the clink of carabiners.

Healy was talking, low and careful. "I'll keep them under, or at least sedated. Keep 'em out of your way.

"Great. We only have a few more days, Healy. We're almost there."

Healy grunted, and Alyssa heard the door slide closed.

Looking down, Alyssa saw an IV in her arm. She groaned, and tried to move to dislodge the needle, but Healy noticed. He stumped over and hit a button. A cool rush flooded into her veins, and her world went black again.

She stayed in this torpor for ages. Days, from what she could tell. The world would come into view around her, and she'd hold on to consciousness for some time, near paralysed, until the clanking silhouette of Healy would appear before another cold rush and darkness.

Then, she woke. Groggily, but something felt different this time. She could hold on to her thoughts again. She looked to her right to where Healy was injecting something into the IV tube. She was about to talk when he put a finger to his lips. She sat silently, feeling an urgent vigour taking over the mire of lethargy. He must have injected her with a stimulant of some sort. It swept through her body, and she turned to Healy.

He stood over her, half-empty syringe in one hand, staring down to where she was held on the bench. Where a few days ago he'd been full of quiet anger, he was now curious. Calm. In his other hand, he had Alyssa's bottle of chalk-white pills. He rattled the container.

"These things," he said, "do they work?"

Alyssa shook her head. "I don't know yet. That's why I'm testing them. If I do it and don't get the palsy then I know it works, and we can submit it for wide trials. If not..." She let the comment hang in the air. They knew what happened if not.

Healy thought for a moment, then grunted and crossed

to Isa's bed. He put the needle into her IV drip and drained it completely. After a few seconds, she started coming to. He waited patiently, checking her vitals and letting her take her time waking up. Alyssa, now fully alert and awake, swung her legs around and sat on the edge of her own bed. She watched Healy as he woke her up slowly and carefully, muttering the soft, soothing noises of a well-practiced carer.

"What are you doing?" Alyssa demanded, and Healy turned around to her and pushed his finger to his lips. She got out of the bed and walked closer to him. He'd sat by and watched while the Blackout team had discussed whether or not to kill the two of them. She wanted answers, and when she was next to him, she hissed in his ear, "What are you doing?"

Healy hissed back. "*We're* waking the girl up, and once that's done, we're getting out of the med bay. I don't want us being seen. Once we're out, I'll explain."

Alyssa decided to risk it and put her arm underneath Isa's shoulder to help her out of the bed. Isa's dark face turned toward her, and she smiled groggily.

"Got them a bit too interested, huh?" she warbled. Alyssa shushed her gently, and she and Healy hefted her under each arm and took her out of the med bay.

"Where are we going?" Alyssa hissed, and Healy pointed to the right with his head. They headed aft for no more than a few metres when the sound of footsteps rang through the hall. Someone was coming down the corridor. Alyssa and Healy dragged Isa through the nearest door and slid it closed behind them. It was a small anteroom office, with a pair of chairs screwed into the decking and well-secured digital holoscreen. The rest of the room was unadorned. The screen showed a complex system of interlinked pipes with green and red indicators, fan and water symbols. It was the control room for the ship's air systems. The kind of place people only showed up to when something went wrong.

Healy propped Isa up on the chair, then turned to Alyssa.

"You'd better talk, and you'd better talk fast," Alyssa said.

"We're going to visit the captain," Healy replied, "I need to tell him what's happening. All that stuff you've been following the last little while? The scarabs? Holding getting pushed into space?" he stopped suddenly. Outside, the footsteps rose to what seemed like a crescendo as they passed directly outside the door.

"Yes?" Alyssa pressed as the sound of walking faded.

"Project Blackout? I was brought onboard about a year and a half ago. I don't know everything about it, but I know enough. They're doing something. Something that will mean the Terrans — the dirtsiders — won't have a reason to send people to space. I want to stop them."

Alyssa didn't ask anything else. She wanted to know why he'd had the change of heart but decided against it. So long as he wasn't drugging her into a stupor anymore, she didn't care why he'd changed his mind.

Healy paused, listening for people walking past. When he didn't hear anything, he said "Come on, let's go," and helped Isa out of her chair. She shrugged him off, now awake enough to move around normally. They opened the facilities manager door and looked both ways down the hallway.

"Okay, we're not as suspicious now Isa's walking under her own steam. We just need to hope nobody from Blackout sees us," Healy said, "We're going fore. Captain's office is this way."

The office was next to the bridge, which was staffed by four people on rotating shifts to make sure the *Sunward Sky* stayed on course. In most cases, Captain Sharma could be found in the office, poring through communications between the ship and the ground, and double checking that the crew and maintenance logs were up to date and on time.

The door slid open almost immediately when Healy knocked. Isa and Alyssa followed the big man in.

The Captain's office was only slightly larger than the other offices Alyssa had seen. Its walls were still white and the storage cupboards bare and essential. Captain Sharma sat behind a screen that functioned as a desk. He was poring over some kind of documentation, but looked up as the three crew members entered, flicking the desk to a generic screen saver mode. He was well-muscled for a long-term spacer, and his presence was one of calm command. This was *his* ship, and he carried himself with a certainty of place that belied many of the other crew members.

He smiled warmly at Healy and the others, but it quickly faded as he saw Healy's expression.

"Captain. This is Isa and Alyssa," Healy said, "Ladies, Captain Sharma."

"Pleasure," the Captain nodded. Alyssa returned the nod, suddenly self-conscious. She had never formally met the man, but his voice had been broadcast across the ship regularly enough that she felt she knew him nonetheless.

"Captain," Healy said, and Alyssa was surprised to hear a waver in his voice, "we need to tell you something and we don't have much time."

Sharma's calm air switched at once. He sat forward, and when he spoke again his tone was clipped and sharp, a strange relic of military precision that didn't seem to fit the ship around him. "I'm listening. Tell me."

Healy hesitated, and Alyssa spoke up. "Remember at launch? The delay with the cargo?" she explained what had happened in the terminal, and everything else she'd unravelled in her time aboard the *Sunward Sky*. Sharma's face was impassive, but she thought she heard a sharp intake of breath when she told him what had happened to Holding. He asked why she hadn't come forward before now.

"I didn't know who I could trust," Alyssa said, "I was worried that outing someone would make me a target."

Sharma nodded and let her continue. She mentioned the machine, the scarab, and the way it had attached to the satellite. As she ran out of things to say, Healy interjected. "It's called Blackout. Project Blackout, and it's been going on for a long time. For the last three years, every satellite that has been up for maintenance has had one of these scarabs attached to it. They're heavy, and they cold-weld to the exterior, so the only way to remove them is to scuttle the entire satellite.

"Each machine links into the satellite's main computer, behind the firewall, and has a trigger on it that will overload and rewrite the host satellite's central firmware."

"These rewrites, what do they do?" the captain asked.

"It depends on the satellite it's attached to, but basically it scrambles them," Healy said, "for positioning satellites, it changes coefficients and time codes, so the calculations that account for gravitational drift will be out of sync. All the satellites will be sending contradictory signals. Devices down dirtside won't be able to reconcile it and won't be able to track. For comms sats, it just fries the broad-wave transmission matrix and hashes the transmissions to it. Communications will be sent back as scrambled noise. It'll take months to decode, if it's even possible."

Alyssa rocked back and leaned against the wall of the office. *Holy shit,* she thought. This operation had much grander ambitions than she'd thought.

Sharma was shocked. The face that had been so calm now looked like it had been punched. "How many satellites?" he asked quietly.

Healy's mouth was a grim line. "Enough to knock out the planet's comms and GPS in one hit."

Isa looked confused and was staring at the colour draining from the faces of the other people in the room. "What is it? What's wrong? So they turn off the satellites?"

Alyssa turned to her, trying to stay calm, "It's the type of satellites," she said, then the Captain filled in.

"If the Earth's GPS satellites are scrambled, then everything on the planet that relies on GPS navigation will go haywire. Self-driving cars, delivery vehicles, drones, nothing will know where it is. Our food and waste collection and transport is fully automated, as are the autopilots on aircraft and seacraft. Spacecraft need to use a different positioning system as they're too high up, so they're fine, but… everything else…" He let it hang in the air.

"Everything will crash?" Isa pressed.

"Yeah. Everything will crash," Alyssa said, her voice hollow.

"The other half is the communications satellites," Healy said, "Nobody will be able to talk to one another over anything but short-wave radio, or physical connections. Which almost nobody uses these days. Satellite comms has been the norm for decades now, it's why we have to be up here in the first place."

The Captain gave a low whistle. "So nobody on the earth would be able to — Jesus."

"That's why it's called Project Blackout," Healy said, "Everything is shut down. You can't travel. You can't get goods or services or even talk to anyone outside short range. Everything gets shut down."

The four of them stood in silence for a moment. It was Alyssa who snapped out of it first. "So, what do we do? Healy, do you know how it's going to be triggered?"

"All I know is that it's a proximity trigger. The initial setup, the first station we put the scarab on, has got a transponder that talks to all the others. When it gets triggered, it sends something off that gets picked up, and triggers the others. It gets set off when we get close to it again."

"Great," said Sharma, "and I suppose we're on our way to that satellite now?"

Healy nodded. "The very same. What I don't know is *how* it's getting triggered. I don't know where the trigger is coming from on the *Sunward Sky*."

Sharma leaned back in his seat, rubbing his hands over his eyes. Alyssa cast a sidelong look at Healy, wondering again what had changed his mind. He'd been involved with Project Blackout. He'd been onside when Alyssa had been caught by the other members, and he'd held Isa and herself captive and drugged for several days. So why the change of heart?

The captain stood, pulling Alyssa from her thoughts. "Come with me," he said and stepped past them out into the hall.

They all followed next door, and Alyssa gulped as she

found herself on the bridge of the *Sunward Sky*. The three people working in the room noticed Sharma's entry and pushed themselves back away from their workstations, rotating in their gimbaled seats.

"Alyssa, Isa, these are our nav officers, Meg, Nicola, and Mitchell. You all already know Healy," they nodded in greeting but didn't ask any other questions. "These three are trying to get to the bottom of a mission-critical problem. You're to provide all necessary resources to assist. Understood?"

More nods. "Good. How long do we have until we rendezvous with the next satellite?"

Meg spun in the couch quickly and checked her instruments.

"GPS Sat 1185 will be on approach in forty-eight minutes," she said.

"Any way of slowing that down?" Sharma asked.

"Not really," Meg said. "Our speed is set by the orbit. We'd have to burn a lot of fuel to change our trajectory, and we don't have it to spare."

Sharma rubbed his chin. "Okay. I'm going to search the ship. Isa, you're coming with me. Healy, Alyssa, work with these three. I want to find that thing before it screws everything."

With that, he turned sharply on his heel and stepped out into the corridor. Isa followed him, and the five left in the bridge were left staring at each other.

Quickly, Alyssa and Healy went over the details of what they were looking for, and the broad strokes of what Project blackout was trying to do. The three navigation techs took only a moment to look horrified before turning to each other and brainstorming. They quickly turned back to Alyssa and Healy.

"We need to check everywhere here. Make sure there's not a physical connection that's been plugged into the nav computer. That's our first port of call. If it's not something physical, we're going to need to check the subroutines on the comms computer, and we're going to have to do it quickly," Meg said to them.

The five of them scrambled around the desks and access terminals on the bridge. There were four workstations with a display screen set into a folded metal cabinet that sat on the floor near the gimballed couches. The couches were on rail mounts that could be pushed away from the controls and locked there. The access panels slid away and exposed a mess of wiring and printed circuit boards that served as the processing and controls for the terminals.

Alyssa, being small and nimble, squeezed underneath the terminals and flicked through the wiring. She was looking for anything that looked jerry-rigged, something that didn't seem to fit the specification of the rest of the computer. When she found nothing, she crawled back out into the main room and shook her head. Meg immediately leapt into action.

"Alright. If it's not a physical bug, it's something written into the comms code. Let me pull it up." Meg's fingers flashed over the console until she found the code repository for the navigation.

"Is there a recent pull request?" Mitchell offered, "A recent upload to the server. Maybe we could find it there?"

Meg shook her head, "Nope. The repository is uploaded in full prior to take-off. Any edits are done without a logged history, we'd need access to the mainframe to do it. If we want to find it, we're just going to have to look through the code,"

She pushed a series of buttons, then flicked her hands across the screen three times, "That's roughly a quarter of the codebase each, work through it on the monitors."

Alyssa and Healy looked at the screen. The time in the corner said there was only about thirty minutes until the satellite was in line of sight. Alyssa's coding ability was okay but not excellent, and there was about five thousand lines of code to get through.

Healy and herself minimised all the subroutines as they flew into place on her monitor. They began working through them, forcing themselves to slow down even though the timer counted inexorably downward. The documentation was spotty. Some routines had text notes with clear instructions and method definitions. Some were clearly laid out with rudimentary notes. Others were a jumble of variables and function statements. They filtered each subroutine, and whispered quietly to each other, explaining the code snippets that the other didn't understand. After a short while, Alyssa turned to Healy.

"Why'd you wake me up?"

Healy, head still in the code, took a moment to process the question. "What? Oh. It was just... you're doing it right, and I realised that."

"What do you mean?" Alyssa closed the subroutine down, pushed the small plus icon on the next one, and groaned. It was a nest of meaningless formulas and poorly named variables.

Healy stretched, frustrated. His long limbs managed to touch the ceiling of the room as he stood up, and the carabiners on his belt clanked loudly.

"What I mean is, I don't hate the Terrans. The dirtsiders,"

he changed the word with the air of an apology. "I'm not like some of the crew on Blackout. Some people *hate* everyone down the gravity well."

"But you don't?" *nothing in this routine either*, she thought, and opened the next one.

"No. I don't hate people for their comforts. I'm too old to be a revolutionary. I just didn't want anyone to have to go through the palsy again. Blackout seemed a way to stop it. Destroy everything, and nobody has to come up here anymore, you know? It's a terrible thing, losing your home planet to a disease you get because of the *work* you do. You take the job and lose your home."

Alyssa couldn't imagine. "I'm sorry," she whispered.

"I know you are," he paused, "I'm trying to help you now because if this medicine of yours works, it might help. Maybe traveling in space can become the adventure it was always *supposed* to be. And maybe nobody has to go through what I've gone through. What nigh everyone else on this ship has gone through. Maybe you can have your homeworld, and you can have your spaceflight. Because being up here?" he looked out the window to the immensity of the star field. "It's almost worth it. But not quite."

Alyssa looked aside from the subroutine and up at Healy. He had a wistful look in his eye, his immense form filled with boyish wonder as he stared out into the void.

She was about to open her mouth when the door to the bridge burst open, and Clarke dragged the captain through the door, holding a needle to his neck.

"You! You couldn't keep your mouth shut, could you?" he shouted at Healy, then pushed the needle closer to Sharma's neck, breaking the skin. "We're *so* close, we're *so close* to the end, and you turn coat. Why? Don't want to hurt them who've hurt us so much?"

"Settle down, Clarke. It's okay," Alyssa said, raising her hands in a conciliatory gesture.

"Shut up, you fucking Terran," Clarke spat, "or the captain gets stuck."

The navigation crew stood with their backs to the terminals, giving the man as much space as possible. Clarke was wide eyed and furious. A small part of her mind noticed the colour of the fluid. Drain cleaner. The same thing she'd threatened Brett with.

"I found him and that skinny little Terran on the way to the main airlock," Clarke was raving at Healy. "I dealt with her, don't you worry about that. Then I had to make sure he didn't know too much. So I asked him," he took the needle off the neck of the man and pointed it at Healy. "What did you do? You told him *everything*."

Nearby, Mitchell was edging into a better position so that he could grab the captain and whisk him away from Clarke and his syringe. He pushed closer, locking his knee next to the corner of the nav couch. He made to sneak forward again and his shoe scraped on the floor. Clarke darted around to face him.

"Don't even think about it, boy!" Clarke said, but Alyssa could see his hands were shaking. Was he scared?

Mitchell spoke. "Clarke, come on. It's okay," Mitchell's voice was deep, trying to soothe, "It's okay. You don't need to do this."

The shaking stopped. His eyes hardened. He pushed the syringe into Sharma's neck. Mitchell cried out and leaped from behind the seat and sprinted toward Clarke. Alyssa shouted and ran to catch Sharma, who was convulsing as he drifted towards the floor. Meg and Nicola ducked away from their stations to assist Mitchell, who was trying to avoid the now empty syringe as Clarke waved it at him like a dagger. Between the three of them, they managed to tackle him to the ground, but he still struggled against them.

Alyssa got to Sharma as he hit the ground. His eyes were already glazed over, and he was shuddering as the contents of the syringe worked its way through his system. He struggled to sit up, to look more fully at Alyssa. When he recognised her, he tried to speak.

"Isa… airlock… she… trapped…"

"Which airlock?!" Alyssa demanded, "Tell me!"

"Aft… systems…" He vomited bile, and his eyes went blank.

Alyssa dropped him. Healy was by one of the navigation terminals, frantically working on something, fingers flying. Nicola, Meg and Mitchell were still struggling against Clarke with limited success. Clarke had his arm pinned by Mitchell, and Nicola and Meg had turned him around and pushed his face against the window. Alyssa saw him move his legs to get leverage, as though he were about to push himself off the wall and throw the other three off him.

Without thinking, Alyssa launched herself into the fray. Clarke tried to twist around, but Alyssa had the element of surprise. She grabbed him by his wrist and began pushing it inward toward his body, angling the needle toward him.

He cried out, swore, and let go of the needle. Alyssa grabbed it before it could float down to the deck, and she pushed the point toward the man's chest. With eyes black as coal and burning hatred, he grabbed at her and stopped her mere millimetres above his ribcage. Alyssa grunted and tried to push down but couldn't get the leverage she needed.

Then the weight of the world shifted. A dull roar reverberated through the hull and the equilibrium of the fight changed. Alyssa flew off Clarke, who fell to the floor. She dropped the syringe, and scrambled to pick it up before Clarke saw it. He grabbed at her ankle and pulled her towards him. She twisted, and he lost his grip on her, and she stood up and jumped on top of him. A press of multiple bodies threw itself onto her back. The three navigation specialists all grabbed her arm as one, and pushed it down towards Clarke's chest. He cried out and pushed with all his strength but the needle moved inexorably down. It penetrated his skin and slipped between his ribs. Meg freed one of her hands and pushed the plunger, injecting nothing but air into the man's bloodstream. It took a moment for the air to travel through him and into his heart. He stuttered, and then began to suffocate. They all held on as he quivered and died in their arms.

Exhausted, the four of them rolled off each other and onto the floor, which was still roaring with the sound of the ships engines. Their breathing came hot and damp and warmed the air of the bridge. The air system hummed loudly to remove the sweat and moisture that had built up during the fighting.

"Oh god," Alyssa sat up. She started shaking, realising what they'd done. Clarke and Sharma's bodies lay inert and cooling beside her and the three navigation officers.

She'd killed someone.

"Don't think about it," Meg said, and grabbed Alyssa's hand. "Don't think about it. We had to. And right now, we need to get back to the subroutines. We only have a couple of minutes to stop the comms."

Healy turned and shook his head. "Don't worry about that," He said, his face carved from stone, "I came up with something."

Meg dashed to the navigation console, pushing Healy out of the way. Her eyes widened as she saw the modifications Healy had made. She stood up straight, and eyed the cold metal of the ship's bulkheads, listening to the engines as the noise thrummed through the metal.

"What have you done?" she asked.

The satellite lay in wait for the *Sunward Sky* to arrive, to slow until it orbit-locked with the satellite. It was waiting to receive a signal in the short-wave transmitter that had been attached to it three years prior. It was a simple flag, autocued and sent out like the "Hello, World!" of early computer programs. The simplicity would trigger a system scramble, but not before it beamed a similar instruction to the next satellite. Each satellite would receive and pass on from one to the next and the next and the next and all the way around the Earth until Project Blackout had destroyed the ability for humanity to rely on space-based communication and navigation.

Shortly prior to the *Sunward Sky* coming into line of sight to the satellite, all of its lights turned off. The ship was running dark, without even the infrared navigation lighting in the hallways. The crew were sent to their quarters, advised to strap themselves down. Told to prepare for an impact. The entirety of the ship's systems were powered down, from the lights to the systems to communications. The engines, which had been placed under a powerful burn only minutes before, went quiet. Everything was silent but the hum of the air systems and the shivering breath of the crew.

The *Sunward Sky* hurtled through space, a multimillion tonne ballistic. Its orbit had declined more than the flight plan suggested. It wasn't going to pass *near* the satellite with its hulking scarab crouched over it.

Inside the spaceship, the satellite loomed large through the window on the bridge, and Mitchell counted down under his breath. Alyssa listened.

Ten.

Alyssa tightened her grip on the gimballed navigation couch, determined not to make the same mistake she'd made on liftoff.

Nine.

Healy was back in the med bay, hunkered down after hauling the two dead bodies into the emergency couch.

Eight.

Isa was strapped into an emergency spacesuit and hiding in the airlock she'd been locked into by Clarke.

Seven.

The other members of Project Blackout were in their quarters, having realised that they didn't have time to storm the bridge. They'd tried to contact Clarke but the radio was jammed.

Six.

Ellyse noticed the lack of engine noise in the ship and realised what the navigation crew had done.

Five.

By turning off the ship's systems, the code that she'd so

carefully planted into the subroutines would never run within the short-range signal that the satellite could pick up.

Four.

Something clicked for Alyssa.

Three.

The shift in gravity she'd felt when she'd been fighting Clarke had been Healy realigning the *Sunward Sky's* orbit.

Two.

They weren't just going to spin *past* the satellite, and have it not be activated because the ship's comms were turned off.

One.

She stared out the window.

A looming blackness, a ceramic and chrome mass rushed at the centre of the *Sunward Sky*, its hulking form silhouetted against a roiling mass of Earth's clouds.

God, it's moving fast, she thought.

The *Sunward Sky* was in a degrading orbit, traveling at an incredible speed, far faster than the relative speed of the geostationary satellite when it impacted in the dead centre of the ship's main column. The satellite and the scarab attached to it rent apart and shattered into a wave of screaming metal, glass, solar cells and ceramic. The nose cone and central column on the spaceship crumpled along a third of the ships length, and the walls, designed for so much resilience to the air forces and resistances experienced in launch, tore like butcher's paper.

The deceleration on board threw each and every crew member into their harnesses, cracking ribs and clavicles and popping lungs. Anything not locked down became a missile, with small objects like glass containers and pill bottles punching through the steel bulkheads and crushing the insulation on the other side. Oxygen and propellant gases blew out the side of the spacecraft at odd angles where the satellite had punctured the tanks, flinging the enormous tonnage of the vessel into a vertiginous spin. The *Sunward Sky* careened through space in a slowly decaying orbit, with all hands onboard either unconscious, maimed, or dead.

On Terra, a distress signal was logged for a satellite, flashing yellow on a screen in the middle of a central system in the desert. It had stopped responding. Keegan saw it, and double checked the location of the anomaly.

He flagged a release for one of the backup satellites to drop in to place, to replace the one that had broken. Then he frowned. He pulled up the folder he'd been steadily working on for weeks now. The list of unusual occurrences around the *Sunward Sky* had grown long indeed. He'd put a flag on it, a private one that would notify him of the ship's proximity to any other anomalies in orbit, but it hadn't gone off.

Something wasn't right. He opened the flag and tried to find the *Sunward Sky*.

It wasn't there.

What the fuck? He thought. A crewed ship shouldn't be able to just disappear like that. Confused, he opened the logs and saw that the *Sky* had gone dark some time ago. Before that, there had been a sustained burn that had taken it off its flight plan significantly, into a degrading orbit at a high speed.

He had a hunch. He mapped out the *Sky*'s path, then

extrapolated it past the point where it had gone dark. Then he pulled up the satellite and mapped its path. He overlaid them.

"Oh, *shit*," He breathed.

PART

TWO

2.1

ADRIFT

The lights in the carpeted hallway sat somewhere between *tastefully ambient* and *too dark to see*, a forgotten miscommunication between lighting specialist and architect. The building was almost brand new, yet the corridor loomed a quiescent hush over any and all activity within. The carpet masked Alyssa's steps, turning them into a series of muted thuds. A door slammed open, then shut again, and a second pair of shoes, heavier than hers, thundered dully after her.

"Alyssa!" Male. Anxious. Angry.

Alyssa walked faster, ignoring the man. He started to jog, closing the gap between the two of them. Alyssa sped up again, but the man still reached her. She rounded on him.

"I don't want to hear it, okay?" she was fuming.

"You can't *speak* to them like that. They're the ones who *funded* your research, they can cut you off," he said, but Alyssa knew he meant *they can cut* me *off*, "In fact, I'd be more surprised if they didn't at this point!"

"I don't care," she turned to keep walking.

"Don't be impetuous—" the man started, before Alyssa cut him off.

"Impetuous? What am I, a child?! You're a coward and a sycophant. I can't believe you didn't stick up for me in there," she gestured back down the hall from the way they'd come.

"Keep your *fucking* voice down," he said, "Those are the biggest investors we've had in the last fifteen years and I'd appreciate it very much if you didn't scream at them down the corridor," he sighed, "or in the conference room, for that matter."

Alyssa's eyes could have burned holes in the man's face, "Don. We've developed a drug that potentially *halts* the onset of Space Palsy."

Don looked at her, impassive. "And?"

Alyssa threw her hands in the air in frustration. "And? Fucking *and?* For thirty years we've been building a series of stopgaps for a dying world. I'm about to go get my reflective parasol out of my locker so that I can walk outside without my skin roasting. The water filtration systems we've developed in the last ten years are nothing short of miraculous, and let's face it they'd better be, because the amount of micropollutants in the water have all but killed the marine life. We need ventilation fans everywhere in this place otherwise the particulates in the air would cake our lungs and stop us breathing.

"The planet is dying, Don. We've killed it. And you and I have found something that might be able to help. Really help. If not the planet then at least it might help us get away from it," she stepped back from the man and pointed back to the hall, "and *they aren't going to run trials*. They're happy to sit there and pull funding because they can't see a return in anything but money. And *you're* pandering to their bullshit," she turned and started walking away again. Don said something, but his voice came out flat and bland, incoherent and repetitive. The voice quacked, and blared, and blared, and repeated. He seemed very far away, and Alyssa tried to turn but she was stopped. Don was gone but the blaring continued. A crisp echo not deadened by the carpet or the carefully placed walls. A metallic edge, alarming… alarming…

It was an alarm.

Alyssa opened her eyes to find herself in the shattered control room of the *Sunward Sky*. Blood pooled and billowed next to her head in the low gravity. The gimballed couch was bent at an awkward angle and crushed to within an inch of its life. It hadn't been designed for impacts at such high speeds and it had been stretched to its limits. Alyssa's arm was bleeding slowly from a gash on her forehead, and her injured shoulder was sore, but she was unscathed aside from that. The alarm blared loudly around her. She could see one of the displays on the bridge screens, the only one not destroyed. Diagrams of red compartments and the words *Oxygen Breach* flashed on the screen. The parts flying off the satellite had punched through the hull from the outside, while parts of the ship had punctured outward from within as the ship had decelerated faster than it had ever been designed for.

Alyssa lurched painfully upward from the couch. The ship was still accelerating, but the gravity was driving her toward the corner of the room. She looked out the window and saw the Earth careening erratically. The *Sunward Sky* was caught in a queer inertial spin and lurching like a maimed whale around its usually solid central axis. Alyssa climbed from the seat and stepped off onto the ground, sliding down the tilted floor and into a corner some metres from the barely functional display. Meg, Nicola and Mitchell were all still out cold, and she pulled herself up to the nav console.

The ship was breached. As she looked at the display, the true extent of the damage became clear. One of the three wings was just *gone*, and the rest of the spacecraft was a mess. Red codes and mando glyphs appeared everywhere, flashing gold in syncopated time with the alarm system. The emergency lighting seemed miraculously unscathed, but ship wide communications were broken, and the recyclers had suffered catastrophic failures. The fact that any supplementary systems were running at all was astonishing, but Alyssa pushed it out of her mind and tried to work with what she had.

I have to get that alarm turned off, she thought, and tapped the display in the vague hope that she could find a setting to make the screeching klaxon silence itself. *Then, I need to stop this fucking spinning.* The lurching gravity was regular but not controlled, so she was constantly being pulled this way and that.

She'd have to try to rouse one of the nav experts. She climbed the wall that had once been the floor of the bridge, trying her best to slip her fingernails into the scant cracks of the grippy flooring. The other couches were arrayed above her, and she pulled herself up them one by one to try to rouse the deck crew.

She got to Nicola first. She appeared mostly unhurt, and Alyssa shook her, gently at first and then with more urgency. Nothing.

Alyssa watched the chest of the young flight officer, trying to watch for signs of breathing. She couldn't see anything.

Her heart sank.

Mitchell was dead, too. At some point during the impact, something had hit him. Well, not hit him. Passed *through* him. The object, whatever it had been, had shot straight through his sternum and left a bloody hole that punched straight through the floor that Alyssa had been climbing up. Only a glob of thick, dark red blood filling the void in his chest prevented Alyssa from staring straight through the man and into the decks below.

She shuddered. She hadn't even known the man, but he'd helped when Clark had attacked. It was such an ignominious way to die, she thought. A stray item, gone ballistic in extreme deceleration and punching a hole through you a million miles from anyone you knew. His face was pallid, and pale and utterly at ease. *At least he won't have to find a way out of here*, Alyssa thought, *He's already out.*

She lurched away, scrambling haphazardly up the floor to the final couch. The alarm still blared in the background and the room lurched sickeningly in an off-kilter rhythm as the ship careened recklessly through space. Alyssa found herself wondering how long it would be before they hit atmosphere. Would they burn up? Would she lose consciousness on the way down? Would she feel the impact as she'd felt the last one, only this time with the full crushing force of gravity on her as the rest of the *Sunward Sky* crumpled, throwing its significant weight straight onto her frame? Would it even matter?

She was very tired. Clinging onto the edges of an air grate with her fingernails, she laid her head onto the flooring on the side. The room seemed far away, suddenly, and she found she didn't much mind if she made it to Meg or not. She stopped wondering about Project Blackout. She stopped wondering if she'd make it home, whether the medicine would work, whether anything mattered at all. It all seemed so pointless now, in a way.

She thought of all the people she'd seen die, or hurt, or maimed or otherwise since she'd been on the *Sunward Sky*. She was a researcher. Why had she decided to do this?

You know why. A small voice in her head said. *Her* voice, though it seemed small and distant. Meg's crash couch was a few scant feet from Alyssa but seemed miles away. The cacophony of the siren went dull. *That's interesting… the tone is all quiet now,* Alyssa thought. It was probably fine. They probably toned it down because the ship was fixing itself. The cold metal grating of the floor was warm, and inviting, and smooth, and she pressed her cheek down into it. One of her eyes turned scarlet as the low gravity globule of blood pouring from her temple grew large enough that it sank into her open eye. The world was a blur of the red of blood and the crisp, meaningless, grey sheen of the floor. Before long, both of them faded to black.

The coolness of the cloth surprised her. A sharp sting of alcohol and a coarse, damp weave of fiber was wiped over her temple and as she regained consciousness she smelled the acrid stench of ethanol pervading her waking mind.

"Alyssa?" the voice was distant but rushing closer like a

train in a tunnel. "Alyssa, can you hear me?"

Alyssa opened her eyes and the cloth immediately went into the left one, wiping away the blood and burning her pupil with the alcohol solution. She yelped, and tried to turn her head away but a wiry set of hands held her as they continued to clear her up. Alyssa wanted to scream but found her throat hoarse and voice almost non-existent. She moved her hands up to feel her assailant, and when she heard a "Settle down. You're alright," she stopped panicking.

Meg. It was Meg.

The alarm was gone. The ship was silent again.

"How did you…?"

"Turn off the alarm?" Meg said. "It's an override switch. Notice we're still lurching about everywhere?" the gravity did indeed still have the drunken lilt Alyssa had noticed before, "I turned off the alarm but we still have the problem. We're in a degrading orbit, and we have no control over the ship. I need to get the attitude thrusters working again but they're fucked. I need your help. How are you feeling?"

Alyssa didn't know how to answer that. She looked at the woman, who was still a blur in a vignette of blood red. Meg was moving about with ease and efficiency, pushing with her legs like a rock climber in order to make her way to different parts of the bridge. She opened a cabinet and pulled out and ampule of fluid, then, holding it in her teeth, pushed back across to where Alyssa lay against one wall and held it out to her.

"Drink this. And while you're at it," she pulled a bandage from her pocket, "put this on your head."

Alyssa tore off the safety cap from the ampule and took

a swig. It was a saline water solution and it tasted awful, but she drank it with a grimace. After that she tore open the bandage and pressed the adhesive plaster to her head.

"What do you need?" Alyssa asked once she'd stopped the bleeding.

Meg looked up from the nav console.

"Right. To control this ship I need to be able to get to the attitude thrusters on each wing. One of the wings is just... fucking... *gone*. So I need to make some adjustments to control for the change of the ship's shape. Normally, I could do it from here but some ballistic must have gone through the emergency adjustment relay, all I'm getting is bad signal response. I need you to go manually switch them for me. I can tell you what to do, but I need to stay here to work them once they're adjusted, otherwise our orbit is going to degrade real fast."

Alyssa blinked. "Okay, where are they?"

"Aft. near the rear airlock for the satellite maintenance hatch."

Isa, Alyssa thought. She'd been trapped down there by Clarke just before he'd come back to the bridge and killed Captain Sharma. If she was going to the rear maintenance hatch, she'd be able to get Isa out of the airlock.

She turned to head out of the bridge.

"Alyssa?" Meg said, speaking barely above a whisper. "Don't let anyone see you. You don't know who's Blackout."

Alyssa nodded and headed out the door.

❖ ❖ ❖

The hallway was a hellscape.

Most of the lights had shattered into a thousand pieces which now danced gaily along the floor, reflecting shards of light that cast kaleidoscopic fractals across the walls. The sound of venting gas came from beyond an automatically closed bulkhead. The room had been exposed to the vacuum and was still releasing pressure. Alyssa took an alternative route via a service corridor.

The ship was nearly empty and rang with the hollow creep of the dead. There was no quiet contemplative silence of the off shift, nor was there the bustle of the active hours. A pall lay over the space, the void and absence screaming silently. Alyssa crept further and further down the corridor, jumping with every creak and pop of the injured spacecraft, wondering if she was being followed by anyone from the death cult she'd discovered aboard the ship in the days before the crash.

Healy had known there was no chance of finding the virus in the communications codebase before the *Sunward Sky* was due to rendezvous with the satellite, so he'd changed the altitude so that instead of floating by and pulling up alongside the satellite, the ship had crashed into it at full speed.

It had been the best thing for a bad situation, Alyssa thought as she staggered down the hallway aft. She was feeling a lot stronger after the electrolyte liquid she'd had, but getting to the other end of the ship was still a lot of work. She pushed one arm against what used to be the floor and planted her feet on either side where the corner met the wall. She reached the aft prep room, where she'd prepped for her first spacewalk, the time she'd discovered the scarabs and seen the co-conspirators that had led to this mess. She leaned into the door, thudding her shoulder against it to get it to open.

She burst through and could see the control cabinet that Meg had described to her in the corner. She could also see the airlock where Isa was held captive. Her eyes were drawn to the small porthole, hoping to see the dark face of the young girl who had been led into so much danger by Alyssa.

Not yet, she thought. She had to get the thrusters working otherwise the whole ship would go down. Isa could wait a few more minutes. She pulled herself to the cabinet and flung it open.

There was a large row of toggle switches, in a series of rows with inscriptions on them. They were the main bearings of each of the thrusters in relation to the centre of the *Sunward Sky.* They were switched back and forth along the rows, with red and green lights, as well as some that had no lights at all. Wing three had no lights on.

One third of this ship is gone, Alyssa could barely get to grips with the enormity of it. She found the series of thrusters that Meg had told her about, hunting them down according to their numbers and locations. She flipped a few of them, hoping she'd remembered them correctly, and the lights switched from red to green. She breathed out. There were two more she had to switch over, and she hunted for them. They were both on the edge of the cabinet and bent at a queer angle. The indicator for both of them was red. She flipped them.

The lights went dead.

Shit, Alyssa thought. Did that mean they were broken? Would Meg be able to get the ship righted again? Or would they slowly pick up speed, hurtling down to their doom on whatever part of the Earth that they were unlucky enough to land on?

Alyssa started to despair, holding on to the edge of the ship, and then she saw the first light flicker green.

Her heart leapt.

She watched intently, willing the other one to follow suit, and after a few seconds it did.

She could have screamed for joy, but instead she turned and scrambled to the airlock.

The ship lurched to life as Alyssa ran. The world turned around her as the floor became the floor again. The gravity was weaker than before, and the ship swayed like an old sloop in a stiff breeze.

Alyssa cycled the airlock, then rushed inside before stopping dead in her tracks.

Isa was in a suit, but it was obvious the young girl was dead. Her legs snapped out at all the wrong angles, and Alyssa could see the sharp edge of a compound fracture where shinbone had punctured both suit and skin. She was crumpled and broken and collapsed in a corner, her nose and face pressed against her helmet. No frost or fog was visible on the inside of the glass.

She was gone.

Alyssa collapsed on the ground next to her, and even as Meg continued to right the ship and get it into some semblance of normal flight, Alyssa wept, holding the lifeless body of the young girl.

2.2

REGROUP

Ellyse's world swam into her vision as the nightmare sound of a klaxon invaded her consciousness. The room was caught in a blood-red monochrome, all hard lit edges and deep blacks that strained her eyes even as the details came into focus. She tried to sit up, but a pressure and a crisp pain slashed across her chest. She fell back with a gasp, then clasped at her ribs. Breathing too deeply hurt. She panicked, trying to move away from the source of the pain but found herself unable to manoeuvre in the dark.

After a short struggle with each movement proving more

painful and more fruitless than the last, she regrouped and felt carefully around her body. It was her safety harness. The straps holding her into place had been fastened firmly and were stopping her from sitting up or moving. Unclipping, she gingerly prodded at the base of her ribs. There was a spongy sensation where it should have been more solid, and the now familiar pain made sense as it screamed through her.

Not good, she thought. At least one of her ribs had been fractured in the crash. There was something wrong with the ship's movement. The normally even press of the artificial gravity was modulating, pressing more heavily for a few seconds before abating, then pressing again in a slow but urgent rhythm. Each time the gravity shifted, her ribs grated against her. The med bay. She'd have to see Healy.

Healy, she thought.

The bastard. He'd always had too much heart. Whenever the team had convened, his voice would sing the loudest in protest. The plan, the ultimate plan, to plunge the planet into telecommunications darkness had always stuck in his craw. Too extreme, he'd say.

No less extreme than the Terran companies that left them up here, getting sick and dying in space with no recourse or recompense or ability to return home.

Apparently, it had been too much for the big man, and he had ruined it all mere hours before their triumph.

All that work. They'd had a few allies on the ground. Doomsday types in bunkers mostly, sought out through backchannels and onion-routed logistics, made good with quid pro quo engineering and supply runs. Their silence was bought with a promise that they'd be safe when everything had gone offline.

The biggest breakthrough had been the scarabs. They had struggled for a long time with how to override the programming in the satellites, but the kind of people who lived in the dark places of secondary networks and encrypted pathways could find the way in with enough time and wideband processors.

From there it was just logistics. Getting the scarab to the launch crater, and then swapping it onto the ship in lieu of some other cargo, making it make weight, and adjusting the logs. It wasn't too hard, especially because most people stuck working in the terminal themselves didn't really care. You show up with a high visibility vest and people don't ask questions. Clarke had seen to that.

Clarke, she thought. She'd have to find him.

If Healy had turned, he was for the airlock. There was nothing else for it. If they made it back to Earth he knew too much, and it would be easy to write it off as an accident otherwise. The big man was much stronger than she was, so she'd need Clarke's help to deal with him. She'd need to rally the other members of Blackout.

With a groan and a hand pressed to her chest in a futile attempt to quash the pain, she pulled herself off the bed and pressed the light panel. The main lights flickered and guttered out and her eyes took another few seconds to readjust to the infrared darkness. Cursing softly, she stepped out of the room and into the corridor into the destruction of the hallway. A nearby cabin door swung open, creaking as though rusted in the strange heaving gravity of the ship. The hall was silent but for the scrapes and moans and catatonic thuds echoing down the fuselage.

She heard the padding sounds of someone else's footsteps echoing down the hall and ducked into the nearest room. She held her breath and ground her teeth against the pain in her ribs.

The footsteps grew louder, and she slid further back into the cabin. Whoever belonged to the cabin hadn't secured their gear before the crash. Personal effects littered the floor, and the open cupboards were a kaleidoscope of ruined belongings. A tag on a backpack read *M. Holding.*

She turned back around just in time to see Brett pass the door. Ellyse hissed his name. He dashed into the room, running into her in the strange gravity. She gasped in pain.

"What is it? Are you hurt?"

She grimaced, "Yeah. Need to go to the med bay. But we need to figure out where everyone else is first. What the fuck happened?"

Brett shrugged. "I don't know. Healy told us to strap in for an impact, but beyond that? I have no idea what's going on."

The last Ellyse had seen of Healy was when he'd been looking after the two drugged girls, Alyssa and Isa, in the medical bay. She had no idea where anyone else was.

"Right. We're going to have to get the rest of us together," Brett said. He pulled a radio from his breast pocket and switched the frequency to the channel that Blackout had been using. Brett tried to hail anyone who might be listening, but there was no response. The chirp of the radio's static echoed down the ruins of the spacecraft's hallways, and the two of them sat in silence as they waited.

"Looks like we're going to have to find them ourselves," Brett said after a few seconds.

Ellyse nodded, then grimaced in pain as the gravity

pressed down again.

"First, let's get to the med bay."

Waugh coughed up a glob of spit and blood. Her left side screamed in pain whenever she breathed. She held her arm against her side as she stumbled up the passageway with its lilting, broken gravity.

When she'd woken up, the gravity had poured her into the corner of her room, and she'd started to climb toward the bridge. When the ship had righted itself and stabilised into its new strange but consistently bouncing gravity, she'd reconsidered. If the gravity had been normalised, it meant that one of the nav specialists was still in the bridge, and she wasn't in the shape for a fight. Instead, she'd started to assess the state of the ship after the impact.

No sooner had she made the decision to head aft again had she found a depressurised section of the ship and had to reroute through the galley and mess. She stopped in at one of the crew meeting rooms to look out the side of the spacecraft to see what had happened to the opposite wing.

What she'd seen had chilled her.

Instead of a looming expanse of black metal, she saw a colossal mess of rent steel and shattered formwork. The huge struts, hoses, walkways and conduit lines that had connected the wing to the ship were no longer the aging but finely engineered pieces of material she was familiar with. In their place was a warped and congealed mess, shattered, stretched and broken. The wreckage that had broken off but had not been flung away by the satellite was slowly drifting out from where the wing should have been in a dark cloud of metallic shrapnel. As she watched, several pieces of twisted conduit hit the window and bounced lightly off it.

Holy shit, she thought, and headed aft as the intercom crackled to life for the first time since the crash. It was Meg's voice.

"Attention all crew. The spin of the Sunward Sky has been corrected and is being controlled through attitude thrusters. The shift in gravity you are feeling is a compensation for the ship weight that has been lost due to the recent collision.

"At this time, movement through the ship should only be attempted if necessary. Repeat, only move throughout the ship where necessary. Greater crew movement will increase the likelihood of turbulent motion due to thruster correction.

"Please note that while the ship is now trimming straight, our course is not. We are currently in a slowly degrading orbit, and at this stage we are assessing options with the current fuel reserves available.

"Navigation will update as more information becomes available."

Waugh wiped her mouth on her sleeve and waited for sounds of disbelief or concern or terror to come from the crew quarters behind her. Nothing was forthcoming, and she staggered on, trying not to think about what that meant for the number of people who had survived the crash.

❖ ❖ ❖

"How do we stop a degrading orbit?" Brett asked after the communication on the ship had gone through.

Ellyse was wincing. "It's mass and inertia. We need to

move stuff off the ship, which means jettisoning whatever we can. We'll start with the cargo hold, but if that doesn't work…" She didn't finish the sentence, and the two of them walked down the corridor without speaking further. They rounded the corner and could see the med bay door as a small shape walked through it. They kept walking toward the room but when they were a few metres away they heard a scuffle emanate from the doorway. A woman's voice cried out and there was the thudding sound of fist on cloth. A series of clinks, like small pieces of hanging metal clanging together rang out, and then silence again.

They both froze. Brett indicated for Ellyse to fall in behind him, and they covered the last few metres to the door. He leaned his back against the wall.

Still silence.

In a quick motion, Brett pivoted out and around the wall, moving just into the room and out of Ellyse's view.

"Stay there or I'll drop you, too," a voice growled.

Ellyse dashed forward and through the door. At the back of the room was Waugh, blood and spit dribbling from her chin, splayed out on the floor with her head to one side. Her breathing was deep and regular, but the muscles on the left side of her body were spasming.

Next to her, the carabiners on his flight suit clinking softly, standing taller than both Brett and Ellyse, with a thunderous look on his face, stood Healy.

2.3

CONTROL

Meg stared at the small control screen in front of her, willing the information she'd been fixated on for the last half hour to change. It was a fruitless exercise, but for the moment it was distracting her from the pain. She wasn't hurt as badly as Alyssa, who she'd sent to reset the thrusters. She could deal with the minor scrapes she'd been lucky enough to get away with.

There was only one screen left on the bridge she could get any sensible information out of. She'd disabled the heads-up display in the main viewing window as it was an extravagance a broken ship with an unknown power reserve could ill afford. The main control panels, the large touch screen desks that had been the main ship interface, had failed when the capacitive displays had been flung through the glass protective casing. She was now operating on a small screen with physical keyboard and input wheels.

She barely remembered how to use them. The last time she'd completed the "compulsory" manual emergency training had been well over three trips ago, probably more than a year on Terran time, and there were no compliance checks being done by the company that commissioned the spacecraft.

The ship was significantly lighter than launch weight, due to the scale of the damage it had incurred on the crash. Its orbit had been thrown off course and it had been sent careening after hitting the satellite. However, with the crew, remaining cargo, and other necessities on board it was still a huge pile of scrap metal moving far too fast, even after altering the spin to get the ship trimming properly again.

Too fast for her comfort. Several hundred kilometres an hour faster than the cruising speed the *Sunward Sky* would normally be doing at this point in the mission. That in and of itself wasn't a problem. An underlying concern was that the spin inducing the false gravity was no longer aligned along the ship's central axis. It was pulsing, throwing things up and down ever so slightly, and with the ship in the shape it was, Meg was concerned about more systems breaking.

Her computation came back. She let out a long, tired sigh.

The screen showed a small image of a blue-green ball, with a small white dot hovering above it. The dot was at the front of a small, solid yellow line. In front of the dot was a dashed yellow line. The dashed yellow line rotated in a tightening spiral around the ball, before the angle abruptly steepened and terminated in a red circle on a large green section on the ball.

They had less than a week to find out how to stay in orbit.

Meg navigated back to the home menu and began a different calculation, trying to fight the panic rising in her stomach.

❖ ❖ ❖

Healy stared down Ellyse and Brett, people he'd once counted as co-conspirators, or colleagues. He was breathing heavily. He would be able to defend himself against Ellyse if he had to, but he knew he'd be done for if they both attacked at once.

"She's okay," Healy said, gesturing behind him to Waugh's prostrate form, "I didn't kill her," she looked like a mess, but the two of them weren't to know it hadn't been him that caused the blood in her mouth. He'd just put her down after she'd staggered into the room demanding treatment for her wounds but threatening to kill him at the same time.

"Listen," he said. Brett and Ellyse looked ready to murder him. "She's out cold, and she's bleeding into her mouth right now. I have to move her, or she'll choke."

"Fuck you," Ellyse spat, but Brett shushed her.

Healy tried again. "Just let me move her. Put her on the doc. Then we can talk."

They considered, and the only sound in the room was the grating gasp of the ship's recyclers. The unconscious woman lay limp in the corner. One of the cabinets on the wall had been rent off in the crash, and a clear, pungent liquid flowed like gelatine across the floor. The throbbing of the sick ship rattled everything around them. Ellyse was gasping, gripping her ribs. Brett stood down and spoke to Healy.

"Ellyse needs help too."

Alyssa's muscles screamed at her, blinded as she was by tears and sweat running into her eyes. She leaned back further, pulling Isa's lifeless form down the corridor towards the med bay.

In some back corner of her mind, a part shut off by fear and grief, she knew that it was useless to take the girl to the med bay. Isa was clearly dead. Her sclera pooled with blood and deep black bruises covered the parts of her body that weren't hidden by the spacesuit's underlayer. Alyssa didn't care. She needed to get her to safety, and Healy and the med bay was the only place she knew to trust. He'd know what to do. Even if it was just to confirm the evidence of her own eyes. To let her know she wasn't stuck in a nightmare and that the only innocent soul, the only friend she'd found on the spaceship was dead.

The corridor was long, and her legs screamed. Isa's body was slight but cumbersome, and recalcitrant to being moved. Alyssa dragged, timing her efforts to align with the lulls in the rotational gravity.

She stopped at a corner to catch her breath. Murmurs and susurrations from other crew members in their cabins echoed down the halls. Cries for pain, cries for help. She couldn't stop. She'd found herself in the hallway where she'd flung herself out, pursued by what she now knew to be the members of Blackout. The locked port on the ceiling and the bulkheads cast deep recesses in the light thrown on the walls. The lighting in this section of the ship was so destroyed, so steeped in shadow that it would have been dangerous to navigate in the unstable gravity, let alone drag a corpse. Alyssa kept on, pulling and grunting and gritting her teeth as she grappled with Isa's limp form, desperate to get to the med bay. The same place that three members of Blackout had Healy pinned.

❖ ❖ ❖

The radio wasn't working properly. It couldn't connect to the broad beam that would allow it to bounce off the planet wide receivers. These were the systems that were usually monitored for comms. Now though, Meg was relying on the shortwave connections to emergency stations that were peppered around the globe, usually not far from launch sites. Like most of the infrastructure that had been deemed nonessential to the operation of the ships, most were decommissioned completely, and those that remained weren't manned at all hours. She was pinging the usual satellite emergency response channels, but only got automated responses, if she got anything at all.

What's more, her orbit was so far off skew now that she was in the shadow of the Earth for almost all the stations and had only a small window in each orbit where the emergency system was contactable. The rest of the time, she was stuck in the Earth's shadow, dancing in the face of danger as the orbit degraded.

She checked the corner of her near-useless screen. The timer was ticking down to when she could hail the next emergency tower. She had a few minutes, so she built a packet of information to send once she got there. Her fingers danced across the ancient, pixelated screen and keyboard controls as she moved the flight record, current trajectory, weight class and distribution of the ship, the full error log, and her work so far in calculating a safe landing vector. She ignored the warning lights flashing yellow and red all over the screen.

Once she'd built the information packet, she ran another calculation, trying to maximise their time on the float by changing jettison release schedules and strategic engine burns. The most she'd managed until now was eight days. She punched in another series of numbers, another round of coordinates. Set to jettison what she could, used a conservative fuel estimate, then hit the calculation.

She leaned back and rubbed her eyes. The deep dread of already knowing the answer, that there was no way out of this, was threatening to consume her. She bit back the panic again, forced it down like so much bile. For the moment, all she could do was keep firing the attitude thrusters to keep adjusting the ships wayward spin. The orbit would stay stable for at least two more days, even in the worst-case scenario.

The computer chimed.

She looked. Again, the dot circled the earth along the dashed line. The orbit became unstable after two days. The fuel burn and jettison of all nonessentials pushed the ship into high orbit, like a shot of energy to an electron shell, but the degradation set in even faster. The simulation had a countdown showing just over six and a half days until the inevitable crash, down to the seconds, which ticked along inexorably.

With each beat of the countdown, Meg tapped her thumb against the side of the archaic screen. The soft *noise* echoed in the room and mixed with the strained thrum of the engines. The numbers loomed until they were her whole world, a countdown so inevitable she didn't know how she'd thought she could escape it. She was out of ideas and now her only choice was one of ice or fire; fling herself from the orbiting station and drift into the void or wait until the re-entry and burn with all the other souls aboard or get crushed by the gravity of Earth.

Her head felt engorged. The sound of the engines, usually so calming to her, a reminder of her control of the *Sky*, became a cacophony and pounded at her skull. The blinking dot of the spacecraft and the ever-changing numbers of the countdown were all she could concentrate on. She was breathing hard, hyperventilating. A sharp edge on the control deck cut into her hand and a bright red streak of blood appeared on the white of her knuckles. She didn't notice.

They were all going to die.

2.4

PATIENTS

"Don't you fucking move," growled Healy, and Brett stopped in his tracks.

They'd spent the last half hour working together in the darkened med bay. Healy had got Waugh into one of the beds with Brett's help, lifting her up into the couch and turning her so that the blood would drain out onto the pillow instead of down her throat. Healy administered painkillers through a drip that would keep her unconscious until he could deal with her again. Then they'd eased Ellyse in as well. Her injuries weren't as severe, but she was still in a lot of pain. She got some drugs too; her eyes glazed over, and the grimace faded from her face.

Brett stood silently and glared as Healy saw to the two Blackout operatives. Healy had kept a close eye on him, and as soon as they were done administering what little help they were able to in the near-destroyed med bay, Brett had made to attack him.

Healy kept talking as Brett regarded him with silent fury. "It would behoove you to keep in mind that I'm the only thing stopping your friends here from dying," Healy said. "Now, don't take that as a threat. I aim to keep them alive anyway. It's what I do. You just need to know it before you try to do anything to me."

Brett was silent and glanced at the bed with Ellyse in it. She was out, eyes closed, breaths coming in short rasps. Brett stared over her supine body at the tall old man.

"Three years. For this?" he said.

Healy snapped up, warning in his voice. "Don't."

"Don't what? Ask why you betrayed us?" Brett's voice was a whisper, hoarse and violent. "Three years, and you turn at the last moment. Why help them?"

Healy didn't respond to the question. When he spoke his voice was flat and level and threatening. "I need to concentrate. Please leave. I am tending to my patients."

"Why? Why help *them*?" he gestured to Ellyse and Waugh. "They're who you betrayed. They're the people you'd worked with for *so long*. You know what the Terrans did to you. You know you can't go home. You know it's their fault," He gesticulated wildly, "and you signed with Blackout to help us. You signed up for vengeance. You signed up to see them hurt. You signed up to—"

"*Don't*," growled Healy, every syllable a whisper holding the threat of a storm, "tell *me* what *I* signed up for. Now *get out. I am tending to my patients.*"

Brett fell silent, and stepped back with his hands raised, heading to the door. As he left, he gestured lamely at the two tables and spat "Why even *help* them then?" before slamming the door shut behind him.

Because, thought Healy, *it's what I do.*

It hadn't always been, he thought as he bent to work on Waugh's wounds. Years ago, he'd felt the same kind of furious zeal that Brett and Blackout now possessed. The kind of screaming fury that the only path he'd been able to take had destroyed his chances of anything like a normal life down on the rock. He'd had friends, such as they were, in the slums.

Most of them had been struggling the same as him. Repeated beatings while sleeping rough on the streets drove most of them to stimulant usage in an attempt to stay awake. High and alert you could fight back when drunk thugs picked you as an easy target. Sober and asleep, you'd wake up with boots in the ribs and blood in your mouth. The addiction was the lesser of two evils more often than not. He'd been on the rock bottom when they found him. Starving, a needle in his arm or a glass pipe in his mouth. They'd offered him a job, in exchange for "rehabilitation".

They'd cured him of the drug problem alright, sending him out of atmosphere away from cruel boots and cold streets. He'd done a rotation as a general crew member and by the time he'd tried to go home and turn his meager spacefarer's paycheck into something more with his life he'd found himself unable to survive on his home planet. The gravity crushed him.

He found it hard to breathe. He couldn't walk without shaking, and even then only for a little while. He was as much a pariah as he'd always been, and so he'd done what they all ended up doing. He signed up for another rotation, and the ship became his home.

He'd railed against it. Fury had filled his every waking moment for years, white hot and hateful. His friends had moved on. They'd probably forgotten all about him by now, the sad teenage junkie who went into the sky and lost the Earth for it.

But that was years ago. The blessing of age, and time, was its ability to dull the aches of existence, and his blazing anger had dulled to a coal. He'd become a ship medic, then undergone as much training as he could, until he was one of the most qualified on any orbital manned ship still in the sky. A sort of catch-all physician.

When he'd been approached by Blackout, furtively, asking what he thought of the way the spacefarers were treated, that coal of anger had been prodded, and the fire had come back. The ghost of the impotent rage had burned in his chest again, and he'd signed on to help bring about what he thought was going to be the end of the world. Total destruction of communication and navigation systems, rendering each person on the surface as isolated as the spacefarers were. A new dark age.

But just as age had dulled the fury the first time, he found his appetite for hatred wasn't what it used to be. He'd gone to the meetings, heard the impassioned speeches about revenge and violence and hatred and found that he was, more than anything, tired. He didn't want the world to burn. He just didn't know any other way to end the cycle of cruelty.

Then Alyssa had showed up. This bright Terran, the kind

he'd always assumed didn't care or didn't know. But *she* did. She cared enough that she was going to test out her medicine on *herself* to see if it wouldn't stop the horrid palsy that plagued everyone he knew. She could *help*. She was not being driven by hate. She wasn't being driven by a lament of her own situation. She knew what was being inflicted and she was taking a great personal risk in an attempt to set it right. She was putting herself in harm's way to help people like him.

And the fact that there had to be more people like her on planet Earth made him stop. He couldn't go through with the plan. He couldn't plunge the world into the dark out of fear. He had to stop it, and the crash had been the only way he knew how.

Now, again, he was alone. He was surrounded by people who wanted nothing more than to do him harm. He was stuck on a shattered machine that had been home to him for the majority of his life. He was scared. He felt alone like he hadn't felt since he'd been on the streets, and he had no idea what would happen next.

But he'd tend to his patients, because that was what he did.

A scuffling sound came from the door, and it hissed and slid open. An exhausted, sweating Alyssa poured through the door and collapsed backward. Something hit her chest. Something frail. Barely clad. Female.

Alyssa looked at him, tears mingled in the sweat pouring from her brow.

"*Help*," she said.

2.5

CONTACT

Keegan was tracking the *Sunward Sky*, building up a flight path from an incomplete image of its movements. He'd see it for a few minutes, and then it would disappear again into the shadow. Normally, he'd be able to use the ship's inbuilt transponder, but he suspected that it had been destroyed when it had collided with the satellite.

For the last several hours, he'd been trying to make contact with the ship. The first time he'd seen it, it had been careening out of control, end over end and looping around the Earth, slowly losing altitude and speed as energy burned off after its orbital anomaly. Then, after it had gone dark for the better part of an hour, it had shown up in the wrong place on the horizon. Where before it had been flipping uncontrollably and following a regular orbit, it now seemed to be in a more regular but still off-kilter spin. Its orbital trajectory had changed as well. Rather than following the flight path it had been set along after its collision, it had skewed further along a north-south axis and was slowly drifting longitudinally.

The change in orbit had made it hard for Keegan to track it, but once he found it again and saw the change, he knew someone was alive on the ship, and someone was in control.

It was at that point he'd called his supervisor again. A swift exchange of words and the supervisor had started to work on contacting the ship's owners and manufacturers, to alert them of the crash. Nearly a day later and he still hadn't been able to contact them. Keegan wasn't part of that process, there were higher ups concerned with the management of the ship, and he couldn't help but be more concerned with the people on it than the inevitable insurance claim.

While the management team attempted to contact the company, Keegan stayed on shift late and when he saw the ship's orbit shift, he'd started trying to contact it. Contacting directly by transponder was impossible; if it weren't he'd have been able to track the ship in the Earth's shadow. By the time he'd figured that out, the ship had gone behind the shadow again.

He'd sworn but put the time where the ship was out of contact to good use. Tapping quickly on one keyboard, he'd isolated a set of shortwave frequencies that he might be able to use. Certain frequencies were locked by different corporations for inter-ship communication, and his radio equipment would automatically skip over those frequencies. The remaining bands were not highly available and had the unfriendly tendency to drop and corrupt data along the way.

When this was a simple voice command, all that would happen would be that the voice would glitch out; you might lose a word or two while the thing recalibrated, but you could still carry a conversation. If you were transmitting data though, it became a huge problem. Corruption in a compressed file meant that the file would decompress into junk, or worse, something actively harmful.

Harm was unlikely, Keegan reasoned. The biggest and most likely issue was that any data exchange would be slow and liable to damage. That, however, was likely an insurmountable issue considering the rapidly deteriorating orbit of the ship. Slow, unreliable data became a huge problem in emergency situations.

Not for the first time, he cursed the way the shipbuilding corporations had set up. Each of them in competition, each fighting for their place in the sky, with no collaboration and actively guarded secrets between them, upheld by corporate espionage and lawyers on immense retainers. He wanted to help these people, but he found his ability limited not by technology but by tribalism. In the interest of profits, these companies had locked down immense amounts of functionality that could have saved lives. As far as Keegan knew, none of the ships could even dock with one another, so an out-of-atmosphere emergency crew transfer was also impossible.

He sat brooding, waiting for the ship to come back around and out of the shadow. The scant open frequencies he had access to were in a list, and he kept all the receivers open and available in case someone tried to hail him.

A few minutes before he expected to see the tumbling

barrel of the ship come back over the horizon, he had a thought. Working quickly, he turned to one of the transmitters, one that sat on a motorised three-axis joint not far from his observation post. He logged its latitude and longitude and mapped it against his current location. Then he plugged in the details of the *Sunward Sky's* orbit, and had the computer transpose it across to the location.

Outside, several miles away, the radio transmitter rotated around and down, pointing to where the *Sunward Sky* was due to appear over the horizon at any moment. It was calm, and in the deserted night it was the sole thing moving in the desolate landscape. Then it stopped, staring away and waiting.

Keegan nodded to himself, adjusting altitude and azimuth data to match the path of the maimed ship so the transmitter would continue to point in the right direction even as the ship kept moving.

He checked his timer. Not long now. As soon as it started over the horizon, he'd hail it with every frequency he had, and if anyone was at the comms, they'd hear him.

Hopefully.

As he pressed the doubt into a small corner of his mind, the timer hit zero. He couldn't hear it, but a series of stepper motors on the transmitter hummed to life, buzzing into the cool night air as it tracked what looked like a small, dark star as it danced across the blue-black of the evening.

Keegan began hailing, not even speaking, simply sending a concentrated packet of data that contained the information about his observation station, the comm frequency to use, and a status query. It was a miniscule piece of data but even so he sent it in triplicate lest the data get scrambled on its way to the ship.

When he'd sent the three copies of the hail, he switched to another of the open frequencies, returned to the header data and altered the comm frequency, and sent it out again. He only had a few minutes until the ship went dark again. He needed to see if he could get an answer.

Adjust header file. Hail, hail, hail. Switch frequency. Adjust header file. Hail, hail, hail. Switch frequency.

For nearly eight minutes he tried this and before long the ship was already well past its apogee and was beginning to descend into the dark of the evening, and Keegan was trying not to get frantic as he raced the clock.

Hail, hail, hail. Switch. Adjust. Hail, hail, hail. Switch.

"Unknown observation station, come in unknown observation station," Keegan jumped and nearly fell out of his chair. The voice coming through his headset was female and the signal was slightly distorted, but it sounded more like equipment noise than an issue with the connection.

"This is obs, we hear you," Keegan gave their station number and his name, then, "What is your status, over?"

The voice was calm but Keegan could hear the tension. "We made contact with a satellite, and it got us good. We're down one wing, and our orbit is destabilising. I don't know how long I can keep the spin stable with the attitude thrusters either. We're lurching about," she gave a brief rundown of the systems and status of the ship.

"How are the crew?" Keegan asked after he'd noted as much as he could about the ship's status.

"Can't tell, really. Unknown casualties. Captain dead. Rest of nav team dead. There's a—" she seemed about to say something else, then stopped and asked, "is this an encrypted line?"

"Negative," Keegan said.

"Never mind," came the voice, "Help us land, and I'll be able to—"

The connection died.

He swore. The ship had fallen behind the horizon again, and he was left with an open, hissing connection. He logged the frequency the woman had made contact on and left it open as he collated the ship's flight data. The orbit was slightly off his last calculations, so he made some adjustments, wondering why it hadn't followed the same path. The transmitter span back to the opposite horizon, facing back out towards where it had picked up the *Sunward Sky* mere minutes before, with a slight bearing change to account for the skew in the ship's orbit.

Keegan flicked all this data to his supervisor, and then made a list of information he needed to get from the woman on comms. Truth be told, he didn't quite know what to do after that point. Gathering information was the extent of his remit while on shift, and rarely had he been required to action anything, far less something as immense as the impending crash of a manned ship. He hoped that finding enough information from the *Sunward Sky* as quickly as possible would mean he could sift through it and find a solution, or at least a course of action. So information was what he would ask for.

After a while, he had nothing to do but wait.

Nearly an hour later, as the stepper motors in the transmitter whirred once again, and the glowing edge of sky on the horizon grew an iota brighter, Keegan leaped into action, ready to ask the long list of questions as quickly as he could. But before he got the chance, the woman's voice crackled again through his headset.

"Alright, comms. We're going dark roughly once every fifteen minutes. Here's what we're gonna do."

Keegan listened closely. It was going to be a long shift.

2.6

TEMPUS

Eleven hours later, Meg was rubbing her eyes and trying to ignore the image of the slowly packaging compression software that had burnt onto her retinas. The countdown was going again. Twelve minutes, sixteen seconds. A few seconds shorter than last time.

Meg watched the progress bar on the compression algorithm tick inexorably upward. She'd scrubbed the flight control data as much as she could, tamping it down to what she thought were the bare necessities. She had to get it to the ground, to this Keegan in the obs station, on an immensely slow connection. As a result, she was running it through a compression algorithm so intense she'd be surprised if he got anything but noise when he unpacked it.

If she managed to beam it down at all. The orbit of *Sunward Sky* was sharpening, and the amount of time spent free of the Earth's shadow in relation to whatever transmitter Keegan had access to was shrinking. When she'd first hailed him, they'd had just over sixteen minutes for each orbit, but a few rotations later and they were down to less than twelve and a half minutes.

Ninety-three percent. She stared at the blip on the nav chart, dancing closer to the horizon. It was going to be tight. The first set of data hadn't even got a third of the way through before the comms array fell into the shadow and she'd had to start over.

She'd sworn loudly at nobody in particular and hit the bulkhead, then spent most of the intervening time before the next broadcast sorting between the essential data and that which could be safely ignored.

As soon as she'd got in sight with the next orbit, she'd been ready.

"This is *Sunward Sky*, do you read?"

"We read you, *Sunward Sky*. Data transmission failed. Presumed to be too much data on the connection."

"Acknowledged. I am going to attempt to retransmit via shortwave on the next orbit. I have scrubbed the data to the essentials for ground crew assistance in resolving an emergency flight plan. Please confirm transceiver is operational and ready to receive."

"Confirm, new data packet ready for receipt."

The next few minutes had been angles and bearings and calibration, then crackling silence again as the ship had sunk into shadow.

The first transmission had failed. Something that had been transmitted had corrupted, and Keegan had delivered the bad news. Each time they transited through the shadow Meg had scrambled through the computer's subsystems, cleaning the data and optimising it to make sure they could transmit the whole thing in the window, adding redundancy where she could so it was more likely to survive being beamed to ground. Each time they tried, the communication window shortened.

Ninety-seven per cent.

She hadn't fed or watered herself since the crash. Her lips were cracked, and she was starting to have trouble concentrating. If the data transfer didn't work this time, she wasn't sure she'd have another chance.

The indicator she'd set up still blinked yellow, letting her know that they weren't out of the shadow yet.

Ninety-nine percent compressed.

She breathed deeply. The orbit of the spacecraft was almost completely out of phase with the spin of the Earth. Of course, the time window would open up again as the ship's orbit came back around from the antipodean side and started drifting back into view of the observation post. However, that would take another several days, and they didn't have that kind of time.

One hundred per cent.

Meg forced her dull mind to concentrate, and hovered her hand over the transmit button. She placed her palm against the rough metal edges of the ship for stability. Dehydration had made her hands shaky and if she sent the packet too early, the header file would be sent into the ground instead of to the transceiver and make the whole file useless.

The disaster area that was the ship's bridge receded into the background as she watched the blinking light.

Yellow. Black. Yellow. Black. Yellow. Black.

Green.

Meg slammed her finger into the transmit button and allowed herself a moment of reprieve. She sank onto her knees. The flight suit scuffed slightly onto the floor and she sobbed silently as the details of the *Sunward Sky's* current trajectory and state were sent to the ground.

"Don," Alyssa gestured, "come have a look at this."

The other lab tech came over and peered at the results that Alyssa had propped in front of her. A series of nigh-incomprehensible scatter plots fanned out across the screen. Each of the plots was set against a soft yellow background with feint lined guides along it in a simulacrum of a physical notebook. Alyssa knew Don found her preference for the imagery of real paper to be quaint, but it allowed her to compartmentalise the file structure more easily than the spew of data that a lot of researchers used. Plus, it looked nicer.

"What?" his irritation was not unusual and not directed at her. The two of them had been working together for years, since before finishing their doctorates, and Don's 'old before his time' schtick had long stopped bothering Alyssa.

"Look," she said. "This latest batch. Electrolytic response is through the roof on it. It has some very weird reactions with alkali metals, and—" Reaching into the air above the desk, she twisted her hands and pulled up a holographic rendition of an amino acid molecule. As she and Don watched, a neural network tried and failed to fold the amino acid into a complex series of protein chains. She pulled another synth-file along and dragged it off its false piece of paper and set it adrift in the virtual 3D sandbox with the hologram. The synth-file loaded, flickered, and then drifted to where the enormous protein chain sat inert. After a few seconds, the amino acids started folding into the protein structure and binding to the synthetic representation of the data that Alyssa had just shown Don. It was folding a lot faster than the neural network had been. And it wasn't making mistakes.

Don refused to be impressed. "Huh. Neat. Now see if you can get it to do it in real life."

He wandered away. Alyssa found herself wondering, not for the first time, if he'd just lucked his way into postdoctoral research. She turned back to the desk and pulled a few more files. She made some adjustments and watched as the protein folded neatly into its component parts, then flickered, reset, and started again.

See if you can get it to do it in real life.

That was always the trick, wasn't it? Alyssa thought. The manufacture of the thing was always going to be the hard part, but she was starting to understand how it might work.

She smiled.

❖ ❖ ❖

"That was the first time I *really knew* I had something," She said to Healy as he administered a saline drip into her arm and watched her quietly. It seemed as though even the ever-present carabiners on his flight suit had fallen silent. He listened softly as she answered the question he'd asked to distract her, but also to find out how she'd discovered the medicine.

"A few weeks later, Don got on board. I'd figured out most of the issues with manufacture, see. Guy never liked doing the work himself, but knew when to jump on a rising star," She scoffed. "What an idiot."

Healy smiled. He wasn't any sort of grand physician or psychiatrist like the kind they had back down on Terra, but he could help a panic attack or sensory overload or shock with the best of them. Alyssa had arrived some time ago, carrying the poor dead girl whose name he still didn't know. She had the kind of blank terror behind the eyes that he usually saw from first time spacefarers when they began to understand that all that was separating them from certain death was scant centimetres of welded metal.

She still hadn't commented on the fact that two of the women that had tried to kill her a few hours ago were unconscious in the med bay decks, nor that the room smelled of burned alcohol from the spill on the other side of the room. She was propped up against one of the cupboards, breathing shallowly, no longer hyperventilating. Her eyes were still glazed and unfocused. The trauma of the crash and finding the dead girl would leave a haunted look in the eyes for a bit longer than usual. It was, after all, significantly worse than the usual fright about being on a spaceship, he reflected.

"I'm just going to get you something to eat. I'm not leaving the room. I'll be just over there," he gestured. "Alright?"

He watched carefully, trying to read her emotions and response. There was a possibility that when he said he was going to leave that she'd take it as a threat of abandonment. If that happened, he'd have to stay in contact with her. To his relief, she nodded. He stood up, clinking and groaning, and shuffled to the small food store he kept in the med bay. Sweet treats and food, like jellies and sherbets, lined the bottom row in vacuum sealed pods, and the top shelf had some nutrient rations. He scooped up a handful of bags from the bottom shelf and grabbed a white pack from the top. He tore off the tab at the top of the white package and held it underneath a water dispenser at the centre of the room. The packet warmed up as its insides fizzed and bubbled. After a few minutes, he grunted with satisfaction and shuffled back to where Alyssa was watching him quietly.

"Here you go," he said, handing her the packets of lollies, then handing her the warm white foil packet. "Best save some of those sweets for after the pottage, Alyssa. I've never eaten it, but I've heard it tastes like shit."

Alyssa chuckled slightly and popped one of the jellies into her mouth. She chewed slowly, and Healy saw a hint of life come back into her eyes.

"They're going to try to kill me still, aren't they?" she said. It wasn't a question. She was just airing a fact she now knew about the world. When Healy nodded, the shadows behind her eyes deepened.

"They were trying to kill everyone,' he said simply. "They, *we*, were a suicide cult, even if we didn't know it yet," he looked out the window at the debris field where one of the other wings should have been. "It might not matter one way or another. If they don't get around to killing you, we might find I've already done the damage."

Alyssa closed her eyes, processing the information. When she opened them again, she put the white packet to her lips and squeezed the sides.

After a second she sputtered, then laughed helplessly.

"That really does taste like shit."

❖ ❖ ❖

Meg's knuckles were white. Her mouth was dry, her skin was filthy, and her hair was greasy and wild where she'd been running her hands through it. Her eyes itched with dehydration and fatigue and she watched one set of numbers creep inexorably up, and another set down.

"Come on," her voice was hoarse. Desperate. The light was still green, still transmitting the data packet down to Earth but it wouldn't stay that way for long. She was staying off comms. The extra data wasn't likely to corrupt the packet, but there wasn't any point pushing her luck.

Ninety-two percent.

"Oh come on you *fucking* thing" she whispered furiously at the terminal. She'd done everything she could with the computer power she had, and the best-case scenario she'd come up with was that in just over a week they were going to burn up over Brazil and spend the last minutes of their lives as a light show for the residents of most of the countries in South America.

Ninety-six percent.

Ninety-seven.

Ninety-eight.

Ninety-nine.

There was a small chime as the file transfer reached one

hundred per cent, and Keegan's voice crackled to life.

"*Sunward Sky* — we can confirm receipt of —"

The comm cut off.

They were back in the shadow. Meg turned and lurched out of the control room.

❖ ❖ ❖

Healy staggered along the corridor, heading to the mess hall as best he could. His usual shortcut through had been cut off, reduced to a hissing mess of pipes and conduits. He'd had to double back around. Alyssa was still in the med bay, now relatively calm. The hunted look in her eyes remained but considering there was a cult on the ship that wanted her dead he didn't think that was unreasonable. He'd walked out to find both of them some food, something that wasn't just emergency nutrient mush or lollies.

He was in the mess, digging around in what remained of the crew locker when he heard someone move behind him. The sharp shot of fear disappeared as he turned and saw Meg, bedraggled, blank eyed, and exhausted, leaning heavily against the doorway.

"Good god, why does everyone in here look like shit?" she said.

❖ ❖ ❖

The first gulp of water had run through her throat and into her, chilling as it went and soothing the thirst she'd been ignoring for hours. After that, she and Healy had sat in the ruined mess hall together and eaten and filled in the gaps for each other, telling each other what had happened at their respective ends of the ship. She had gasped when she'd heard Isa's plight, and Healy had done his best to mask his anxiety when she detailed the hours she'd spent trying to get the information to Keegan.

"Don't worry, Heals," she said through a mouthful of food. Healy looked at her quizzically. She waved around at the general destruction, "The crash. Don't worry about it. If I were you, I'd have done the same thing. Lesser of two evils, right? I mean, fuckers had an option we didn't, they just had a simple code they could transmit. I couldn't have figured out how to fix the software in time. Fuck no. Best thing to do when someone threatens you with a rock is throw a bigger rock. And this ship is a big ass rock."

He hadn't seemed convinced, she thought as she made her way back toward the bridge, but it was true. He'd done the only thing any of them could have in the time they had available. The fact that he was haunted by it was probably good, she thought, but on balance? Still the right move.

She felt better after food, water and a stack of caffeine pills. The hunger and thirst had disappeared, and the itchy tiredness behind her eyes she could keep at bay a little longer. She got back to the bridge with about five minutes to spare and organised her questions for Keegan. She would have just under twelve minutes this time around, so she'd have to make it sharp if she wanted any answers.

The light flashed. Yellow. Black. Yellow. Black. Yellow. Black. Green. She moved to thumb the intercom, but it was her turn for a voice to interrupt her.

"*Sunward Sky*, come in *Sunward Sky*. Keegan to *Sunward Sky*, come in *Sunward Sky*."

"*Sunward Sky* here, go ahead."

"We've run an emergency calculation with the data you've sent us, *Sunward Sky*. We have a time saving jettison manoeuvre for you to undertake. Please see transmission data."

A file had appeared on the screen, sent in triplicate. One of them had come through without corrupting. Meg thumbed it open and pored through it.

A time save. That's all they were getting. A series of jettisons to be made in conjunction with burns at specific times over the next thirty-six hours, and that would give them a few more days before the orbit degraded again.

Then what was the plan? Send a rescue ship? It seemed unlikely the company would bother. Why send more people up to space to rescue those that might not even survive a suboptimal re-entry anyway?

Meg realised Keegan was still talking.

"Aberration in the orbit that we can only explain through a mass of propellant that hasn't been accounted for—"

"I'm sorry," she cut in, "Say that again."

"We couldn't match the data you provided with the orbit that we're recording, using the thruster information you've sent through. There's something else causing the ship to shift in its orbit."

Meg froze. She knew all the thrusters were either working as they should be, or they were shut down. Alyssa had seen to that earlier. There were only two things that could be diverting the ship's course from the one she'd set it on. Leaking fuel, spraying rapidly expanding liquid mix into the cosmos.

Or oxygen.

2.7

JETTISON

The door Brett was searching for was buried beneath the wreckage. A series of metal ducts, cable trays and more gnarled and rent metal than he knew what to do with lay between it and him. He grasped a broken piece of conduit, placed his legs against the small section of undamaged surface and yanked, frustrated. It did nothing but exacerbate the throb in his knee that had grown steadily worse since he'd woken from the crash.

Someone shuffled down the hall behind him. Brett turned, half expecting Alyssa or even Healy, but no. Just another confused crew member wandering dazed around the ship.

"What— what happened?" she asked.

Brett gave his best conciliatory smile and spoke warmly and kindly.

"The ship is currently in lockdown," he said, "I think it's best if you go back to your cabin. I believe the crew on the bridge gave the order some time ago."

The woman nodded vaguely and drifted off, unsteady on her feet. Brett watched her until she rounded the corner to the crew cabins, then turned back to the mess blocking the doorway.

He pictured the ship layout in his mind. He was trying to get to a storage space where he and the other members of Blackout had secreted an emergency cache onto the ship. There were freeze dried rations, several carts of water, medication, first aid, and a small cache of heavy-duty tools.

This door was too far gone for him to use. The heavy lifting he could deal with himself, but it was likely that some of the cabling was live. He didn't want to risk electrocuting himself. He kicked the back of a warped and burned piece of panelling in frustration, then cursed as the shock went up his foot and resonated in his knee. He'd have to double back quite a way to get around, past the crew quarters and the med bay.

The lights flickered, guttered, and went out for the last time as he left. The automated lighting system was starting to short out.

❖ ❖ ❖

Alyssa felt her mind switching back on. It was as though

her peripheral vision was returning, except it was her ability to think, to get away from the fog of shock. The world had gone blurry and faint and grey and black. All she'd been able to think about was Isa, plucked from nowhere and sent to space only to die for reasons nobody would ever understand. Then she'd got to Healy. He'd sat her down. Talked to her. Made her feel like something was being taken care of, that things might be alright even through the black cloud of her worry. He'd fed her, made sure she drank water. Most of all he'd been there, ready and waiting for her to come back to the present. Back to the situation. Back to herself.

She almost wished she'd stayed in shock.

She was sitting in the corner of the destroyed med bay. The only other two people in here were the women from Blackout who, when they woke up, were going to try to kill her. There was at least one other person on the ship who was out to do the same, and he was a lot bigger than she was.

She stood up. Her knees threatened to buckle. The wavering, inconsistent gravity made her feel nauseous and she bent forward, overcome by vertigo.

Across the room, Waugh stirred. The screen monitoring her condition chimed and lit up a pale green. The glow from it reflected dully into the destruction of the room. Alyssa froze, watching as the woman began to wake up.

"Fuck fuck fuck fuck *fuck*," Meg paced back and forth across the control room. The jettison package from Keegan was nothing but a stopgap to increase the time until *Sunward Sky* hit atmosphere. She kept swearing as she manipulated the robotic arms that were used to load satellite arrays and manoeuvre cargo while on the ground. Now she was programming them to shunt as much of the remaining cargo out as possible. It was a combination of fly-by-wire and guesswork: the cargo manifest was supposed to be an accurate model of the ship's contents, but she didn't know how accurate it was after the crash. Not to mention, at least one of the crates had been replaced by one of the scarabs.

She'd also attempted to hunt down the leak but wasn't able to find anything while staying in comms. The instrumentation was shot, with both oxygen and fuel registering as just over one hundred percent capacity.

There were sealable baffles inside the tanks that would allow them to shut them into separate partitions. In theory, she could close each of them off and maintain integrity and flow to the unbreached areas. She'd sealed all the baffles but she had no way of telling the extent of the damage, or if the seals were working at all. The sensor arrays weren't responding either. There would have to be a visual inspection to see which tank the leak was coming from. If it was fuel, there was a chance they'd need to decrease their estimated descent time. If it was oxygen, they'd need to adjust the amount of time they still had where the crew had air left to breathe.

Either way she needed to know what they were dealing with.

Healy.

Healy would help.

She ran her eyes over the jettison schedule once more. There were three occurring over the next few hours. The first was in twenty minutes or so. Satisfied that the emergency procedure was adequately organised, she headed back toward the mess.

❖ ❖ ❖

Alyssa watched as Waugh stirred in her sleep again, unable to take her eyes away, frozen like a wild animal under torchlight. Waugh moved, then groaned and stilled again. Alyssa knew she should be running, but she was caught, trapped in fear. Maybe Alyssa could talk to her when she woke? Find a way to communicate and reason with her.

Not likely, she found herself thinking. Waugh's arm shifted. Another soft sound escaped her lips. And still Alyssa couldn't will herself to move.

❖ ❖ ❖

The human need for food and water made certain spaces locus points, and that remained true even as humanity had made its way out of the atmosphere. Healy sat in the mess and watched a few of the remaining crew members filter in to find what remained of the ration stores. He saw three of them at an empty dispensary. One of them held down the chute where the food should have been appearing while another pushed a skinny arm up into it to clear a blockage.

The quiet desperation for food overrode the survival instinct of the most imminent danger. Even the decaying orbit of the ship couldn't stop it. It was about survival, a sort of base pragmatism that held on long after meaning and reason dissipated. It was remarkable, Healy thought. He had in the last few hours had his own meaning and reason for existence fall from around him. No longer was he some revolutionary, he too was now operating on mere survival instinct. He couldn't —

Someone grabbed his shoulder and wrenched him

around, jerking him from his reverie.

"We need to get them back to their beds. Now," Meg said.

"What? Why, what's happening?"

"We're clearing some cargo," she was whispering now and leaned in conspiratorially before continuing. "There's another problem too. I'll tell you after we clear the room, I don't want them to hear. We've got twenty minutes before the first jettison shunt, so we need them out now. Come on."

His search for meaning was over, at least for a moment. For now, his meaning was to get people back to their rooms. And then there would be something else. And something else. With every step along his path, he was reaching out and not knowing whether the ground would be there to meet him. If he was lucky, he'd find something underfoot, some new reason to keep going.

Together, he and Meg approached the trio at the dispensary.

"There's going to be a fairly large acceleration shock that goes through the ship," Meg said, "As it is, we're not sure how the ship is going to handle it. We're in pretty rough shape. We need you all in your cabins because it's the safest place for you to be."

The man who had been holding the chute open stood and sized himself up against Meg. He was taller and stockier than she was, but he was dwarfed by the clinking form of Healy. He backed down, and the other two followed suit. They shambled out of the room.

"What did you want to tell me?" Healy asked, but Meg pointed to the opposite side of the mess. A young, thin woman was seated at a table, staring, unseeing. Meg approached.

"Hi, excuse me?" Meg said, "I'm sorry, but we need you to get out of here. There's a—"

"Do you know what's below the wreckage just fore of the cabins?" the woman's voice was quiet and dreamlike. Almost distracted.

"What?" Meg asked.

She shrugged. "Earlier. There was a man, away down—" she pointed toward the aft of the ship, fore of the cabins, toward a stowage compartment. "He seemed to be trying to get through a wall. It was covered, broken stuff everywhere. He told me to go back to my cabin."

Brett, Healy thought, and he had a suspicion he knew what he was trying to access.

"I'm not sure who it was you spoke to," Healy lied, "but it sounds like there's something we should be checking out. Where specifically did you see him?" when she told him, Healy shot a dark look at Meg. She didn't know about Blackout's cache. He turned back to the young woman. "Thank you, now would you mind getting back to your cabin? We're looking at only a few minutes before we have to make the course correction manoeuvre."

Course correction manoeuvre was the wrong phrase, but it sounded better than *dumping a heap of cargo into space.*

"Come on," Meg said to Healy, "the jettison *should* work automatically, but a lot of stuff is broken. I don't trust anything to work properly on this ship anymore."

Alyssa didn't *want* to move. Too much had happened in too short a time. All she wanted was to sit and let her head clear. She hadn't had time to even begin to process Isa's death. She was only just out of shock from the ordeal of waking up to a spaceship having torn itself apart. It was a lot to deal with. Her body was still shaken, bruised.

Waugh made a noise and rolled over to face her, eyes open. Alyssa froze, but Waugh didn't react. She was still unconscious, eyes wide and unseeing.

It was time to go. Alyssa lurched up from the ground and slipped quietly from the room. The groan of the door seemed to echo through her skull and out across the med bay floor but both women stayed unconscious. She snuck on tiptoes away from the med bay and down the corridor for some distance before giving up and running as fast as she could down the corridor toward the bridge of the ship. She couldn't run as fast as usual because of the odd rhythm of the gravity. Still, she was moving at a reasonable pace when she rounded a corner and collided with Brett as he was making his way back to where she'd just come from.

❖ ❖ ❖

By some miracle, the controls that operated the cargo hatch on the central bay of the *Sunward Sky* had not been damaged in the crash. The small pocket of air that was inside the cargo bay rushed out, carrying the soft remainder of a hydraulic groan as large pistons pushed the hatch open. Inside the ship the sound joined the noise of the creaking superstructure and settled in with the other sounds of the ship's ailments. It lasted several minutes while the colossal maw opened. Finally it stopped, and the hull resonated with only the other screaming systems of the dying ship. As the

Sunward Sky careened around the blank empty above the Earth, its cargo bay lay open.

The jettison was coming.

❖ ❖ ❖

Brett grabbed Alyssa by the hair, pulled her to the ground and leapt on top of her. Alyssa tried to fight back, but she was no match for his strength. He straddled her across the chest with his legs, pinning her down with his weight. The fluctuations from the ship's off-kilter spin made his bulk press onto her intermittently and force the air from her lungs. His face was a cruel twist of rage and he slapped her cheek before grabbing her throat. Alyssa managed to dodge out of the way a few times but eventually his thick fingers found her neck. She grasped at his hands in a futile attempt to pull him away.

"Couldn't just leave well enough alone, could you?" he spat.

Alyssa pulled at his hands, trying to keep them away from her windpipe.

❖ ❖ ❖

In the cargo bay a red light flashed, and a set of alarms began ringing, warning nobody and going nowhere. A six-axis robot arm span down and released a set of straps on a conveyor holding several tons of construction materials and tools. With a short, sharp jerk, the arm swung to the back of the conveyor, and the magnetic clasps holding the pallet to the ground released. In the same moment, the robot arm groaned, pushing the jetsam away in Meg's last-ditch effort to correct the *Sunward Sky's* degrading orbit.

❖ ❖ ❖

Alyssa felt the pulsing gravity shift, just a little. Brett's weight on her pulled back, and she heaved against him. Surprised, he let go of her throat and shot to the ceiling. Alyssa felt for a moment as though she was floating, dancing away with the change of inertia from the cargo being thrown out. She pushed off the ceiling of the corridor with her hands and watched Brett as he struggled to do the same. She hit the ground and he swore at her, clawing to get back within range.

Gravity shifted back again, and she watched him get thrown down to the deck, winded. She forced herself up unsteadily on her legs and took off toward the bridge, leaving him gasping in her wake.

2.8

PRESSURE

Alyssa burst through the door to the ruined bridge, breathing heavily. Healy and Meg span to face her, eyes wide with surprise and fear. Alyssa slammed the door shut behind her.

"Lock it," she gasped, and Meg leapt toward the controls for the hydraulic deadbolt. She had no idea whether it would work, but she didn't get an opportunity to find out before Brett slammed into the door, kicking it open at the same time as Alyssa slammed her weight against it and closed it again.

Meg swore and yelled "Healy!" but he was already moving. His lanky, jangling frame dashed towards the door where Brett was now using his greater strength to prise it open. Alyssa was pushing but her feet slipped across the slick deck, pushing a pile of broken parts across the floor with her foot.

Healy thumped his own weight against the inside of the door, jerking it back and causing Brett to cry out in pain as his hand got jammed against the bulkhead. Somehow he managed to keep his grip.

Alyssa and Healy pushed against the deck and kept him at bay, but he was slowly forcing more and more of his arm through the door, preventing them from shutting it completely so that Meg could push the lock mechanism. Alyssa's strength was fading. She wasn't going to be able to hold on much longer.

Meg looked around the rest of the room. She took in the decks, and the broken HUD panels and the mess of wiring, trying to see something obvious she could use to deter him.

"Healy, you fucking traitor!" Brett yelled breathlessly through the door. He seemed to be holding on out of sheer spite, and though they couldn't see his eyes, Alyssa could imagine the dead violence in them, the same that she'd seen every other time Brett had been called in to do Blackout's dirty work.

Healy grunted heavily as the door slipped again and Brett pressed his advantage once more. The majority of one of his arms was in now, as was one of his boots.

A flash of steel clanged against the bulkhead and Brett cried out in pain. Meg had appeared next to the door, brandishing a pipe that had fallen during the crash and had been laying next to the med kit on the floor. Alyssa hadn't seen Meg pick it up, distracted as she was by the effort of pushing the door closed.

Meg brandished the pipe. "Get your arm out of here or I'll break the fucking thing off," her voice was flat and dangerous.

Brett grunted, "You wouldn't."

For what seemed like a long time, Meg just stared at him, eyes like thunder. Brett met her gaze. Alyssa gasped and continued to fade, and Healy pushed against the door, redoubling his efforts to compensate for Alyssa's waning strength.

Meg swung and connected with Brett's arm, and Alyssa heard the wet sound of metal on flesh. Brett screamed and pulled away, running down the corridor. Healy slammed the door shut and Alyssa collapsed, catching her breath.

Meg threw the pipe down and pressed the door lock button. There was a hydraulic thud, then nothing. Healy pulled the door. It opened.

"Shit," Healy said.

Alyssa looked up from the floor. The effort of holding the door closed and running away from Brett, combined with the sickly, limping movements of the ship was making her feel ill again.

"Can we keep it closed some other way?" she asked, but Meg was already moving.

❖ ❖ ❖

Brett stumbled along, cursing into the empty hallway and trying to ignore the pain in his arm. Meg had hit it hard, but he didn't think it was broken. He could still move his fingers, which was a good sign. *It still fucking hurts though*, he thought as the ship lurched around him.

The lights in the secondary corridor were flickering as he entered, and the infrared emergency strip light had come on. The corridor was a kaleidoscope of jarring tonalities, and the horizontal through lines along the walls and ceiling were disrupted by emergency hatches and, in one place, a gaping hole filled with a snarling mess of wires and ducting. He felt the shift in gravity from the ship's spin again, and paused in the middle of the empty corridor.

The ship was slowly tearing itself apart, and the strained sounds of metal and ceramic joints being stressed to the point of shear ricocheted down through the ship's innards. With each beat frequency ebb of the gravity the shaking sound of the slow demise of the *Sunward Sky* eked through the oxygen and made a silent cry to the space beyond.

That wasn't what had stopped Brett. He was thinking about what had happened during his scuffle with Alyssa on the way to the bridge. He rubbed his arm absentmindedly. When he'd been fighting Alyssa, the gravity hadn't shifted slowly, he'd been suddenly knocked clear by a large shift. There had been enough of a change that Alyssa had managed to fling him toward the ceiling and then bounce up herself to escape while he reoriented.

That couldn't have happened because of this kind of slow, rhythmic shift. It was more like a cord had snapped, a sudden jolt against the ground. That would only happen for two reasons. Either something had fallen from the ship, or it was a deliberate jettison. Either way it didn't bode well.

He stumbled further down the corridor and hid in a maintenance room. If anyone from Blackout was still active, they would know to meet here.

If it was a deliberate Jettison, the ship was falling, and Meg was taking emergency manoeuvres. If the ship was falling apart, he didn't want to think about it.

He'd have to wait and see if it happened again.

"What?" Alyssa's voice was flat. Not surprised or alarmed, just tired.

"Yeah, it's not good," Meg jabbed her thumb toward the ruined display. "I can only get rudimentary readings from about a third of our systems from here. I know we *have* oxygen. I know we *have* fuel, but I can't tell how much of each."

"So what does that mean?" Healy said.

"Well, we're drifting from our flight path. There are three more jettisons scheduled, and we've got a thruster program that *should* be keeping us in the sky until we can mount a proper rescue. But with this leak, it's impossible to get rid of all the variables we need to.

"If it's a fuel leak, the thrusters might stop working, or they might not. It depends on how bad the leak is. If it's oxygen, we might have to spend a couple of days not breathing before we touch rock again."

Alyssa froze. "What?" she said, trying to hide her sense of rising panic.

"I know," Meg said. She seemed to have taken on an almost Zen-like calm. "It's really not ideal."

"You *think?*" Alyssa exclaimed. She could tell she was losing control of her emotions, but she felt detached from them at the same time, as though she was watching herself lose control. The crash, the death of Isa, her own injuries and now this? It was too much. Her breath increased in frequency and decreased in depth. Hyperventilation. She was panicking.

Healy grabbed her. "Hey. Hey. Look at me," he said, and pulled her out to arms reach, holding her by the shoulders. He stood there for a minute or two, staring carefully at her until she met his eyes. "This is a bad situation, but we need to find out *how* bad, and we need to do it now before it gets worse. Okay?" he spoke clearly and calmly to Alyssa. After a moment she nodded.

They turned to Meg, "Okay, where do we need to go?" Alyssa asked.

"Okay," Meg said, flicking to a map on the ruined display, "Down the main corridor, there's a hatchway. Under spin, it's in the ceiling. It's a service corridor to the central part of the ship. Healy, you probably know about it." He nodded. Alyssa recognised it, too. It was the hatch she'd snuck down to the cargo bay.

"Aye, it leads to the main stowage."

Meg nodded. "Yes, but you're not going there. Go past it, then turn fore. There's a hydraulics section that's cordoned off from the rest of engineering by a series of bulkheads. When you go in there, there are three triple sealed tanks. One is an oxygen-nitrogen mix for breathing, there's a liquid hydrogen, and another liquid oxygen for the fuel tanks. One of them is burst. It should be obvious which one when you get there. I can't trust any radio communication, so you'll have to leg it back here."

Alyssa nodded, head spinning from the barrage of information. Healy looked grim.

"That service corridor isn't usually accessible under gravity though, is it?" he pressed.

Meg sighed. "No. No it isn't. I'll have to put us on float. You won't have long."

❖ ❖ ❖

Waugh's stocky form had stepped tenderly through the doorway into the maintenance room not long after Brett had settled down. Ellyse had followed, watching the woman in front in case she collapsed. Brett had rushed them both in, lay them against the wall and made them as comfortable as the maintenance room would allow.

Brett didn't know if anyone else in Blackout was still alive, and he didn't have any reliable way of contacting them anymore. The comms in the ship were still down. Unless anyone else came, it was just the three of them.

He didn't feel the shift in the rolling tumult of the gravity straight away. The lightening load on his bones happened gradually enough that gravity fell from him. It was a gradual pick up of the wind in an alley; the rising heat in a cup of boiling water, where it wasn't noticeable until it was unbearable. Over the course of minutes, his body went from being rhythmically pressed into the ground to being oddly bouncy. It wasn't until the rhythm lifted him from the floor of the room that he realised. He floated, surrounded by tools and cleaning products that had come loose in the crash.

The spin had stopped, and there was only the lurch of the ship careening, unaccelerated, through space, left to lend weight to those in the room.

Brett grabbed a handhold and pushed himself over to where Waugh was holding herself.

"What now?" he whispered to her, as the rotating wing

arrays of the ship softly *clicked* into place.

"Go, go, go!" Meg pulled the door to the bridge open and moved out of the way to let Healy and Alyssa through.

They spat out of the bridge and into the hallway, parallel to the floor. Healy led, and the carabiners on his suit rattled as he reached in front of himself and into the welds in the corridor, pushing himself along it, accelerating a little more each time.

Alyssa wasn't as skilled and fell behind, but not by much. She caught up with him as he pivoted at the right-angled corner that led down into the spinal corridor of the ship. She found herself wishing for the dexterity of the older man. As he neared the corner he pushed almost lazily against the wall, just enough to spin himself around to meet the top corner of the corridor with his feet and cushion his deceleration.

Alyssa tried to copy him but pushed too hard and sent herself careening head-over-feet toward the corner. She crashed into Healy, who, expecting her clumsiness, had braced himself softly. Carabiners smashed into the side of her body, where they were cushioned by her vac suit. He pushed her off him, to the top side of the wall at the end of the corridor and checked the timer.

"We've already lost a minute. Let's go, we're stopping about three quarters of the way down this corridor!"

With that, he pushed off again, launching deftly and finding cracks to use as makeshift handholds in the corridor. Alyssa followed him.

As they approached the hatch in the ceiling, Healy,

rather than pulling himself down the corridor, began to tap it lightly with his hand. Once again, Alyssa nearly ran into him before realising what he was doing. By gently touching the wall, he was introducing friction, which slowed him down.

She copied him, barely doing more than grazing the wall, and she felt her momentum slow. A few times she pushed too hard, and she bounced into the corridor, but instead of overcompensating she allowed herself to drift over and then began the process again on the opposite wall.

Together, they came to a near halt just short of the hatch. Healy lodged a foot against the ceiling bulkhead and pulled against the opening to the hatchway. It groaned, and a deep sucking noise permeated the corridor. Healy blanched and pulled the hatchway closed. The noise stopped.

"Hard vacuum out there. There's a breach."

"What do we do?"

He took a deep breath, thinking for a moment. The timer on his helmet was backward, but Alyssa could see they were down to seventeen and a half minutes before Meg turned on the artificial gravity again. Time seemed to simultaneously slow down and speed up as Healy's eyes rolled up and his mouth moved as he calculated something in his head. The counter ticked. Then he spoke.

"Alright. Size of the hole and the amount of pressure we're dealing with, I think we should be able to push the thing closed from the other side. That way we won't be leaking air we can't afford to lose."

"Do you know how much air we'll lose when we'll go through?"

Healy shook his head, "Hard to say. Hopefully not too

much. The other thing is what we'll have on the other side of the corridor to push against."

"How so?"

"Well, from here, I could close it fairly easily. It opens outward, so I can pull on the hatch and push against the ceiling with my legs. Use the leverage. Other side is a corridor. I can't remember how far away the hand and foot holds are from the hatch, so I don't know where we'll be able to stand. And we'll be pushing, while being sucked away from the door. It won't be too much, but it will take both of us, between the positive pressure and no gravity."

Alyssa got the picture. She took a deep breath, then felt a pang of anxiety at how few breaths they'd all have left if this went wrong.

"Alright," she said, "let's do it."

Sixteen minutes ticked over in Healy's display.

The two of them pushed against the walls they'd drifted to and positioned themselves on either side of the shaft. Working together they twisted the handle on the hatchway. Alyssa tried to quell her hands from shaking as the knurled steel handle turned and a deep whine of evacuating air rushed past her. She looked to Healy.

"Ready?" he looked grim. "You first."

He let go of his side of the hatch and it blew fully open, leaving an empty maw for Alyssa to enter. She pulled herself around and pushed with her arms into the centre of the corridor. She accelerated.

And then kept accelerating.

The sound of the air around her disappeared as it

vanished into the vacuum, and she found herself flying too fast down the service hatch. The venturi effect of the air rushing into the corridor was stronger than she'd expected, and she was now careening down the hallway.

She reached for the hand holds on the side wall of the tunnel, but she was moving too fast. She managed to pull herself up, but her ribs blossomed with pain as she swung around and crashed into the tunnel wall. The sound of vacuum silence was fast approaching, with only a faint whisper of the evacuating air resonating through her gloves where she was holding the ship. Outside her helmet there was nothing.

She looked up. Healy had come through in a far more controlled fashion than her and had pulled up outside the hatch. He was holding his feet against the wall, but there was nothing nearby to push against and he wasn't able to close the hatch. Alyssa could see but not hear the air rushing against his suit, disturbing the carabiners, setting them rattling violently against him.

She began to climb back up toward the hatch to help but was unsure what to do. She was a good deal shorter than Healy and she wasn't going to be able to reach the door from the foothold on the other side of the tunnel.

Healy had a slight grip on the hatch, but it was doing little more than providing a third point of contact for balance, and he didn't have the leverage to close it. He was stretched awkwardly between the rapidly draining oxygen of the corridor and the hatchway and the cold edge of the foothold. A bridge between safety and the unknown.

A bridge, Alyssa thought, and she knew what to do.

She kept climbing toward the hatch and started to feel the gentle push of the wind slowing her down. She kicked more firmly against the footholds to push herself along. When she got close enough to Healy, she grabbed him by the leg to get his attention. He looked down in alarm, but she waved at him with her free hand, then gesticulated a climbing motion. He looked confused for a moment, then understood and nodded. He reached up with his other hand to get a better grip on the hatch instead of trying to force it closed.

When he had a good grip, he nodded again. Alyssa began to climb up Healy's body, wrapping her fingers through the myriad carabiners that littered his suit. She hooked two fingers through each one, pulling herself like a rock climber along his body.

Before too long she was at his shoulders, and she twisted up and sat on top of them. From where she was, she could see the corridor of the ship they'd just come from, spreading out at ninety degrees from the service shaft she and Healy were in. Looking at it from this angle gave her vertigo even though she knew intellectually that there was no *up* in a low-g environment.

Healy was too tall for her plan. She was back in the corridor, and to close the hatch, she'd have to swing it shut and leave Healy in the shaft by himself. She needed him to move down. She tried to yell at him, but the air had thinned, and he couldn't hear her. She leaned down and gasped as her ribs burst into a line of pain again, and she pressed the glass face of her helmet against his.

"Kneel down!" she yelled. Healy looked perplexed but then he understood. He let go of the top of the hatch. Alyssa grabbed it, and he knelt. With her newfound leverage, Alyssa could force the hatchway about three quarters closed. The air howled out of the now diminished gap, and she felt her elbows lock as she hit the limits of her reach. She swore.

"Healy!" she yelled, "Stand up again!"

Healy couldn't hear, and she couldn't bend while she held the hatch in her hands. Her ribs flashed in pain, and her arms were going to give out if she didn't do something.

She yelled again. "Stand up! Stand up!"

Healy looked up and saw what was happening, saw Alyssa struggling to make the last few centimetres to close the hatch, and he stood up. Alyssa slammed the hatch shut and twisted the handle until she felt the seal lock into place. The howling wind died around her, replaced by silence and the sound of her heavy breathing. She gasped and closed her eyes, letting go of the handle and letting herself drift.

Healy grabbed her almost immediately and pressed his helmet up to hers.

"We've got less than eleven minutes. Let's go."

2.9

TIME

Meg shook her head to force herself to concentrate on the timer clock as it ticked inexorably lower. At any moment, Alyssa and Healy would come bursting through the door. All she wanted was for it to be over, for the timer to end and for the two of them to be back so she could reactivate the spin gravity.

She hoped they were nearly at the tanks. If it took them any longer to get there they wouldn't get back in time before she had to spin the ship back up again. They'd be added to the list of casualties of the *Sunward Sky*. Just another pair of dead astronauts.

At this point, she didn't even particularly care whether it was the oxygen or fuel tank.

Except she did. It made a difference to the ship's ability to continue along its trajectory. If it were fuel, they'd need to reevaluate the jettison schedule to make sure it was possible to keep the orbit from degrading too sharply. She didn't think it was possible, but they might be able to optimise the jettison and burns with whatever reserves they had left. If she was really clever, she might be able to get the ship down without it burning up in the atmosphere.

If it was oxygen it was a different story. They could have hours. They could have less than hours. She breathed in, trying to stay calm. Once that failed, she swore, repeatedly, and clapped her open palm against the surface of the console in impotent frustration, sending herself reeling away from the console in the null gravity.

"Come *on*," she gathered herself. She watched the line that demarcated the ship's decaying orbit. Watched as it dipped below the projected line that leap-frogged around the Earth with its proposed jettison points overlaid.

A small chime twittered in the nav room. Meg was confused momentarily before she made the connection. They'd fallen out of the shadow of the Earth and into range of the emergency team she'd been talking to. Keegan. That was his name. She pushed herself across to the comms, glad for the distraction.

"*Sunward Sky*, come in *Sunward Sky*. *Sunward Sky*, come in," his voice spat across the bridge, tinny and fuzzy.

"This is *Sunward Sky*, go ahead Keegan," Meg said, steadying herself with one hand against a ceiling handhold and the other on the comm array. Her legs shot out parallel to the floor behind her, swaying as though in a breeze.

"*Sunward Sky*, you are approaching more steeply than according to projected trajectory. Please note that current trajectory will likely result in critically dangerous conditions for crew."

I fucking know that, don't you know I fucking know that? Meg thought but didn't say. She thumbed the comm to explain the situation.

The cargo bay was a completely different place from the first time she'd seen it, Alyssa thought, trying not to get too distracted as she flung herself further toward engineering. Before, the gigantic bay had been closed and near dark, full of whispers and secrets from the conspirators from project Blackout she'd followed in before the crash. Now it was a liminal space. The enormous gangway hatch yawned open. The curve of the Earth, deep blue with sickly orange clouds, was visible on the left side from where Alyssa craned her head, bobbing and weaving and looping around as the ship's gait continued to wander. Robot arms lay poised next to scrape marks on the floor where cargo had been flung out to force some extra lift for the doomed ship.

The rest of the space was a cavern that felt like a mausoleum. Large containers strapped to the floor formed tectonic breaks in the central drum. They looked like places where people died. Tombstones, waiting for victims.

A shudder ran down her spine as she sped along. The air from the main corridors of the spacecraft was long gone, and she could hear nothing of the outside world. Just the anechoic rasp of her own breath as it fogged the visor of her helmet.

In front of her, Healy reached out and tapped against the columns on the side of the bulkhead again, braking in that strange way she'd seen when following before. Alyssa tried to copy but tapped the wall too hard and she almost sailed past the railing, over the gangway and into the drum of the cargo bay. Panicking, she overcorrected and pushed against the columns on her right, which sent her crashing into the wall. Healy was ahead and the air had evacuated out. He couldn't hear her and continued his more nuanced deceleration.

Swearing to herself, Alyssa pulled along the steel grating of the floor to get herself moving again and watched as Healy continued to slow down as he approached a large rectangular hatch. Its corners were rounded, and it was even more worn out than the rest of the spacecraft. The word *engineering* was all but gone, only visible by way of slight darkening where the painted lettering had protected the steelwork for longer than its uncoated counterpart adjacent. The yellow warning stripes that had once ringed the doorway and the hazard symbol at its centre were also nothing more than vestiges, bright yellow burnished down to a dull brown over the course of years.

Alyssa approached cautiously. In the back of her mind, she was beginning to panic at the lack of time remaining before Meg would have to spin the wings up and she and Healy would be locked in the drum. Healy turned as he reached the hatchway, seeing how much Alyssa had lagged behind for the first time. He didn't beckon. There was no point.

He opened the hatch to the engineering deck and left it ajar for her to follow through. Alyssa adjusted her braking to match, trying to pass through the door slowly rather than coming to a complete halt. When she got through to the other side, she looked around.

If the cargo bay was a mausoleum then the engineering

bay was the end of the world.

❖ ❖ ❖

"*Sunward Sky*, please confirm, you are venting pressurised fluid of an unknown description?" Keegan's voice was flat but unable to completely rid itself of his fatigue and concern.

Meg confirmed, "Yes, and it's knocking us off course," she glanced nervously at the timer on the display as it danced slowly downward. Less than six minutes now. "Currently attempting to ascertain damage and nature of fluid vent. Expecting an update in six minutes or so."

More than that, She thought. The timer was how long they had to get back through the hatch. It would take another minute or two to get back into the bridge.

If they made it.

❖ ❖ ❖

Alyssa hadn't seen the engineering deck before the crash, but one thing was clear: It hadn't been locked down to the same safety standards that Healy and the crew in the wings insisted on. Tools and maintenance equipment floated in the air around her between flashed out digital panels and emergency analogue backups. Stainless steel piping protruded from the floors and walls, all connected by a wellspring of sensors and wires sending readouts into the panels. Some of them still blinked with red, blue, orange and green lights in obfuscated patterns that she couldn't fathom.

She saw another pipe, larger than most. It ran up from just behind the hatchway, protruding from the ceiling and kinking at waist level to run along the forward wall of the room. About three quarters of the way to the corner, a large spigot broke the line. Jutting out perpendicular was a spigot handle locked in the closed position.

Someone was impaled on the handle of the spigot.

They were snapped over the pipe, and the handle protruded through the small of their back, crusted in a thick layer of dried and frozen blood, crystallised into a scarlet so dark that it was almost black.

The story was written in the bloodstains on the walls and in the sickly way their body had folded. The impact of the crash had thrown them against the pipe. From the knees down the legs were bent at unlikely angles after being crushed against the wall, bones snapped against the steel plating that separated engineering from the cargo bay. Compound fractures split their skin, bones dyed with the same shade of deep black blood that marred the handle of the spigot. The face was simply gone. The person's head had kept moving after the body had been stopped by the pipe until it had smashed face-first into the wall and disintegrated.

Alyssa could see three sets of bloodstains. The first was the initial, violent splatter from the impact on the wall, spraying outward in an explosion of instantaneous violence. The second was the pool of low-g blood billow which had incidentally touched the wall, large smears here and there over the top of the first, darker and deoxygenated. Then finally there was the sharp, broken splashes from when the pool of blood had been driven to the floor again as the ship got underway.

She blanched and did everything she could to avoid vomiting in her suit. How had her life come to this?

❖ ❖ ❖

Don sat on the desk in front of her. His arms were crossed in incredulity, a doubtful expression on his face that Alyssa could have sworn hid a sneer. She was resisting the urge to reach out and slap him. This was Don at his most frustrating. The reshuffle to the team structure had come a few weeks earlier. Alyssa had missed the email after she'd collapsed on the couch, her mind full of measurement calibrations and other data, but she'd found out soon enough. Don had gloated into the room the next day, waiting barely a minute before declaring his latest promotion. *Head of department, can you believe it?* he'd said. Alyssa could, especially when she considered the number of friends Don had in other, similar positions around the University.

Now, she was his direct report, and his research goals had shifted away from the esoteric and interesting to the directly pecuniary. This posed a problem for Alyssa's research into the palsy. She'd already gone through all the grant applications and any investors she could get to entertain the notion, but nobody wanted to buy it. She'd had problems enough with getting the work approved even up to this stage. The last round of funding hadn't even given her enough money to hire a lab tech, leaving her alone in the lab late at night, recording results and writing up methods. Don didn't care about the project. Spacers couldn't afford the drug, therefore there wasn't a market, therefore there was no project. In his mind, the finances were their own morality.

She opened her mouth to speak but he cut her off.

"Look, it's all very admirable," he said, managing to sound magnanimous through dripping sanctimony, "but the money has run out. There's really nothing else to do."

"Ask for human trials. We can manufacture enough for a limited trial."

"No," he said firmly, "I'm not wasting our money on this. It's been denied. We have better things to work on."

"Better things?" Alyssa was trying to hide her rage. "Better things? What better things? Every single marker is indicating this could be a *life-saving* medication."

Don sighed, "I'm not going to argue with you again."

"The fuck you aren't," Alyssa said, "you're betraying your responsibility, to the university and to the research that we do."

"Responsibility? I'm not the one spending university resources on a dead-end project without approval or funding. There must be a purpose to this, an end goal," he said.

"There is an end goal," Alyssa said, still fuming, "Life. Saving. Medication."

Don shrugged, "Who's going to buy it? We can't just pump money into a bunch of minimum wage space jockeys out of the good of our hearts."

"Yes!" Alyssa cried in exasperation, "God, yes, we can! That's what research is for! It's not for lining pockets of the people who've already wrought so many ravages upon us. It's to raise the floor of the human condition. That's what the end goal is. That's what I'm proposing," She reached her arms out on either side of her in a vain attempt to make herself seem bigger, to make her ideas seem better. To make him *listen*.

He didn't listen.

Days later, Alyssa decided that if nobody was willing to invest in the people who kept their systems working, she'd do it herself.

For months, she worked into the evening. She skimmed materials from the lab. She dropped test results from other experiments, claiming lab accidents as the reason things were going missing. She came in the early hours of the morning to manufacture the pills full of the drug she had so much hope for. It didn't have a name. She would pore over the results from the tissue tests, looking for evidence that it hadn't worked. That it wouldn't work.

Finally, she had enough. The pills were small, and chalky. Nothing like the smooth tabs or capsules of a professional high-production pharmacy. Her tabs were ill-shaped and prone to snapping, but she kept them in a container in the pocket of her bag. She snuck them from the lab.

She got the confirmation of her crew status on the *Sunward Sky* two days after she quit her position at the University.

Healy crashed into the wall next to her, softly, but the sight of him brought her back from her shock. The broken corpse of the engineer was still there but was pulled from Alyssa's view as Healy wheeled her around. He pressed his helmet to hers and his voice echoed through the visor as he yelled.

"We have to go!" he pointed back out the door toward the way they'd come.

"What? What about the engineering room?" she shouted back.

"I've been!" came the reply.

How long have I been staring at the body for? She thought. The trauma of the last few hours was catching up to her, and she wasn't thinking clearly.

"Was it fuel or oxygen?" she yelled, but Healy was already moving. Pulling himself along the corridor as fast as he could, with an urgency she'd not seen in the man before.

Oh god, she thought. *How much time do we have left?*

Meg glanced at the clock. Less than two minutes. The next jettison was due any second now, and it *had* to happen. She hoped the jolt wouldn't affect Alyssa and Healy.

Alyssa yelped as the robot arms inside the cargo drum sprang into life. The six-axis machines grabbed the containers and began flinging them with shocking speed out of the bay of the spacecraft.

She felt as though she'd been stuck in a dolly zoom. The spacecraft's gangway leapt toward her as the ship accelerated. Neither she nor Healy had expected it, and they had to brake unexpectedly to slow down before they overshot the tunnel to the hatchway.

Healy flew past the hatch and turned around and crawled back. Alyssa could see him cursing through his helmet. Behind him, the cargo bay lay open, and the Earth shone darkly in the night, illuminated by the stars. There were twenty seconds left before the ship's gravity would reengage and the hatchway would be forced to close.

They weren't going to make it.

❖ ❖ ❖

Meg watched the timer as it continued to count down. Her hand hovered over the command to restart the ship's spin.

Five seconds.

She had to press it as soon as it hit zero. They couldn't afford more time in null-g without control. Every second she tarried would spell potential catastrophe for anyone injured, especially if they had internal bleeding.

The timer hit zero.

She told her hand to press the button, but she couldn't make it move. There was some broken part of her brain, like the wiring between the command and the action was split and fraying. Locking them out of the wings at this point was a death sentence. It seemed cruel, somehow, to not know if they had made it across the line in time. The number began to count upward. Meg watched, frozen, as the numbers grew larger. She had to press the button. *Had to.* She couldn't wait any longer.

Something connected in her mind, and she slammed her hand on the control, sending herself flying to the ceiling. Around her, the mechanical growl of the ship's large motor resonated through the hull. As the spin increased the sense of up and down came back, and gradually she floated to the ground.

She didn't know if they'd made it. And she still didn't know which one had breached. Oxygen, or fuel?

Of the two scenarios, running out of oxygen was worse. The major issue with a fuel leak was how to optimise the jettisons on the ship to allow the escape pods to enter the atmosphere at the right angle. Too steep and they'd burn up. Too shallow and they'd bounce off the atmosphere and get flung back into orbit. With an unknown quantity of fuel, she had no way of knowing if her calculations would hold up along the flight path they'd planned. At any point, they could run out, and then they were stuck with whatever re-entry angle they had.

The major component of an oxygen leak was dealing with how to breathe when there was no air.

So, oxygen leak was more pressing. She started running calculations, trying to estimate how long a theoretical oxygen supply would last.

A loud crash sounded behind her.

She turned to see Healy and Alyssa piling into the room, not even stopping to take the time to close the hatch behind them. Meg crossed to the hatchway and closed it, turning just in time to see them remove their helmets. Healy looked grave, but Alyssa was white as a sheet and starting to quiver. Meg grabbed her and pushed her firmly to the ground. Alyssa stared blankly and Meg told her to stay down before turning to Healy.

"You shouldn't have waited," he said.

"I know. But I did, and now you're here. What happened to her?" she jabbed a finger at the woman staring vacantly at the wall.

"There was a body in engineering. What was left of one anyway," he said. Then, more gravely, "the leak."

"Which was it?" she asked, bracing for it, "fuel or oxygen?"

She thought she'd been prepared for the worst-case scenario, one where they had scant time but at least the fuel reserves for a relatively safe landing. The entire time she'd been thinking that the situation was a binary, that it was going to be fuel *or* oxygen spraying into space. But she hadn't even considered what came out of Healy's mouth.

"Both," he said, and his face was ashen.

2.10

Meg's mind immediately began to spin, and her breath thudded into the air with flat terror. They had to get everyone out *very* fucking soon lest they run out of air, but she'd been planning on making thruster manoeuvres. She couldn't count on that if the fuel tank was ventilated as well. She let out a long, tired sigh. Alyssa was hyperventilating, dithering around the room looking for somewhere to put her helmet. Healy clinked around after her, trying to slow her breathing and gently taking the helmet off her to place in the storage locker that they'd got it from. The rattling bones of the ship were everywhere around them. Meg thought Alyssa could probably have left the helmet on the floor; one more piece of litter would hardly matter. Meg crossed to the console and began punching in numbers, more out of habit than anything else. Behind her, Healy knelt to Alyssa. She was still breathing hard, but starting to calm down, and was muttering something to the man. Something about a handle, and a puncture, and blood. In front of Meg, the calculation finished and drew the now too-familiar graph of a broken and failing orbit, pulled up several times by small bursts of items flung from the rear of the ship. The angle of entry was too steep, the speed of entry too great. She sighed again. Behind her, Healy made to talk, and she snapped.

"Get out of here, both of you!"

"What? Why?" Healy asked.

"Because," she said, "we have no fuel, we have no air, we have maybe two possible options for re-entry without being burned alive, and it's my job to figure them out, and you're distracting me. There's a crash room at the end of the corridor. Go. *Now*," she added when Healy looked like he was going to argue.

He thought better of it and pulled Alyssa up from the ground. She was woozy, still in shock. *No wonder*, he thought, *for someone who's spent her life in a research lab she's been through a lot.*

They stepped out of the room, and the clack of Meg's keyboard faded as Healy and Alyssa headed further along the hall.

The crash room was little more than a cot, a small larder of snacks and stimulants, and an emergency comm. It was designed for crew members to be able to sleep for short periods of time on shifts without having to head all the way aft to their quarters. It was only designed for one person, but they could both fit if one of them lay on the bed.

Alyssa, still not processing everything that was happening, groaned as she fell into the gel of the safety cot. "I can't believe this is happening. I can't believe it. I can't believe it," She kept repeating the phrase as though it were a mantra.

"I know. We're going down," Healy could scarcely believe it himself, "we're going down, and a lot rougher than we thought. Elsewise we're going to have to learn to breathe vacuum. Even on the ground it isn't going to be easy. Space Palsy has most of us in its grips pretty tight. Even yourself will feel the effects of it by now, unless your science experiment works."

Alyssa looked grim. She reached inside her jumpsuit and pulled out the pill bottle. It was lined with the dust from the ill-formed and powdery medication she'd made for herself. It was still about a quarter full. "I guess we'll see," she said. For a moment she pondered the container, then Healy watched her put it back in her suit.

He hoped for her sake that it worked. The treatment after a long space run was a grim affair. Water suspension tanks for weeks, followed by simple exercises with weak resistance bands if he was going to be spending any length of time on Earth, and in his advanced state he'd have tremors and nerve damage for the rest of his life. He knew some long-term spacers who needed breathing assistance and pacemakers when they got back to Earth, which usually meant medical debt and servitude.

It was going to be hard. But it was going to be easier than breathing oxygen that wasn't there.

Alyssa seemed finally to have roused herself from her state of shock. "If there's going to be an evacuation of the ship, should we let the rest of the crew know?"

❖ ❖ ❖

"Attention all crew. The Sunward Sky *has sustained irreparable damage, and an emergency evacuation will be taking place. However, the timing of the evacuation is critical to ensure the escape is as safe as it can be. We are making preparations now. Please remain in your cabins for the time being."*

Brett leaned back from the door, smirking incredulously. Waugh grinned back, but Ellyse only grimaced.

"We go back to Terra and most of us won't survive," she said. Her breathing was still laboured. The autodoc at the med bay hadn't been running at full capacity and Ellyse was still pale.

She was right. Whether through re-entry shock or the slow gravity crush, it was going to be hard for the crew. Brett tried not to let his eyes linger on her injured body. He didn't know whether or not it was concern for her own life that had driven her to comment.

They sat in silence again, and Brett felt a deathly pall fill the room as they each considered their own mortality. He breathed. There wasn't much to do but wait for the evacuation. They'd been considering attacking Meg and Healy and Alyssa before the announcement, but now it seemed pointless. The doom was coming for everyone on the ship. They'd get to the life pods, just the same as everyone else.

The life pods.

He turned to Waugh. "When we go to the pods, how likely is it that the Terran lot in the cabin is going to be there with us?"

"What do you mean?"

"They'll announce, right? They'll tell us all it's time to move, but *they'll* be in the nav room still, figuring out entry coordinates and everything. They'll be the last people to get aboard the ship, right?"

Waugh nodded, "So?"

Brett jumped up, propelling himself off the floor as the ship's gravity fluctuated. He walked to the shelving at the back of the lockup and started muttering to himself. He grabbed a long row of hose, and a cylinder of something Waugh couldn't see.

"What are you doing?" Waugh asked.

Brett told them, and a few minutes later the three of them left the hideout, heading toward the emergency bay. Brett pulled a small trolley along with him.

❖ ❖ ❖

The emergency procedure was taking longer to calculate now. Meg had overridden all the inputs for fuel and oxygen and manually calculated a series of approximations to push the programmed ship off course. Given enough time she was confident she'd be able to reverse engineer the calculation to find out how much oxygen they had left, but she didn't want to waste time on it. She'd find that out once they did run out of oxygen, and by that point the answer wouldn't be particularly useful to them.

The display updated and showed the procedure for evacuation. One jettison, one fast burn, and the calculated success rate of survival for the escape pods.

Her stomach dropped.

The calculated survival rate was just over fifty per cent. Even taking every chance, using every piece of emergency landing acumen she could muster, only one in two life pods would punch out of orbit and into a safe landing vector.

It was the best she could do.

She pulled out of the bridge and raced down the hall to the crash lounge she'd sent Healy and Alyssa to. They followed her back to the bridge where she talked through the strategy. Alyssa looked dazed, and Healy's face grew darker and darker. When Meg finished, she looked at the other two. She was completely drained, unable to even feel distraught at the situation.

Alyssa spoke up, voice shaky but firm, "Is there anything you need us to do to help?"

Meg shook her head, "Nope. I just needed someone to know what was happening. I needed you to know that I tried my best. I really did," Shame welled up inside her, white hot and full of self-loathing.

Alyssa grabbed her arm, "I know you did. Nobody in their right mind would say otherwise. It's all anyone can ever do in situations like this."

Meg breathed in, steeling herself. Alyssa held her hand on her arm, and she felt Meg's body relax as she came to grips with the situation. After a few minutes, she spoke.

"Alright. We're gonna have to let the ship know. This burn is going to be soon. Once it's done, they can head to the escape bay."

"I'll do it," Alyssa said, crossing to the comm. She thumbed the control, and her voice burst across the ship.

"Attention all crew. We have calculated a landing vector for

the life pods. I repeat, we have calculated a landing vector. Please be aware that there is a further burn required to prepare the ship for its landing. This burn will be starting shortly. Please remain in your cabins until such time as the burn is complete. After this time, move to the escape pods for evacuation."

The rumble and thrust of the ship's engines didn't build slowly. Instead, a roar and a rush, a gigantic sprint and a leap forward, burst to life all around the survivors. The sound of the two remaining engines and the stabilisation calibration that Meg had done tore through the hull. In the nav room Healy, Meg and Alyssa pressed themselves into the corner, holding on as their bodies were ravaged by the high-g acceleration. In the cabins, those who were still alive were sucked into the protective layer of their beds and torn askew by the fighting forces of the ships rotation and thrust in a single moment.

Waugh, Brett and Ellyse had only just managed to complete their work, and they had shoved their equipment back into the trolley and behind them before the burn started. They, too, had hit the floor.

The burn lasted three minutes and fifty-four seconds.

The sound died as rapidly as it had begun.

The weight released from Ellyse's chest, leaving her gasping on the floor. She sucked at air that had been such a struggle to get in, then coughed as her body adjusted back to the low-g environment.

She was dreading the return to Terra. Her brief visits

back to the planet were spent in immersion tanks and soft gel beds when she could get them, and even then the gravity hurt. She stood up from the floor and tried not to think about it. Brett was already up.

They were in a long corridor and surrounded by the circular hatches that hid the escape pods. The one closest to Brett was open, revealing a secondary door. The inner hatch was solid steel, with robust locking mechanisms around the edge and a heavy hinge. It was only wide enough for one person to crawl through. Its external handle was inset and built out of burnished metal that glinted coldly in the lights of the corridor. This second door was the hatch for the pod itself. It was utilitarian and designed to maximise structural integrity while still being useable as a door. In theory it was able to withstand a terminal velocity impact with the Earth.

Brett closed the hatch that was attached to the ship. This one was larger, with a triple layer of thickened glass inset into a small window. With the door closed and the pod still in place the panel was black dark. Only if the pod had been deployed would any light enter through the window.

They'd just made modifications to the escape pod, and he turned the wheel on the shipside door to lock it down. As he did so, the airlocked hatchway to the corridor groaned open.

The remaining crew members shuffled into the evacuation corridor, looking sick, pale and scared. They had no idea what had been happening, having been locked in their crash couches. They stared expectantly at the three of them.

"Hi," Brett said.

❖ ❖ ❖

Meg was still sitting at the display, fingers moving furiously over the input pad. Alyssa asked what she was doing.

"Just checking something," Meg said. Healy looked over her shoulder and onto the screen.

He stared for a few seconds, then said, "Oh," se seemed entranced by the screen for a moment, then turned to Alyssa. Alyssa was feeling lightheaded and found herself panicking about a lack of oxygen.

"It's nothing major," Healy said, then clarified, "well it is, but it shouldn't affect us directly. The ship looks like it's going to touch down on the ground, not the ocean. Likely to land just inland of the coast."

"What?" Alyssa exclaimed.

Meg's fingers continued to fly over the keypad, "It's not ideal. A ship this size, you wouldn't want to be nearby. Huge impact crater. It's okay though, it looks as though the final jettison can be shunted forward til not long after the escape pods drop, which should shallow out the orbit enough to make the ship land offshore."

Alyssa had to control her breathing and kept imagining their air running out as she did so.

Meg continued typing, then started the computation. Time hung in the rapidly toxifying air around them, limp and cold. Nobody spoke while Meg's makeshift computer program calculated. When it chimed that it was complete, the three of them jumped to run back to the screen.

Alyssa couldn't parse the information. The graphics were rudimentary, all looping catenary curves and blinking dots. She studied Healy and Meg's faces, trying to understand whether the result was satisfactory or not. They looked grim, but eventually Meg nodded.

"That'll do," she said, "we'd better get to the bay."

There weren't many crew members left. The escape pods held four people each, in principle, in the same two plus two arrangement of horse-drawn carriages and cars, yet another design inheritance that humanity had taken with them into space.

In a normal evacuation, a decision would have to be made. The escape pods could only accommodate two thirds of the full crew allotment on the ship. *Typical*, Ellyse thought as she helped the sick and injured people on board through the nearly too-small hatchways in the bay. Who aboard would have decided which third of the crew were to be left to die in the spacecraft?

It was an academic disappointment in this case. The crash had killed so many that the remaining crew could barely fill the escape pods. Despite this, Brett and the others were spreading the remaining crew among the pods. The crew members were told that it was to avoid overloading the pods, which was true, but Brett had an ulterior motive.

A tall, gangly woman who Ellyse had been helping turned to her. Her eyes were wide, and she was shaking with a combination of shock, hunger and fear. Her skin was pale, pink and blotchy from a long lack of exposure to sunlight.

"I haven't— I don't know if I'll make it," she sank to the floor. Her legs were shaking so badly that she couldn't stand, and the hand Ellyse grabbed as she knelt was astringent and bony. The shakes from the palsy were wracking her body, and the fear of being back in permanent high gravity was causing those latent tremors to amplify. She was terrified.

Ellyse grabbed her shoulders, not unkindly, and looked into her eyes, "What's your name?"

"Anya."

"Ok, listen to me Anya. Are you listening? You're going to be okay. You've not spent much time dirtside for a while, but that's alright. Emergency services are going to be there when we get to ground. When you get down, the gravity is likely to make breathing hard, but emergency will be there soon. Ask for steroids and immersion tank treatment. Alright?"

Anya nodded.

"What are you asking for?" Ellyse repeated.

"Steroids and immersion tank treatment," she said.

"Good. Now you've got your own pod here. You'll be safe," *I hope*, she didn't add, as Anya crawled inside.

Ellyse sealed both the inner and outer hatch and turned to Brett and Waugh. There were three pods remaining without any of the other crew in them. Ellyse and Brett went into one. Waugh crawled into the other.

The air was getting thin.

❖ ❖ ❖

Meg led the way and thumbed a timer on her suit. The low thud of the first escape pod dropping ricocheted through the ship, and Alyssa and Healy stumbled behind her.

That's one, she thought, and pressed forward. The air was starting to taste staler. She fought the urge to quicken her step, but they still had several minutes to get to the escape bay. She counted the pods as they dropped, relief flooding her with each thud. She blocked out the calculated success rate of the landing and the fact that only half of the crew would survive the shock of the impact. She'd worked hard to get the survival expectations even that high.

The second-to-last pod dropped just before they entered the bay. Meg went first, followed by Alyssa and then Healy. A small trolley full of unfamiliar equipment lay in the corner, but her eyes were fixed on the sole remaining pod. Through every other window, the harsh remains of blunted sunlight streamed and cast a spatter of golden light on the raw steel of the floor.

The outer hatch was tighter than she expected, and her arms began to burn with fatigue after only a few moments. *The oxygen must be low,* she thought. The hatch finally gave.

"Meg," Healy said. His voice sounded far away as she pulled on the heavy steel. She ignored him. "Don't, Meg," he said. "It's too late."

She turned to look at him. His face was set in a hard line, and Alyssa was squatting on the floor next to the trolley. A length of hose connected an unlikely looking handheld object to a gas bottle and a small but powerful ion battery. She caught hold of the tangy scent in the air, and the block of solid rod stowed in a cylinder on one side of the trolley. It was melted and burned on one end.

She span back to the door, and in the dark steel saw rich purple and black residue and bright chrome scars along the edge of the seal.

The escape hatch had been welded shut.

2.11

CRASH

Keegan couldn't believe it. The data he'd started gathering after the launch of the *Sunward Sky* had finally broken containment. Someone higher up the food chain had taken his freelance reporting, all the strange data packets being sent in bursts and his comms with the Nav officer, and sent out an alert. The tale of the *Sunward Sky*, the unknown and uncared for ship that had become crippled and was about to hit the Earth, had spread like a duststorm.

Now, far from his small, uncomfortable office in the middle of the desert, communing via ruined satellite link,

Keegan was in a helicopter, racing to find which drones were rescue drones and which were news feeds trying to be the first to a story.

The machines were all nearly identical, four or six wing models with cameras and satellite connections. But there were differences. The official rescue drones transmitted encrypted data, which showed up scrambled on a raw feed Keegan had by his side. The news feeds and content streams, on the other hand, would show up clear as day.

The rescue drones were also methodical, moving in patterns to efficiently cover the ground so they could create a real-time map of the ocean and register anomalies that might represent the fall of an escape pod. The vidfeeds just searched at random. Once Keegan realised that he was able to zoom out and see the rough, circle packed path that the rescue drones were forming, and pick the anomalies. He'd check if the vid feeds were unencrypted, and then scramble them if they were. The story was going to get out, but at this stage they could do without the distraction of news crews.

Not that it mattered. The Atlantic was now playing host to a horde of visual and location data that was spewing across the globe. The very systems that the *Sunward Sky* was supposed to maintain were becoming clogged by opportunists rubbernecking at its downfall.

Keegan couldn't quite believe it had been him, his independent report from the control station that had made this rescue attempt possible. The company responsible for the satellite had gone completely silent and hadn't, as far as anyone knew, communicated with the *Sunward Sky* or the media since the news broke. He sighed with discontent, and punched the button to scramble another batch of news feed drones. Keegan looked out of the right side of the helicopter.

He could see the patchwork of drones break up and swarm to the east.

A voice cut over the radio, directed at both Keegan and the pilot of the heli, "Got a new radio burst from that Nav Officer, Meg did you say her name was? Approximate landing data for the pods," Keegan asked where they were. "Looks like they're going to be spread over a few hundred square kilometres, falling in the next few minutes. Hang tight, wait for the call to rendezvous. The last thing you want is to be taken out by the podful of people you're supposed to be rescuing."

The line went dead, but then a direct connection came through for Keegan. He let it through and heard the same voice as before.

"Keegan. There's a complication to this that you might have to deal with."

There are parts of a spaceship falling from the sky, Keegan thought. *How many more complications could there possibly be?*

"Most of the people on the ship are long term spacers, which means cases of Space Palsy are going to be extremely prevalent. Most of them aren't going to be able to stand up or walk very well. A lot of them won't be able to at all."

Keegan blanched, "Are you serious?"

"As a street fire," the voice said. "Now, it's not impossible that some of them will have trouble with air and blood circulation."

"What?" Keegan had heard of Space Palsy but wasn't familiar with its symptoms.

"I'm just saying, it's possible."

"Okay, and if the possible happens, what do I do then?"

"Hold on," there was a silence on the line, and when the operator got back it sounded like they were reading from a file. "Space Palsy is a difficult condition to work with while on Earth. Suggest use of medicinal narcotics for acute pain relief and immersion tanks."

Keegan couldn't believe what he was hearing. "Narcotics? You want us to administer *narcotics?* When we scrambled, we didn't plan for that. I'm a desk jockey normally, I only got the call up because I found out about this crash in the first place. There's no morphine on the chopper, and what the hell is an immersion tank?"

"It's like a tank of water. You put them in it, I guess, and—"

"Okay, okay, I get the picture. I'll figure it out," he shut off the comm.

Immersion tanks. He looked out at the boiling ocean, devoid of life, toxically saline and filled with litter from hundreds of years of ecological mismanagement. The sun was hot enough to burn in less than ten minutes. They could immerse, sure. But they'd be poisoned for it. And that's if the sea wasn't so rough as to drown them first.

❖ ❖ ❖

Over the span of six minutes all bar one life pod had jettisoned from the *Sunward Sky*. By the time the last one had released from the hydraulic clamps that held it, the first was beginning to breach the upper atmosphere. The angle of approach on two of them was too shallow; they broke orbit and drifted into the empty void of space.

Three malfunctioned. The age worn and cracked tiling

tore off and the friction burn of entering the atmosphere at terminal velocity ripped the pods apart. Their remains were never found. The constituent parts of the pods caught fire in the atmosphere and disintegrated. Only the smallest pieces survived, falling as specks of barely noticeable dust across a world already choking with it.

Three more pods came in at too steep an angle. The parachutes broke when they tried to open, tearing and providing nothing but a brief halter to the descent. They hit the water with enough force to snap the brittle bones of every palsy-addled traveller inside.

One of those people was Waugh. Her final moments were an all-consuming roar and a pain that burned every neuron of her mind. The impact of the water was a release.

In the days to follow, the pods that no longer read life signs from afar would be recovered. The bodies would be removed. Burned. Nobody would be notified.

The remaining pods had breached the atmosphere at the goldilocks angle. They'd flown straight. They'd held together. The parachutes had neither torn nor failed to fire. Each of them landed in the water.

Meg's calculation had beaten the odds.

The jerk when the parachute opened felt like his lungs had been shot into his nasal cavity, followed by them being wrenched back into place by the impact of the escape pod into the water.

Brett had only been in space for a few months. In that time his muscle mass had gone catabolic. It had atrophied. His blood volume had reduced, his connective tissue and nervous system had degraded. He'd been aware of all of this in his head. He'd known that his servitude on *Sunward Sky* presented a risk to his ability to live his life on Earth. The hours of his labour and his ability to function under gravity were the untold wages demanded by a life in space.

He'd known it was happening, but the reality of the situation hadn't struck him until now as he landed back on Earth. He was pressed into the back of the landing couch. His clothes weighed heavy on his skin, as did the clasps on the safety harnesses. He felt light-headed and his peripheral vision was murky and dark.

Ellyse, in the seat across from him, was far worse. She'd been in space for years, with very few dirtside breaks. The couch was sunk low, and her eyes were closed. The sound of the ocean lapping against the hull rang out as a series of dull metallic slaps. It was quiet, and over the sound of the waves Brett could hear Ellyse's breathing, low, shallow and rasping.

He unbuckled quickly. The straps clinked loudly against the edge of the seat with an immediacy he was no longer used to in full gravity. Dark spots filled his vision as he stood up, drowning out his view of Ellyse. He stopped moving and waited for the blood to rush back to his head. The pod lurched underfoot as he moved around, shifting in the waves. The small stabilising muscles he used to rely on had degraded, and trying to balance in the pod was difficult. Still, he managed to stagger over, bent low to fit under the pods tiny ceiling, twitching ever closer to the bed of the last remaining member of Blackout that had been on the *Sunward Sky.*

When he got to her he didn't know what to do. He didn't want to try mouth to mouth resuscitation or to pump on her chest. He wasn't sure if her body would handle it, the extra pressure in addition to the gravity. In the end, he just grabbed her hand, to reassure her that someone was there. Her mouth was moving. She was saying something, low and urgent, repeating the same thing over and over to herself. Brett turned an ear toward her. Her voice only just broke over the gasp of her lungs.

"Keep. Breathing. Keep. Breathing. Keep. Breathing"

He knelt next to her, still holding her hand. "That's it. Keep breathing. Good."

There was nothing left to do but wait.

The seal on the outside of the pod broke, and Keegan steeled himself against the rush of air when he opened it. Inside, he saw that only one of the seats was occupied, and he wondered again why so many pods had been sent down only partially full. He was halfway in before he saw the second person. A man, kneeling at the edge of the crash couch, holding the hand of the woman stuck there. He was muttering a mantra to her. The woman's lips were blue, and Keegan couldn't see if she was breathing from his vantage point at the hatch.

As he descended, the man registered the sounds that had been happening behind him. He turned around, and his concern dropped away and became a scowl. He pointed urgently to the woman, "We need to get her into water."

Keegan moved gingerly toward the two of them, nodding, "We're working on it. There are immersion tanks available not too far away, but we can't put her into the ocean. It's too rough, and besides—"

"How far away are the immersion tanks?" the other man

interrupted.

"They're onshore. They're being organised by search and rescue," Keegan was feeling extremely out of his depth. Fieldwork wasn't something he did a lot of.

"You don't have them? She's going to suffocate!" the man spat, "Do you have anything to help her breathe, or did you just open that hatchway to watch us die, you fucking Terran?"

Keegan rocked back and thumbed his comm to the pilot, "Yeah hi, we need an evac as soon as possible. We've got a crew member with severe breathing difficulty, and we need to get her to an immersion tank."

His radio spat to life, "negative, Keegan. We're halfway back with some of the other crew, going to have to go via the shore. Fifteen, twenty minutes at the earliest."

"From shore?" the man was furious now, "You lot are fucking useless, aren't you?"

Keegan ignored the remark, turned to him and asked, "Is anyone else coming down? Are there any more shuttles to land? Do you know how many more pods there are?"

The man looked away for a moment. He'd made sure that the last pod wouldn't come down, and he'd deliberately scattered the crew among too many pods so that Healy and the rest couldn't return. He looked to the woman lying in the chair, her hand resting gently in his. It wasn't clear if she'd make it another twenty minutes.

"I don't think there are any more," he said.

Healy stood, struck dumb and with a slowly growing fury, staring at the welded seams that were sealing the door to the escape pod. He couldn't believe it. After everything they'd done, Blackout had managed to sabotage their escape. They couldn't unweld it, even with the torch there. The seal on the door could have been compromised, something they wouldn't know until they were in the void, and it was too late.

Healy and Meg frantically discussed options. Alyssa was silent, and beginning to feel lightheaded as the air grew noticeably thinner. The conversation went on without her input.

Can we manoeuvre? No, we don't know if we've got enough fuel reserves, and we haven't got time to check.

Can we strap into our cabins? No, the ship isn't designed for landing impacts. You saw what happened in the crash, a lot of people died. Meg was trying not to look at Healy as she said it, aware of his discomfort at having sent the ship on its collision course.

They made a decision, and without another word they started to sprint down the corridor towards the other end of the ship. Alyssa's legs were burning, and dark spots appeared in her vision. She was gasping as she asked where they were headed.

"Remember the launch room, when we took off?" Healy said. Alyssa could hardly forget. She could still feel the way her arm had snapped, pushed down by the force of the launch.

"Yeah, I remember," she was struggling to keep up, running out of breath and exhausted. Healy and Meg were breathing harder too, but they seemed less fatigued than she did.

"The officers have a launch room too," Healy said, "but

they're built tougher than the cabin couches, or the couches in the launch room. More robust, see."

"Why's that?" Alyssa said.

"There aren't as many officers," Healy puffed as he loped along, "plus, they were the couches that were put in ages ago, when the ship was being tested. Test flights were only manned by essential crew. And this is an old ship, so when it was tested, there were no spacers. They were all Terrans— dirtsiders," he corrected himself quickly, looking apologetically at Alyssa, "it's not like them to put *themselves* at risk."

Alyssa shook her head, forcing herself to concentrate, trying to ignore the staleness of the air and the thought of the evacuating oxygen tank. There was something about what Healy had just said that didn't seem right, but she couldn't grasp the thought. Before she was conscious of it, she'd stopped in the middle of the hall to think. Healy and Meg didn't notice and continued running. She called to them, and her voice echoed sharply down the corridor. The other two turned to her.

"What is it?" Meg said, "Come on, we have to go!"

"What aren't you telling me?" Alyssa said. Her mind was foam and cloud.

"What do you mean?" Meg said.

"I can't think properly right now. What's happening in this room. This launch room for the officers. Tell me what I don't know," she swayed with the ship.

"It's affecting you faster than it's affecting us," Healy said, "Our bodies have a lower oxygen demand than you do because of the palsy. It means you'll start getting lightheaded just before we do," he held his hand out and Alyssa saw that his usual tremor was now a violent shake as Healy began to suffer the beginnings of oxygen deprivation, "We're telling you everything. I promise. Okay?"

"Okay," Alyssa set off down the hall again. She still had a paranoid unease about their plan and felt as though she was missing something. They reached the forward end of the ship and turned right into one of the rooms just off the hallway. Suddenly, Alyssa understood what she'd been missing.

They were standing in an airlock.

"Why can't you just put her in the ocean?" Brett spat.

"Because it's toxic," the Terran said, "and because it's rough. If we put her in there, she might hit her head on the pod and drown. Or she won't, and she'll die from being submerged in the ocean."

'If we don't do something she's going to die anyway!"

The man nodded, then thumbed his comm and started talking to whoever was on the other end.

Behind them, Ellyse's breathing was soft, yet desperate.

The air was noticeably thin now, but there was a short-term oxygen supply in the suits they were putting on. Alyssa stood in a daze thinking about the jump.

The jump into the void.

Alyssa jerked herself back into motion and pulled her helmet over her head. She fiddled absent-mindedly with the clasps on her gloves as she gazed out the window that looked across at the only remaining wing of the ship. Enormous rings rotated around the central shaft, with what remained of corridors and broken structure flying off into the night. From her reference point it looked as though the centre of the ship was spinning, but she knew it was stationary and the wing structure she was in was rotating. She could see the second wing, the remaining wing, not far from her.

That was where she was going to jump, without safety lines or thrusters of her own. Just her aim and blind, desperate hope.

"Why can't we just stop the rotation and go through the ship, the way Healy and I did when we were checking engineering?" Alyssa asked again.

Meg's voice came through the radio in a chatter, "I don't know if doing so will knock us off track, and if we go off course at this point, I don't know if we'll survive, or if we have any fuel to get us flying straight again."

She'd suited up far faster than Alyssa had been able to. Healy's carabiner-laden suit was already a flight suit and only needed minor adjustments to make it airtight. The two of them turned to her. Alyssa's head was clearer now that the suit was feeding its oxygen to her. She nodded, understanding. The act of slowing and stopping the rotation of the wings could mean that its course got disrupted. It made sense now.

Alyssa patted her pocket. The container of homemade pills was still there. The airlock in front of her hissed as Healy wound the wheel to open it. Alyssa tried not to think of Isa, broken and empty in a place just like this at the other end of the ship. Her breath felt ragged as she stepped into the lock.

You can do this.

"Alright, listen here," Meg addressed her and Healy at once, "this is a free flight. We don't have any guylines or ropes or cables or anything that can reach all the way across to the next wing, where the officer deck is. So we're going to be jumping.

"We're jumping from here to an equivalent room across the other side," at this, she pointed across. Alyssa followed the direction of her finger and saw the rounded rectangle of a door with an inset window of blackened glass on the opposite wing.

"It's important to, listen to me! It's *really important* that you don't aim directly for the door when you jump. We're spinning. If you jump straight across from here, the Coriolis effect will get you. You'll jump, the ship will spin away from you, and you'll spend the rest of your life in the vacuum," she checked her oxygen meter. "Which will be around fifteen minutes before you suffocate."

Alyssa checked her own oxygen supply. Sixteen minutes, it said. Not a lot of reprieve from the dwindling atmosphere onboard.

"To counteract the Coriolis effect, you have to aim *below* the door, so that by the time you reach it, the wing has spun *down* to meet you," Meg lowered her hand to just below the bottom edge of the ship's wing, to a mess of steel sections and joints, "Aim there. That should give you plenty of room and allow for you to slightly misjudge without it being a catastrophe. Are you ready?"

Alyssa nodded, nervous, then realised that she was facing away from Meg, and they were both wearing helmets. Meg couldn't see her nodding.

"Yes," she confirmed. Healy did the same.

"Alright," Meg slammed the airlock cycle, and a rushing

sound permeated the room as the air evacuated.

The hatch opened.

Alyssa blanched. Removing the outer layer of the spacecraft, the skin that stood between herself and the vacuum was an immediate and visceral thing. The suit puffed out as the internal air pressure pushed out against the vacuum.

"Healy, you go, then Alyssa, and I'll follow behind," Meg's voice was much calmer than Alyssa felt.

The thump in her heart grew louder and almost drowned out the throb of the dying ship emanating through her feet. Healy turned, facing away from the doorway, pointed at the spot below the ship's wing, then crouched and jumped.

He drifted off, and Alyssa watched him as she lined herself up to take the leap. Staring out into the space between the wings, her heart leapt into her throat and her legs turned to jelly.

When she'd boarded this ship, so long ago, she'd dreamed of a spacewalk. To dance, careless and alone as a tiny speck in an endless universe. Then she'd seen Holding murdered and she'd seen the scarab graft itself onto the side of a satellite and she'd realised that the void she'd so desired was just as fraught with the foibles of humanity as any other place. Looking out now, it held a silent threat, where the ship was still safe to her.

In some small corner of her mind, she knew it wasn't true. The ship wasn't safe, no matter how the thrum and sway of the engines convinced her otherwise. The ship was doomed, and it was only familiarity and her mammalian expectation of being grounded and connected to something that meant it felt safer to her than to anywhere else. It was nonsense, and if she waited longer the ship would tear itself apart or the thinning oxygen would dissipate entirely.

She steeled herself, crouching against the wall of the ship, then felt the silence and the stillness envelope her as she sprang into the void.

Her aim was true, and she watched the wing she'd aimed at rise to meet her. Behind it she saw the cosmos laid out, resplendent in its enormity, the infinite and the divine spinning dizzyingly around. The open brace of the Earth's curvature framed the entirety of the rest of existence. She was a mote. A speck, leaping with nothing but blind hope between one side of an insignificant structure to another, a structure wrought from the minuscule materials available on the one world where humanity had, for the smallest time, flourished. Everything she'd done, from the fight for survival to the stress of Project Blackout's sabotage to the problems with engineering to the ship and ground control and even her research, it all fell away from her for a moment. It was all so small in comparison to the broken convalescence of reality that lay in unwarped majesty in front of her.

The universe was cold. They only had each other.

She watched the hatchway rise up. Suddenly it jerked and the entire ship lurched away from her. Healy, who was almost to the other side when it happened, hit the door and bounced and he frantically grabbed a handhold, but he was already shifting up and out of sight along with the rest of the wing as Alyssa watched.

"Shit!" Meg's voice was frantic, "The final jettison!"

Alyssa immediately understood what had happened. When Meg had measured the descent, it had looked like the ship was going to fall on the land. To stop that happening, she'd modified the timing of the jettison, shifting it earlier in the flight to push the flight path to last just a few minutes longer. In their hurry to escape, they'd mistimed their jump, and the jettison had happened as they were floating between the wings of the spacecraft.

Alyssa swore to herself as the door she'd been aiming at screamed past her. The edge of the wing was rapidly approaching. Before she knew, she was a meter away and nearly sweeping out of her reach. She thrust her arm out, trying to reach for one of the guiderails that were crisscrossed over the hull. She fought the urge to close her eyes as she stretched herself as far as she could go, willing herself forward and upward and wishing she had some way of changing her trajectory.

She hit the edge of the rail at the second joint in her fingers. She hooked on and her body rotated around its new fulcrum. As she slammed into the steel of the outer hull, she felt a sharp pain in her leg.

She didn't care. She'd made it.

"Alyssa!" Alyssa's radio crackled with Meg's voice. She turned. Meg's trajectory was even further off course than hers had been, and she was set to pass below the bottom edge of the ship's gigantic wing and fall to Earth.

Poised as she was, Alyssa wasn't able to reach. She didn't have the arm span and the rail was at an awkward angle.

Folding over at the waist, she reached down with her feet toward the rail she'd been hanging on to with her hands. Without thinking, Alyssa jammed her boot between the rail and the hull and turned it ninety degrees to spin away from the Sunward Sky and stood up into nothing, throwing her hands up and reaching out to Meg.

Meg, for her part, had seen what Alyssa was doing and

was reaching toward her as Alyssa stood up and put her hands in the air. Meg caught Alyssa on her forearm and Alyssa pulled her straight down toward the steel deck, crouching to try to minimise the rotational inertia from their collision. She bent back, giving with the movement of the ship and holding on as Meg slammed into the hull. A crack appeared in Meg's helmet, and rapidly cooling air exploded outward in hissing puffs of cold steam.

"Get inside, Alyssa, go!" Meg let go of Alyssa's arm and grabbed onto a different guide rail. She was on the outside surface of the wing, spinning rapidly around the core and being thrown outward by centripetal force. Likewise, Alyssa had to climb upward to get to the hatchway. Healy was crouched in the airlock, laying on the ground above her and reaching down to her. She ignored his hand and climbed the extra few feet, pouring herself into the airlock and gasping with exhaustion and relief.

A few moments later, Meg's arm appeared over the edge of the airlock entrance and both Alyssa and Healy grabbed her and pulled her onto the deck. Her helmet hissed and ice crystals were forming around where the impact had broken it. Inside the visor was a cloud of fog. She pulled her leg to the side just in time for the door to slam shut and the airlock to begin its cycle again.

Alyssa leaned against the wall as the sound of the ship came back with a hiss of air venting into the airlock.

Meg's helmet smashed as she tore it from her head and threw it against the wall.

"Fuck," she said, "I can't believe I forgot about the fucking jettison."

Healy and Alyssa said nothing. With the suits off, the

sharp stale taste of the failing systems on the ship were all the more bitter. Each breath was a gasp that felt more insubstantial than the last.

"Come on," Meg said, "Emergency pod."

The inner door to the airlock opened and the trio staggered down the hallway. The next door was on the other side and led into a well-reinforced room with no windows out.

Alyssa had seen a launch room like this when she first walked onto the ship. When she'd first boarded in the hope that she might be able to do something to help the people who were forced to live their lives on a ship like this. That room had been spartan and fitted with badly maintained launch beds and fittings. The crew had been crammed in side by side like so many cattle. Their expendable nature was written in the broken amenity and cold air of the launch room.

This launch room was well appointed. All the equipment was still old and poorly maintained, but it was obvious that at some point it had been, if not luxurious, then at least made of sturdier stuff than the one she'd suffered at launch. The couches were more solid and robust, spaced farther apart, and there was a suite of disconnected wiring from a long-gone entertainment pod.

It was an opulence long discarded in favour of pure utility. The systems had been ripped out, and any and all services or infrastructure that wasn't absolutely necessary had been degraded and ignored. Even the essential systems had been left too long and now operated at a point of near failure. That which had been whole had been slowly mined until only a husk remained, ready to be punctured or crushed at a moment's notice.

Wordlessly, Healy, Alyssa, and Meg found a crash

couch, strapped themselves in, and waited. The air grew thinner around them, and Alyssa felt the stale feeling grow like a slick on her skin. She tried not to think about the ship's orbit as it degraded, falling closer to the ground with her in it.

She dug in her pocket and pulled out her pills. The reason she'd come here in the first place. They were chalky. Fuzzy. Vague. A leap of faith, or something like it. They were white and bright, not like the froth and dark that was beginning to encroach on her vision. The ship roared, but was it getting louder? Was it the engine, or the noise of atmosphere she heard, rushing against the hull?

She put the pills next to her. The ship was crying, or screaming. Millions of parts in harmony torn apart by cruel violence and perpetuated by a cascading set of failures.

Relax, she thought, *Sunward Sky is falling. You won't need to worry soon.*

She shook her head to clear it, and failed. The sound from the hull was definitely there now. A cacophony. A lullaby.

Alyssa closed her eyes.

2.12

LEGACY

Keegan tried, he really did, and so did all the other workers on the rescue teams. They did what they could to drive off the network drones from the newsfeeds and livestreams, but their efforts proved nearly futile. Before long the machines were swarming through the air like the locust plagues of the past, buzzing over the crash sites and darting around the survivors as they were pulled into boats and helicopters. The emergency evacuation of the *Sunward Sky* was the most streamed topic on every network. Entire datacentres were flooded with imagery of every pod and every survivor, video feeds of every angle, the vision from a million mechanical eyes.

Before long, anyone who had ever worked on a spacecraft, or near one, or had studied orbital mechanics for more than an afternoon, was dragged onto vidscreens to be interviewed by pundits who breathlessly, earnestly, and inaccurately estimated the chain of events that had led to the crash.

On the first day, as the survivors were being transported, the night began to fall. The majority of the drones didn't have night cameras and couldn't see the dark grey carcasses of the escape pods in the ink-black of the choking sea. Newsfeeds began replaying footage from earlier in the day, and the speculations began. Nobody directly involved with the *Sunward Sky* from Earth could be contacted, and the victims of the crash were either sick, infirm or dead.

A solitary drone, flying close to the water and matching the zigzag movements of the official drones, followed one of the rescue helicopters as it returned to the shore. The drone operator watched as the helicopter landed at a concrete box warehouse. It looked like a bunker writ large, with tilt-up concrete walls, gigantic roller doors and blacked-out windows. The building was retrofit with batteries, heat shielding and what looked like a set of enormous water filters. Each filter had a pan that lay open to the sky, runoff tanks designed to expose the water to the ultraviolet radiation of the sun. Workers in sunsuits were scrambling around, hacking supplementary systems onto the side of the pans and frantically cleaning the rest of the systems.

The drone flew up high enough to capture the entire facility and watched. The rescue helicopter it had been following wove its way over the tanks and battery arrays toward the doors at the other end of the facility. The workers on the ground barely reacted as they fought to connect a series of thick hoses to the side of the water filters. As the doors opened, the helicopter moved in. Several hundred meters above the building, the drone motors stopped. It dropped through the air like a stone, then the rotors fired up again, this time in reverse. The motors screamed and the drone shot downward through the air, manoeuvring and aiming for the closing door. It shook, threatening to tear itself apart against the friction of the wind and the operator watched the status indicators blink red on their heads-up display.

The drone blew through the door with mere centimetres to spare, and immediately braked to avoid hitting a series of baffle walls that had been set up opposite the landing pad. The operator swore loudly as the decelerating drone hit one of the walls before pushing itself up and away from the ground. The flashing red indicator for one of the wings went solid, and the response from the machine became sluggish.

The drone rose to the ceiling of the space, above the height of the baffle walls, and sped low across the makeshift drop-in ceilings that spread across the room. It navigated through the trusses of the roof, dancing through the gaps until it reached the main hangar.

The drone operator nearly let go of the controls.

In the back half of the hangar was a series of grimy water tanks, lit by the musty sunbeams struggling through the blacked-out windows. Each tank was the size and shape of a standard bunk, glass sided and held together with bolts and epoxy. They were stacked three levels high on gangways with umbilicals sprouting from the top and bottom. Several were cracked, little more than angry shards of glass surrounding empty steel frames. Most lay empty with days and months and years of grime built up inside them. The glass fronts, once clear, were caked and opalescent with filth.

A scant few were filled with water. If the water had been

clean when it was pumped in, it was no longer. It had absorbed the disuse of the tanks and become a dank, murky, choking colloidal mixture of the muck that had rested in the tank for so long.

There were bodies floating in the tanks, visible through the translucent water and the filthy glass. Each of them was stick thin with a respirator obscuring their face. They looked like ghosts.

The operator thumbed the drone's controls, and the machine moved closer to the tanks. The water looked noxious; it was little wonder that there was so much frantic activity outside. The people in the tanks were limp, exhausted, and barely conscious.

In front of the rows of tanks, on the ground, a dozen more people lay on the blackened concrete. Volunteers were walking between them with breathing masks, pressing them onto their faces to allow the survivors to breathe more easily for a few scant seconds before they moved on to help the next person.

Two more volunteers stood on the gantry with hoses, trying desperately to fill another tank. The hose was clogged and degraded and the water coming out of it was a sickly green-grey. The asphyxiating survivors of the *Sunward Sky's* crash were about to be plunged into toxic liquid in an attempt to save them from the gravity that pressed their lungs closed.

The drone operator quickly began flying around the space, zooming in on the volunteers, the survivors, and the disarray and conditions in the rescue centre. A security team came for the drone and tried to snatch it from the air, but the operator dodged high, capturing the entirety of the space. A few seconds later a worker in the high-visibility orange of the search and rescue crew came out and scrambled the drone with an electromagnetic pulse device. The drone sputtered and died, and the video feed stopped.

But by then it was too late. The drone operator had been streaming the entire time, and thousands of people were watching. The pundits and media personalities, who for hours now had been rerunning imagery of the pods falling, jumped onto the new video like wolves. They ripped the stream, cut it and replayed it and spat it all over. The tale of the demise of the *Sunward Sky* turned quickly from that of an unfortunate disaster to one of gross negligence.

The media cycle continued, unabated, and the grainy images of ghostly spacers in filthy survivalist conditions was all that anyone was seeing, anywhere, on any of the feeds they followed.

That is, until the *Sunward Sky* itself fell.

A ship the size of the *Sunward Sky* was only designed to return to Earth in a reverse lift-off. The aerodynamics were supposed to self-correct, baffling winds and course correcting with the thrusters so that the ship could land back on the same landing pad it left from. It wasn't *supposed* to re-enter the atmosphere in any other manner.

The *Sunward Sky* careened through the thickening air mere hours after the rest of the escape pods had fallen through the atmosphere. The pods had made a meteor shower and a media shower that had shocked the world and now everyone watched as the *Sunward Sky* suffered its death throes.

As it fell the friction of the air around it heated up the already blackened panels. A wavefront of compressed and rapidly heating air built up at the nose of the ship. Eventually it burst into flame, and an orange-red tail stretched behind it. Vidfeeds caught the gigantic man-made meteor from every direction as it tore its way to the ground. Its two remaining wings were still being rotated by the ship's centripetal gravity system, and the eccentric rotation that had been plaguing it in orbit quickly became catastrophic when combined with the wind currents tearing around the hull. The ship began to tumble and a trail of broken steel members and conduits and ductwork and panelling flew off and burned up behind it as the ship tore itself to pieces.

After hours of feeds of sick spacers and rehashed footage of crashed pods, the burning wreckage was the crescendo that the media frenzy needed. The sky was a pyre, and the video footage of it was intercut with images of gaunt spacers, thrown far and wide using the very satellites that the *Sunward Sky* had been charged with maintaining.

Inside the ship, Meg was pressed into her crash couch, drenched in sweat as the room heated up. The fresh air outside the hull roared through the superstructure of the *Sunward Sky* but couldn't penetrate the hull. She could barely breathe. The oxygen in the ship was all but spent. A small part of her mind recognised that she'd need to open the access hatch as soon as the ship finally hit the Earth to let fresh air in. But for now, at the speed they were falling, the oxygen outside was as dangerous as the lack of it inside.

Her tongue felt thick in her mouth. There were only a few minutes left to fall but the horrific noise in her mind and all around her made it impossible to tell how much time had elapsed. It was an instant that held an eternity. She had been born into the terrifying roar that surrounded her and she would die here. White noise was all she knew. All she'd ever known. She breathed but felt no satiation from it, such was the lack of oxygen. Her mind was going fuzzy, and the static seemed to match everything else in her existence. On and on it went, interminably.

Until it didn't.

What remained of the ship hit the ocean and decelerated from terminal velocity to nearly zero in an instant. Meg felt her ribs crack as she was thrown forward into the harnesses, and the roaring sound stopped, replaced by a sickening gurgle as the ship began to sink. They were at the front of the ship and they'd hit the water first. Meg panicked; if they were submerged underwater they wouldn't be able to do anything. They would have made it down to Earth, only to be starved of oxygen by a few scant meters of water.

As she lay, holding her ribs and panicking, a shockwave ran through the structure of the ship. It lurched and began to tilt upward, having struck an underwater outcropping. The front of the ship tilted up until it burst back out of the water, and the tail end, thrusters and the aft of the ship sank into the sand.

Eventually, the ship came to a creaking halt.

Meg could barely think straight, but she started moving immediately. The room was tilted at a sharp angle, but she could see the broken and harsh clouds of the sky on one side of the thickened window near her. The window on the other side was underwater and peered into a dun-coloured murk.

She unstrapped herself and tried to ignore the pain in her chest. She fought against the gravity as it weighed on her. It was exhausting. She'd managed to maintain a semblance of muscle mass using a set of resistance bands in her cabin, but exercise wasn't the same as the constant, cloying press of the world bearing down. As she moved to the window and the supply kit that she knew lay beneath it, the combination of thin air, pain, and gravity made her heart race. By the time she arrived she was gasping for oxygen that wasn't there.

She pulled open a cupboard by the door and grabbed the emergency drill. She picked it up and pressed it into the window with shaking hands. The hardened acrylic had at some point been a smooth, flawless feature of the *Sunward Sky*, but it was now scored and scratched. She pressed the drill bit into a scratch and pulled the trigger.

It made short work of the window, and a containment alarm went off inside the cabin as fresh, oxygen rich air made its way through the hole. Meg pressed her mouth to the hole and sucked, feeling the oxygen fill her lungs and finding the desperate, animal need for breath relax from her. After her lungs were full, she held her breath as she drilled more holes. The drill was heavy and hurt her arm but she kept going, punching holes in the spacecraft she'd called home until she couldn't physically lift the drill any more.

The pressure in the cabin was lower than the air outside. As a result, the fresher, oxygenated air rushed into the space.

Meg staggered back to her couch, legs flailing and wobbling beneath her, and fell. She turned to look at her crewmates. Healy was gasping, unable to move. His muscles were too atrophied.

Further away, she could see Alyssa.

She wasn't moving.

The rescue team arrived half an hour later. Keegan was exhausted. He'd been helping ferry people back and forward for almost a full day now. His eyes itched and his hands tremored.

He and another rescue worker had to cut into the bay next to the window where Meg had drilled the holes. The screeching sound of the saw against the hull of the spacecraft woke Meg up. She watched as they cut their way in, and then saw a man's head. He turned to his colleague and she heard him yell "Three stretchers!" before pulling himself into the cabin and making his unsteady way down the sloping floor toward her. She recognised his voice from somewhere.

Meg didn't remember what happened on the way out. It was all shifting lights, a small stretcher, and then the cacophony of a helicopter and the sickening sensation of full gravity movement. Before long, the noise stopped, and Meg found herself laying on the ground in a warehouse full of filth.

As they lay her down, the young man who had picked her up and carried her out on the stretcher walked past. He was talking quickly over a headpiece.

"Noone else on the ship proper. There weren't any more when we got there. No, just the two of them. We retrieved the third but she didn't make it. A stroke, I think. Yes, I know."

He kept walking, stocky and steady of foot, across the acrid floor of the warehouse. Meg began to shake, then sob as she realised what had happened. Alyssa, after making it almost all the way through the entire ordeal since the crash, had died on the way back into the atmosphere. The thin oxygen and a lack of food and water, along with the stress, had taken its toll.

Meg sobbed quietly to herself. Healy was laying next to her. Ignoring the pain in her arms, she lifted herself up and commando crawled to him. An accretion of black, oily dust covered her flight suit as soon as she moved off the stretcher. She saw the rest of the hangar. The tanks full of filthy water, with emaciated humans bobbing in them. The people walking around administering oxygen to survivors who lay gasping on the floor. The people they skipped because it was too late to help them. The immersion tanks, all occupied or not fit for humans. The emergency equipment that was out of date, or badly maintained, or broken.

They didn't care about us up there, Meg thought, *why did I think it was going to be different down here?*

Healy's eyes were open, but just barely. Small slits, peering out from a craggy face.

"Healy?" she said. He grunted softly. "Did you hear what that man just said?"

He could barely move his lips, "No. everything is too loud. Too heavy. I can't. Breathe."

"I know. I know," Meg said, ignoring the burning in her own muscles. She dropped her voice to a whisper, then leaned down to him and said, "I'm so sorry. Alyssa didn't make it."

There was a long silence. Then Healy, with great effort, sat up. His carabiners, rather than safety devices and softly clinking adornment to his suit, were now a millstone holding his body down. He sighed heavily, then turned and crawled on hands and knees to Alyssa.

When he got there, he was stock still, just for a moment. He was above the young scientist's body, staring at her. For a moment, Meg thought he was going to bend down to kiss her forehead, but he didn't. Instead, his lips began to move. He spoke so softly that Meg couldn't hear more than the deepness of his voice and the sensation of his brogue. It was a prayer of some sort.

Once he was done, it was obvious what even that small

amount had taken out of him. His face was sheened with sweat, and pale. Before he collapsed, Meg saw him reach down and briefly hold Alyssa's hand. She thought she heard the words *thank you*.

She saw something in his hand as he pulled away, a bottle of some kind. He slipped it into his breast pocket, and then his strength gave out. He rolled onto his back on the floor, gasping. The sweat on his face was a death mask, and his skin was so pale it was almost grey.

"Hey!" Meg called to get the attention of the staff on the floor of the hangar. "Help! He needs help!" One of the staff rushed over with an oxygen bottle and a respirator. She pressed it to his face, and after a minute Healy stopped hyperventilating. His features, still pale, began to harden. There was a rage beneath them, and a dark look in his eyes. He still couldn't speak and still had trouble breathing, but he began to say something into the respirator, softly and urgently, repeating it like a mantra until the staff member noticed.

"What?" she said, but Healy couldn't speak any louder.

He kept repeating it, over and over, urgently, until the staff member took the respirator off and leaned down to press her ear closer to his head.

"Project Blackout. Find Brett. Find Ellyse. Find Waugh. It was them. They know what happened. Project Blackout. Find Brett. Find Ellyse. It was them. They know what happened. Project Blackout."

The tank was filthy. Grains of muck and grime swam on her skin, and the water felt like an oil slick being rubbed against her body. The world outside, Terra, the space she'd never be able to properly inhabit ever again, was a broken mess of grey-white liquid smoke.

Ellyse knew that she must stink. She couldn't smell with the respirator on her head and submerged as she was, but the filthy water and broken-down filtration system was recycling the same oily, sweaty, aged water in and out of the tank repeatedly, miring her in gunk that she knew would take forever to get out. If she ever got out.

She didn't remember how she'd got here, but she was glad that she'd made it into immersion. Her lungs felt lighter, and she was alert due to the oxygen-rich feed she had coming through her respirator. It was eerily quiet. Below, on the ground, she could see the blurred outlines of the other survivors, and she sent a silent prayer of thanks that she wasn't on the ground.

As she floated, a rhythmic thud began to thrum through the water as a small team of people came walking along the gangway toward her. They stopped outside the tank. They looked like security. They surrounded the tank and stood imposingly. They knocked on the glass. The noise reverberated through Ellyse's skull, and she turned to face the one who had knocked. He was blurred, but the tablet screen he held up to the glass explained everything.

Brett hadn't needed any special assistance after the crash. He'd been on Earth for several years prior to the launch of the *Sunward Sky* and so his muscles, while degraded, weren't as bad as the rest of the crew. He could still stand easily enough. He could walk.

He was one of the lucky ones.

He cast his eyes angrily around the hangar from the anteroom just outside the main floor where the rest of the survivors lay. *Typical Terrans*, he thought. Too much to ask that they keep the emergency facility well run. To make it habitable in the event that the worst did happen. Just let it fall into disarray, let the expendables rot and lay on the floor. He wished he could say he was surprised.

A voice from behind him called his name. He turned. The Terran that had picked him up from the life pod, Keegan, was standing in the doorway along with several security guards. Brett felt his heart quicken.

"What is it?" he said flatly.

"Does 'Project Blackout' mean anything to you?"

Brett wheeled away from the small group of Terrans and looked out into the hangar. It took him a second to find him, as he was a fair distance away, but he spotted Healy, lying on the ground covered in the ridiculous carabiners on his flight suit. He'd survived the crash.

Brett took off at a flat run, away from the guards and out of the door into the hangar. His leg strength wasn't what it used to be, and he was slowing down. Security was behind him and gaining fast, but he'd reach Healy first.

He jumped over the prone bodies of the other survivors and stumbled slightly. He was going to kill him. It didn't matter what happened now. He was going to kill him and he was going to make sure it hurt before the Terran security team got to him. He'd destroyed everything.

Five meters. There was a woman in his path, lying face up on the ground. He jumped.

Something hit him in the leg, and he pivoted in mid-air and cried out in pain. He landed awkwardly and sprawled on the ground next to Healy. His left wrist, which he'd used to catch his fall, stabbed with sudden pain. He turned to look at how he'd stumbled.

It was Meg. She'd seen him running and had stuck her hand up to trip him on the way. She was holding her forearm and grimacing in pain, but her eyes were locked on Brett, staring at him with a look of satisfied vengeance.

Ignoring the pain in his wrist, Brett hoisted himself up and staggered over to where Healy lay and landed a single, furious blow onto the old man's cheek.

There was a deep cracking noise as the brittle cheekbone fractured, and a gash split across Healy's face as Brett fell furiously onto him, winding up to hit him again. The second blow broke his jaw, and several teeth flew out, yellow-white stars against the grimy black ground.

Brett didn't land a third punch.

Security caught up to him and tackled him to the ground. One pulled a set of cuffs from his belt. Brett tried to fight back, but he was no match for the pair of them after his stay aboard the *Sunward Sky*.

"You *fucker!*" Brett cried, struggling futilely and furiously as he was cuffed and dragged away. "After all the work we did! After all we achieved! You *fucker!* You sellout! Now you're going to rot down here, instead of up there! Is this what you wanted?"

Healy was barely conscious, laying on the ground in a rapidly growing pool of his own blood. Despite this, he managed to smile. A grotesque mockery of a grin split his bloody features, and he stared at the Project Blackout member being dragged away at the same time as another set of security members walked across the gangway where Ellyse floated in a tank of grime.

"You can't make anything better," Healy managed to mumble, "if all you want is to destroy. That's what you never understood."

Brett's cries of rage echoed across the hangar as the security team dragged him out, and Healy fell into unconsciousness as the medical team rushed over.

The drone that had flown into the hangar and broken the story of the treatment of the spacefarers was the stone that started a landslide.

Over the following months, a series of investigations looked into the treatment and demographic of people that were taken into spacecraft such as the *Sunward Sky*, and the working conditions and expectations that they were subject to after signing up.

The investigations uncovered entire rackets and corporate rings that were tasked with finding drug addicts, homeless, lonely and disenfranchised people to serve as indentured slaves on the maintenance ships above the orbit of the Earth. A string of companies were charged with human trafficking. The media was in a frenzy, and the *Sunward Sky* became a catchcry for the revolution of spacefarer's rights. The footage of the rescue, the reports of the conditions aboard the spacecraft and testimonials from the survivors all served as a crushing indictment of the corporation that owned the ship. Add to that the company's continued silence, and the government quickly built a case for its dissolution. Of the directors, most were jailed, though some were found dead, by coincidence in cities where known crew had family members. No official connection was ever found.

Healy spent a long time in hospital, but eventually he was discharged. He was able to lend a lot of assistance to the investigation into Project Blackout and his role aboard the *Sunward Sky*. With his help, the rest of the scarabs were located, each leaching parasitically to the side of a satellite, burrowing into the controls and waiting for the command to scramble the world's communications. Each was carefully extricated from the satellite it was attached to and sent down to Earth. Project Blackout came to illuminate the night sky in a series of metallic meteorite showers.

Brett and Ellyse were interrogated. Ellyse never gave them anything. Her fury at life aboard the spacecraft and the damage to her body left her unwilling to betray Project Blackout, the one piece of agency she'd had in her adult life. Brett, on the other hand, for all his bravado and bluster, broke down in the face of the interrogations. He'd managed to glean enough information simply by his proximity to others in the project on the ground level to know where the Scarabs were manufactured. He knew one of the Earthside coordinators, and from there Project Blackout's operational base was routed, broken, and dismantled. Brett, Ellyse, and the remaining members were jailed.

The *Sunward Sky* protocol was enacted and signed into law. It was a special edict that detailed the length of time and the length of respite that workers could manage in low gravity environments to limit the effects of the Space Palsy.

Nearly a year later, Healy and Meg sat quietly in a courtroom, not for the first time. They had both grown used to sitting and waiting in their wheelchairs for their turn to give evidence, or depositions, or lend their story in some other way to various legal proceedings. Their testimony alone had led to the majority of the crew aboard the *Sunward Sky* to be exonerated. They had given statements to governing bodies to argue for further rights for space travellers. Their own condition, healthy people driven to being bound in wheelchairs by the work, was used as evidence of the corporation's cruelty for years to come.

Despite that, there was still one question that hadn't been answered, after all the suing and countersuing and hearings and media frenzy.

What had happened aboard the *Sunward Sky*?

Healy looked at Meg as the other members of the chamber shambled in. They were both seated in the front and centre of the room, in the wheelchairs they'd been assigned. Healy reached into his pocket and thumbed the container he'd secreted away there. Alyssa's medication. It was empty now but for a chalky residue. The lid had cracked, breaking on the impact with the Earth, and Healy found himself running the top of his fingernail over the imperfection in the surface. It was all he had left of her. He'd missed the funeral, a small affair two weeks after the crash for her and all the other victims. He'd been too far gone after Brett's attack, but he knew he'd never be able to forgive himself for missing it, despite being in hospital.

As far as he was concerned, they were only here because of her. Alyssa had been a young woman with nothing to lose who had come aboard to *build* something. To take a risk on herself for the sake of everyone. For people she didn't know. Even for people who wished her harm. Alyssa, the one who had raised the alarm on the scarabs. Who had convinced *him* that doing something hard to make a stranger's life better was worth so much than working to make the people he'd hated lives worse.

Alyssa the med researcher, the Terran. The spacer.

He heard announcements over the loudspeakers as the chamber filled with people. He was used to it now, the pomp and ceremony he'd never been afforded before the catastrophe. Camera drones whizzed past, and large, static cameras adorned the corners of the walls. Everywhere he looked there were the unreal eyes, behind which were millions upon millions of people waiting to hear the testimony of Meg and himself.

Meg was poised to tell the technical details he wasn't across. How the crash had happened. How she kept the ship flying straight. The tanks and the spin gravity and all the rest of it. His part of the story was something else entirely.

The camera lights all turned on. The black glass faces winked at them, and red warning lights indicated that they were live.

Reaching into his other pocket, Healy pulled out a smaller vial. This one was unbroken, and still full. It held similar but more robustly made chalky pills than the container he'd got from Alyssa.

He winked at Meg, and she smirked at him. Then he popped out one of the pills and put it in his mouth, in full view of the cameras, and washed it down with the glass of water on his desk.

His name was called less than a minute later, and the room went silent. A staff member started to move the microphone down to the level where he could reach it from his wheelchair, but Healy waved him off.

Gripping the side of his wheelchair with both hands, he kicked the foot stands away and placed both feet flat on the ground. He pressed down, carefully at first, then with more confidence. The room was dead still, and he heard nothing but the rustle of his clothes as he stood up. He shook slightly. Standing was still an effort, but he wasn't going to do this from the chair. He stood, full height and proud, staring out at the crowd.

He reached into his pocket and felt for the small container with the cracked lid. Alyssa's pills. He pulled it out and placed it carefully on the evidence table in front of him.

The microphone whined slightly as he adjusted it and he stared keenly into the dark eyes of the cameras and of everyone who was watching from around the world, using the very communications systems he'd spent a lifetime maintaining. He looked one more time at Meg. She nodded.

He cleared his throat, and began to speak.

THANKS

FOR READING

Thank you for reading *Sunward Sky*. This book, from go to whoa, took four years to complete, and in that time I had so much help from so many people. No book exists in a vacuum, and we should disavow ourselves of the notion that writing is a solitary experience. The quiet hours at a computer are only tolerable because of the love of friends and family who show their support. Here are a just a few of the people who have helped me.

Mum, I'd be nowhere without your encouragement and the way you've shared your love of language and science fiction. I think my obsession with spaceships can be traced back to you bringing Star Wars home on VHS in 1994.

Lachie McNaught, you've always been the first to congratulate me whenever I've managed to complete anything. You're a great friend and have been for a long time. The mango chutney was great by the way.

Jon Stubbington, your artwork, professionalism, and repeated enthusiasm to work with me has been an incredible help to build my projects.

Tim Bowker, for being the first reader and listener of my writing. Someone had to believe in me first and it was you. I haven't forgotten.

To the writers on Voidspace for the daily polls and nonsense talk, and who are a constant source of solace when I'm feeling the words aren't coming out right.

To everyone who listened to the low-quality bedroom microphone first draft of this story, it wouldn't have happened without you.

And of course, to Prue, who encouraged me to finally take the time off to rework the podcast into the book you now hold in your hands. I love you.

For all who have read this far, I have one final favour to ask if you'll permit me. The works of indie authors such as myself live and die on word-of-mouth recommendations. We lack the marketing and funding available from big presses, so we rely on readers to spread the word. If you enjoyed this book, it would be incredible if you could help get the word out there. Tell a friend, pop it on Instagram (tag @henryneilsen_writer if you do!), review it on Goodreads or Amazon or whatever you like. It feels like a small thing, but it really does mean the world.

I've got many more stories to come, and I hope you're willing to come along for the ride. Subscribe to my Substack (henryneilsen.substack.com) for updates.

Thank you so much.

Henry Neilsen

ABOUT THE AUTHOR

Henry Neilsen is a Melbourne-based writer, musician, environmental designer and nerd. He is fascinated by technology and the stories we tell each other about technology, both in fiction and real life. He has a number of fiction and non-fiction writing projects, which can be found on his website:

www.henryneilsen.com

Substack: henryneilsen.substack.com

Instagram: @henryneilsen_writer

Bluesky: @henryneilsen.bsky.social

Goodreads: www.goodreads.com/henryneilsen

9 780648 942634